About the

Bryan J Mason wrote this novel in London in the late 1980s, but reluctantly put it away in a drawer after his agent narrowly failed to get it published. He dug it out every ten years or so and each time he did was surprised to find that he enjoyed reading it and still found it funny. At last, he decided to try and get it published, after making some changes, including firmly placing the action in the late '80s and early '90s for today's reader.

He has worked as a brush salesman and rent collector, made sound effects for BBC Radio and been a tax inspector and occasional actor. He writes regular theatre reviews for *StageTalk Magazine*.

Shaking Hands with the Devil is Bryan's first novel. He is currently working on one featuring a Jewish detective investigating a series of serial killings in Northern Ireland during the Troubles, called *An old Tin Can*.

He lives in Bristol with his wife and has two children in their twenties.

SHAKING HANDS WITH THE DEVIL

Bryan J Mason

SHAKING HANDS WITH THE DEVIL

Vanguard Press

VANGUARD PAPERBACK

© Copyright 2021
Bryan J Mason

The right of Bryan J Mason to be identified as author of
this work has been asserted by him in accordance with the
Copyright, Designs and Patents Act 1988.

A CIP catalogue record for this title is
available from the British Library.

ISBN 978-1-80016-154-2

*Vanguard Press is an imprint of
Pegasus Elliot MacKenzie Publishers Ltd.*
www.pegasuspublishers.com

First Published in 2021

**Vanguard Press
Sheraton House Castle Park
Cambridge England**

Printed & Bound in Great Britain

Dedication

For Mary, always with love.

Acknowledgements

This novel is entirely a work of literary imagination and all characters are fictitious with any resemblance to real persons, living or dead, purely coincidental. However, having said that, many of the names and places referenced have featured in various notorious crimes.

This work would never have seen the light of day without the guidance, support and occasional exasperated pleas from my first literary agent, the late Carolyn Whitaker at London Independent Books. Publication some thirty years after she read the first draft is testament to her effusive encouragement, belief and advice which I will never forget.

I am not omniscient, but I know a lot

Who holds the devil, let him hold him well,
He hardly will be caught a second time.
Johann Wolfgang von Goethe, 'Faust'

Shaking hands with the Devil
Smutty schoolboy slang for masturbation

PART ONE

BEFORE AND DURING

CHAPTER ONE
RED

The arm slowly came away from the body with a sucking sound, reminiscent of that made by a leg being reluctantly wrenched from an undercooked roast chicken.

Sinews snapped, flesh puckered, and an opaque, sticky mucous-like liquid squirted up into his face and hair. Blood began to pump from the incision like a procession of rampant angry red ants while the cadaver's mouth suddenly and alarmingly fell agape and began gurgling in the most grotesque fashion.

Clifton Gentle woke up in a panic, the sheets on his bed saturated not in blood, but in the sweet sweat of his labours. The labour of dreams. There had been a time when he attempted to write down particularly fascinating dreams each day upon waking, but that had been in his adolescence before he found out that no one else found other people's dreams remotely interesting. This one meant something though, and he needed to think about it in a bit more detail to work out exactly what it was. Perhaps it was a means to an end? And if so, what an end.

As he got out of bed Clifton mulled over the possibilities on offer. Whilst shaving, washing and brushing his teeth without either method or precision, the day slowly began to unfold in its logical and well-worn pattern. Here he was in the upper rooms of a three-storey house in North London, washing his upper body in the late 1980s. It was all so terribly systematically symmetrical. He noticed that his nipples stood strangely erect in the cool morning air, and were also pointing slightly upwards. It occurred to Clifton that all should really be well with the world at this particular time, and that amid this strangely apposite geometrical upturn the current chaos of his life ought to be a short-lived and minor aberration.

Sitting on the lavatory a minute later, he read a Walt Whitman poem from a well-thumbed collected edition that always sat yellow and stained on the curling linoleum floor.

'For my enemy is dead, a man as divine as myself is dead,

I look where he lies white-faced and still in the coffin —

I draw near...'

The lines, as ridiculous as all poetry can be, condensed just about everything that was wrong with Clifton's life on this particular drab Wednesday morning. He was bloody confused.

But first there was breakfast. He couldn't very well be expected to set about this sort of business on an empty stomach. His breakfast had lately become a fairly miserable affair; a spartan grey meal of habitually burnt toast and strong brackish tea left too long in the pot. He missed the breakfasts of his childhood, lovingly prepared by his doting mother and consisting of the full works with sizzling back bacon, perfectly poached golden eggs, glorious field mushrooms and sweet crimson-red tomatoes bursting open at the seams, all of it served up in a soothing rosy glow with dainty flowers in a chintzy vase on the jolly tablecloth.

Turning on the radio, he cheered up a bit. The news broadcast droned on, the presenters apparently unconcerned whether anyone was taking the trouble to listen or not, while bumptious and chatty voices told tales out of school about murder and folly 'at home and abroad'. Clifton smiled to himself, reassured that there was an element of confusion elsewhere in the world and leant across to the radio to turn up the volume for the daily weather forecast. He hadn't thought about the weather yet, just as he didn't every day until the broadcast came on.

Hitherto, it had been nothing; 'the sky' at most, but in England the weather forecast became the first important thing to happen, the chief topic of the day and the greatest reality of a million moments. It affected everyone in some way or another. After all, everyone cared about what it was doing outside. Even murderers.

'A beautiful day,'

'Beastly,'

'It's trying to come out,'

'More pissing rain!'

Michael Flanders and Donald Swann had written a comic song in the 1960s in which every month was characterised by some kind of intemperate punishment or other such as hail, fog or slush. Weather in England is by its very nature pessimistic; it never rains, but it pours; it never shines, but it does have occasional sunny intervals.

As the pattern for the weather became established and was officially designated, so became Clifton's day.

'With persistent heavy showers over most of London and South East England well into the evening,' read a sonorous voice. Good. People were less likely to be about, and what he was going to do later on that night required complete and absolute privacy.

The rigid and unerring format of the BBC Radio 4 morning news comforted Clifton, who was usually in need of some sort of bolstering first thing, even if it came in the form of an ersatz routine of a magazine-style radio programme. He knew that in two, or at the outside three minutes, the sports news would come on. That was always his cue to go to the bathroom, leaving the radio chattering away to itself in the kitchen while he brushed his teeth, scraping black specks of toast from between his molars. When he got back in the kitchen the round-up bulletin would come on followed by the parliamentary report. There was nothing to doubt the natural progression — it was as sure and safe and guaranteed as night follows day and death follows life: all was as it should be.

The presenters were interviewing bystanders who had witnessed the latest IRA attack on the UK mainland which was then accompanied by Margaret Thatcher's usual breathy condemnation. The Home Secretary Douglas Hurd warned that Britain was facing the threat of high-level terrorist activity and that the IRA "must be extirpated". Clifton wondered what 'extirpated' meant, although he could well imagine. There was also a lot of excitement about the Cheltenham Gold Cup and a horse called Desert Orchid, but none of that interested Clifton. Turning the radio off he scanned the kitchen, making sure nothing was out of place. He had already made his bed and straightened everything up. He'd been in the bathroom and seen what was in there. And he didn't like it much. The vacant, somewhat bored expression on the latest one was reason enough to finish him off in the first place, but he was becoming even more tiresome in his current deceased state.

Clifton picked up his black imitation leather attaché case from the hallway. Inside, as ever, were the familiar contents: one tuna and mayonnaise sandwich on granary bread made the evening before, a reporter's notebook with a silly picture of a monkey smiling on the front cover and a blue biro pen. Stuffed at the bottom, wrapped up in a plain brown paper bag, were a clean pair of grey British Home Store Y-front underpants. Popping back into the kitchen, he picked up a postcard

17

featuring a photograph of Big Ben from the badly stained Formica worktop, before tapping on the rim of the goldfish bowl, momentarily scaring two carroty-grey fish.

Leaving the flat, he shut the door, banging it loudly to deliberately annoy the elderly neighbour in the downstairs flat who never dared to complain. After popping the card addressed to his parents in the post-box across the street and buying his newspaper from the news-stand outside the grubby Underground station, Clifton fell headlong down the escalators towards the platform for his daily dose of purgatory. Once on board the Tube train, squashed up against fellow travellers in extreme discomfort, he was unable to read his paper, which hung limply by his side and was slowly torn to pieces in the crush. Inhaling stale odours emanating from equally sour bodies pressed up against him, Clifton pondered on the lives that these people led; lives probably extremely different from his own. Yet what made these people so different? After all, they commuted on the same dirty, overcrowded Tube train each day, had the same sort of jobs, wore the same sort of clothes, and looked equally dissatisfied. Yet they were different, and in ways they would neither imagine nor understand. At least not for the time being anyway.

Forty gruelling minutes later, he tumbled out of the hellhole posing as an underground station and trudged towards an unimposing sludge-coloured government building in which he worked as a senior administrative officer in Human Resources. Whilst not being particularly good at his job, he wasn't too bad, and was at least better than two or three of his immediate colleagues. As far as his manager was concerned, he was a fairly competent member of staff who didn't cause any trouble. A great deal of Clifton's day was spent on the telephone, arranging for unseen invoices to be sent to another equally unseen arm of the Civil Service, where they were grudgingly and inaccurately scrutinised by a man called Wax. Clifton had never met Wax who in turn didn't know that Clifton, his post or his entire section even existed.

Much to Clifton's considerable surprise, he was both respected and liked at work; office contacts found him occasionally amusing and witty with no pretensions for promotion. At six foot tall he always commanded a certain amount of attention, but to counterbalance this he wore clothes of a lamentably bland nature. Greys and browns pervaded the palette of his wardrobe, although an occasional heroic blue or mustard yellow shirt might surface at times of laundry shortages. Otherwise, he stuck to polyester and cotton mix drip-dry white shirts with a grey or sickly cream tie which looked like something nasty had been spilt down it. His shoes were invariably light tan. At home, in the bottom of a chest of drawers, Clifton had twenty-three and a half pairs of identical grey, knee-length elasticated socks.

Seated at his desk, he focussed on the days and evenings of labour ahead of him, before recalling the last line of the Whitman poem he'd read earlier.

'…I draw near,

Bend down and touch lightly with my lips the white face in the coffin.'

Clifton smiled a thin smile, picked up the telephone receiver and made his first call of the day.

CHAPTER TWO
BLUE

Another thick file flopped down onto Detective Chief Inspector Dave Hicks's desk. He groaned loudly and rather theatrically before looking up; an expression of woeful disgruntlement painted all over his large, bearded face. The young PC who had delivered the papers on his instructions promptly turned round and walked back to the post room, smirking to himself. DCI Hicks picked up the file and flicked it open. The contents consisted of a number of handmade cuttings culled from local and national newspapers, together with an awful lot of badly typed memoranda called things like 'Incident Report, No. CXXXVIII'. They were packed for the most part with irrelevant and misleading details of ill-doing in North East London. Stuffed within its tattered pages were reports of domestic violence, minor burglaries, petty muggings and various misdemeanours reported in Dave's patch over the last eighteen months. There were also a number of details concerning the recent spate of horrible human mutilations that so far showed no sign of stopping. Dave started leafing through the papers, attempting to resemble a man on top of the situation. He was Dave Hicks from Hackney Marshes, local boy made good; occupation self-styled unconvincing wide boy and full-time policeman.

'Hicks from the sticks, that's me,' he'd say to anyone who would listen. He was the ideal policeman; he worked long hours, was conscientious, obsequiously subservient to his superiors, always willing to take anything on, and consequently disliked by most of his colleagues. He'd managed to climb up the slippery pole of success until here he was, at the comparatively young age of thirty- four, a detective chief inspector in a busy and extremely villainous part of North London.

He'd already solved countless crimes, assisted in no small part by the efforts of his team.

'My boys,' he would say, 'are following up my leads.'

He made sure that he was constantly in touch with both the superintendent and detective superintendent, and at times also with the chief constable himself. Dave was assiduous in giving up-to-date reports on all cases likely to be of interest to the local press.

'I expect a breakthrough' was as good a catchphrase as any. If a breakthrough *did* materialise it wasn't generally due to DCI Hicks, but his superiors weren't to know that and probably cared even less.

With suspects, DCI Hicks encouraged strong talk and rough handling, together with a heavy use of amateur dramatics in the interrogation room. Small theatrical skits were played out every week before fascinated audiences, and featured the full repertoire of pleading, cajoling, physical threats, weeping, wailing and full-blown hysterics. Alibis were invariably broken down and confessions 'extracted' from the villain whose unhappy lot it was to be placed in Hicks's own theatre of the absurd. It was said that many of his collars gave themselves up just to escape being in his company, but that was not only unfair, but also dismissive of Dave's proven interrogation talents and his extraordinary devotion to duty as well as his fondness for creative role playing.

'I've got him bang to rights!' Dave would invariably announce and unlike some, he *always* got his man.

And now he was hunting for this current nutter who was cutting up bits of bodies and dropping them off, piece by piece all over the place.

'That's bloody rude,' Hicks said. 'No one's going to nause up my manor!'

Look at what he'd already achieved in the short time he'd been around. Violent street crime was down by fifteen per cent from the previous year, burglary at twenty-three per cent and the overall clear-up rate was an amazing fifty-one per cent. Put that against the record of Dave's immediate predecessors and it was nothing short of a revolution in crime prevention. In hardly nowhere else in the country, let alone the metropolitan area, was a senior policeman able to boast a comparable record. As a consequence, he'd been made much of in the division's glossy annual report. Dave made sure of that by volunteering to be on the editorial panel. He was already a familiar and regular face on the local TV news bulletins, and this enhanced his media-savvy profile.

'We are on this case like a boner fido bloodhound,' he asserted to millions of bewildered viewers across the London area, 'and my men are barking at the leash.'

The lads and lassies in the division never ceased to be amazed by the DCI's aptitude for falling on his feet while passing himself off as a heaven-sent genius and saviour. If it wasn't for the dangled juicy carrot of abundant overtime much of the conspiratorial muttering about 'dropping him in it for once' would have had more substance.

Anyone associated with the press was especially courted. Reporters were routinely allowed easy access to enter the police station at will, picking up confidential slips of paper left around accidentally on purpose. Many of the hacks were granted an 'exclusive' interview with the great man himself. An insight into modern crime detection was always guaranteed, and Dave prided himself on being on first name terms with each and every one of the reporters.

'Morning, Bill!' he'd bellow across the station car park to John Duffy, chief reporter on the *Hackney Gazette*, and virtually a daily visitor. Dave Hicks was good copy and always worth a banner headline.

'Don't worry, boys,' he announced in the midst of the hunt for a perpetrator of recent sexual assaults. 'We're going to grasp the balls by the horn.'

DCI Hicks was at last getting to the bottom of the file. He couldn't find anything that might be classified as a clue in this case: just the usual hotchpotch of everyday foul play — nothing out of the ordinary. Dropping the folder and spilling papers across his desk he stared slightly absent-mindedly at the worn poster pin up of a semi-clad young lady left on the wall opposite his desk by his predecessor.

What sort of maniac was this man? So far, the police had recovered a number of body parts that the chaps down at the pathology lab said belonged to 'at least six different people'. Hicks wondered where the rest of the bodies had got to. They had half a dozen, possibly more, partial corpses in the freezer, all of them chopped up into various pieces, forming a sort of grisly incomplete jigsaw puzzle. Among the parts were arms, feet, tops of thighs, hands, torsos and a few heads, one of which appeared to stare in a particularly insolent manner at whoever was viewing it at that precise moment. As he glanced down at the dossier again, the cadaverous face and thin, rangy figure of his superintendent appeared, rapping briefly on the panel of the door as he strode in. Dave leapt to his feet and saluted. He always saluted.

'Good morning, Mr Chief Superintendent.'

'Morning, Dave. And yet again by the way, it's not Chief and not Detective Chief, just Superintendent. Any news?'

'No need to worry, I'm on top of it, sir. It's all in the bubbling pot. I feel that it's only going to be a matter of time now.'

Superintendent Haigh looked worried.

'What have you got to go on?'

'If you recall, sir, I sent you an interim report last Friday.' He hesitated. 'Perhaps you had time to surmise it?'

'What? Oh, yes, of course I did, but I couldn't make head nor tails of the blessed thing, which is why I've come down here today. Look, Dave, you know the press are on my back about this business day and night and I need to hear directly from you what's going on.' He paused and tried to look sincere, overdoing it somewhat. 'I want to know what you think, Dave.'

Hicks swelled and at first could only stare at his superior officer in wonderment.

'Sit down, sir, and I'll get you a nice hot cup of something.'

Superintendent Haigh sank, easing his narrow, world-weary joints into the ragged chair, sighing deeply while Dave hurried out of his own office and barked a few orders about coffee. At length he came back and sat down at his desk, beaming like a child.

'I've got the girl to get you a nice cupofchino from the café next door, sir; it's so much nicer than the stuff from the machine.'

'Bugger the coffee, Dave! What I really need is to understand what the hell you're doing to catch this maniac. What the devil are you up to?'

The detective chief inspector pursed his lips, stood up from his chair and for a second considered saluting again, before thinking better of it and instead walked over to a large incident map on the wall with various, red-flagged pins stuck into it.

'This map shows the area in question,' he said, pausing for Superintendent Haigh to turn around and look suitably impressed. 'Each pin represents the position where a part of a body has been located.'

The superintendent seemed a trifle more comfortable. Dave hit him with his master stroke.

'And I believe… that the murderer must be a local man because of the small area involved and the reliance upon the knowledge of the local geography this entails…'

The superintendent was getting excited.

'Yes?' he said encouragingly.

'…and that not all the identities of his victims are known to the police at the moment because of the physical difficulties pursuant to the process of positive identification. However, I also believe,' said Hicks, with a suddenly assumed sing-song rhythm in his North London accent, 'that we will do so, and that such identifications will enable us to carry out enquiries that will surely lead to our man.'

He walked back to his desk, smiling broadly, and sank down into his chair. There was a short, sharp moment of chilling silence followed by an explosion, sounding like that made by a frozen chicken being dropped into a sink full of washing-up.

'Is that it?' shouted the superintendent, aghast. Hicks looked puzzled and a touch crestfallen.

'Yes... sir. What else did you want?'

'Well, Dave,' began Superintendent Haigh with more than a hint of sarcasm in his voice. 'I don't really think that's going to cut it with the press boys, do you? I know you've demonstrated a knack for pulling rabbits out of hats in the past, but I can't honestly see where you are going with this one. What orders have you given the division, for God's sake?'

Hicks quickly recovered his composure and puffed himself out to full girth.

'To boldly go where no man has gone before. To use everything in our powers to catch this maniac: grasses, door-to-door enquiries, patterns of behaviour among known villains, good old-fashioned police work, threats, looking in bins and,' he added in a conspiratorial touch, 'utilising my own excellent contacts amongst the local media.'

Haigh looked even more worried.

'Now you know my feelings about the press,' he said. 'They're more harm than they're worth. Poking their noses in, getting in the way, printing confidential information as well as total rubbish…' He sighed again, catching the ever-gleaning keen eye of Hicks. Would whatever he said to this man make a difference? And what was the alternative? 'But if you're doing the best you can, I suppose you'd best carry on for the time being. Just bloody well keep me informed on how things are going. ON a daily basis please! And if anything of any real significance turns up, then let me know as soon as you do.'

He got up out of the fraying chair, strode past Hicks, who again saluted, and walked out of the office at high speed, colliding with the young WPC carrying a polystyrene cup of scalding, hot coffee. As he walked down the stairs, attempting to wipe the brown stain off the front of his uniform, he heard the detective chief inspector's voice bellowing down the stairwell.

'Don't you worry, Super, we'll give it our best shot across the bowels.'

***

The alarm on his bedside clock rang out. In the morning gloom of his queen-size comfy bed, Dave peered at the luminous glowing green digits. Six fifteen. Time to get up and catch criminals. Almost immediately he became uncharacteristically depressed. The nutter was still at large, apparently able to kill at will and dispose of bodies all over the place and until Dave could solve this case, he would just remain one amongst a growing crowd of keenly ambitious policemen in the bulging Metropolitan Police area. But just think, if he cracked it, it would make him a star.

It was definitely worth going for in a big way.

'The world will be my lobster,' he muttered on the way to the bathroom.

Dave washed his face, blinking in the piercing bathroom light, and peered approvingly at his familiar features in the mirror. Nice and neat and tidy; a button nose, bright blue eyes, and short, mousy hair atop his head setting off that marvellous full beard.

'A man's face,' he said and smiled.

He liked to see a beard, well at least on a man. It was, well... manly. Drying his whiskers, he applied a generous amount of an aftershave called 'Zeus Juice' to his cheeks. Finally, after much combing of his hair, which was admittedly very thick and luscious, he placed a pair of bright blue plastic spectacles on the bridge of his nose.

'I hate dull colours,' he'd told his colleagues the first day he walked into the station sporting them.

Their eyes scanned over his plain grey suit, grey tie, off-white standard issue shirt and shiny grey shoes, and then back up to the almost fluorescent frames.

He ate a breakfast of sizzling back bacon, two sausages, black pudding, triple poached eggs, fried slice, mushrooms, kidneys, baked beans and badly burnt toast. As a big man he liked a big breakfast. He also liked a big lunch, a big dinner, a big tea and a big supper.

He sipped at his black coffee ('no sugar, sweet enough, ha, ha, ha'), farted and left the flat; his shirt buttons straining against his now full belly. He lived alone, although in the same street as his mum who still lived in the family house.

'I've got to have my independence,' he said.

Mum came over to cook for him three evenings a week and he went over to hers about three times a week. Mum also cleaned the flat, did his laundry, mended the fuses and fetched all of his shopping.

'He's too busy what with going to work and catching criminals, and anyway he prefers me to do it for him; I know best,' she said to her friends when they told her that the great lunk was big enough and ugly enough to do it himself. Dave arrived at work after listening to the news on the car radio. The bulletin led with news about increasing numbers of East Germans trying to flee the border into the West, but then later mentioned the nutter's case again, only this time omitting Dave's name. If only he could break this one, the sky would be the limit. He would be Hicks — Master Detective. The latest in a long and distinguished line; Sherlock Holmes, Philip Marlowe, Hercules Poirot, Frank Cannon and Crockett & Tubbs all rolled into one. He could be greater than all of them. He pondered what he was going to do to further the case that day on the drive to the station, having to carefully steer around the enormous piles of rubbish kicked into the street by passing oiks the night before.

One thing had so far eluded the media: a ubiquitous name for the murders. They'd been variously dubbed the 'Bits and Pieces murders', the 'North London murders', and the more alliterative 'Bodies in the Bins' murders, but no one name had so far captured the imagination of news editors that it was omnipresent. Perhaps in time it would come to be known as the 'Dave Hicks Case'? Arriving in the station, somewhat cheered by his daydreaming, he called an immediate briefing with all the officers in his division. They trooped in, giving sideways looks to each other, not exactly relishing the day's work ahead of them.

'Right, boys,' Hicks started, 'I want action and I want action now. This whole thing has got to stop, or at least it's got to get going.'

There were looks of confusion. Dave interpreted the silence as respect.

'What I mean to say is this.' He banged his fist very hard on the table and just managed to hide the startled wince of pain. 'We've got to be seen to be doing something. The super requires it, the gentlemen of the press require it and' — he paused for dramatic effect for a few seconds while eyeballing each one of them — 'I require it.'

He looked keenly into each one of their tired, bleary eyes.

'I'm arranging daily press conferences and I want each and every one of you to turn this into a Major Event. I want you to go out to Joe Public, the man on the street, and to the narks on your manor. Threaten whoever you have to. Show them we mean business on this one. Let them know we're closing in and that when we catch this nutter, we won't look too kindly on anyone who knew something about it and didn't let on. This nutter must have friends or family who can see he's a bit bonkers and who might want to grass him up. He might even slip up himself. I want us to be there when his slips up so we can debag the rotter.'

As far as Hicks could see, everyone was suitably buoyed up by his inspirational speech and as he strode out of the office, he felt pleased with the lift he'd given to team morale. One officer, in the same dynamic mould as Hicks himself, stopped and turned towards the detective chief inspector.

'Excuse me, sir, when's the first press conference due?'

'Half past four,' said Hicks, 'just in time for the teatime news.'

***

Hicks left the station at eleven thirty, after munching through most of a packet of milk chocolate biscuits and set out to do some sleuthing on his own.

'They stalked their prey, the greats, that's what they did,' he muttered, steering the large red Volvo along the cramped, untidy roads that made up his North London manor.

'Looking for clues' is what he would have said to anyone who asked what the hell he thought he was doing.

Mercifully, the question was not posed.

One by one he visited each of the sites where the body parts had so far been found: an apparently random journey through the less salubrious areas of a locale that was already approaching being categorised as 'the dregs'. It hadn't experienced any interest from yuppies and others making money on the coattails of a suddenly affluent London and was pretty much as it had been for decades: a dump with pretensions of complacency.

Dave ticked off each of the sites. A couple of rubbish tips, an abandoned greyhound stadium, a deserted alley behind the Eastern Hospital, a bin beside a dried-up pond in a wreck of a recreation ground and an area of waste ground behind an advertising hoarding. They were all out of the way places in the midst of the teeming confusion of Hackney life. Whoever had thought of disposing the portions of cadavers certainly knew the area well and had chosen these little hidden areas of mediocrity with care.

The main thing that worried Dave was what had happened to the missing bits and pieces, and particularly to most of the heads which had so far remained undetected. Parked in a grimy alleyway still redolent with the stale smells of urine from drunken pubgoers the night before, he sat in the passenger seat, trying to imagine where the nutter might try to hide grisly sections of a human body; to see right inside the killer's perverted mind. Dave knew that this was the sort of thing all great detectives did.

After a moment's tortured consideration, he decided the missing parts could possibly have been hidden in a more secluded area than the parts already found. This was clearly a brainwave. He thought on. The nutter might still have the parts about him, desperate to retain some sort of sick hold over his victims in death, like a trophy. It certainly was a possibility. It was also likely that some bits may have already been uncovered but remained unreported to the police. Dave was aware of the distrust some people still felt about the police force; that was why he was a champion of open policing. Speak nicely to people and they'll respect you; Mum had told him that. Alien as it was to Dave Hicks — man of the people — some policemen could be downright rude to members of the public. Perhaps the bodies had been found after all but left to rot by people who didn't bother to inform the authorities. He took out his notebook, 'My aide de memo' as he called it and began to write.

1. Areas not usually frequented by the general public

2. Still with the murderer/nutter

3. Not reported and already found

Putting down his pen Dave thought again and scribbled down another possibility.

4. Dogs

He looked at his wristwatch. Two minutes past two.

'Time for lunch,' he announced, in what he considered to be butler-like tones, then awkwardly shuffled over to the driver's seat and started up the car. He drove quickly before striding up the garden path and calling out as he opened the front door.

'What's for dinner, Mum?'

A tiny woman rushed out at him from the kitchen, flushed with excitement.

'Hallo, love. I've been keeping it warm for you.'

She led him into the dining room where the table was already well stocked and neatly laid. A starched white linen tablecloth, gleaming knife, fork and spoon, a cruet set, mustard pot and sauce bottles all perfectly arranged at easy grabbing distance. A table fit for a prince.

Prince Dave sat down, running a plump finger over the cloth with pleasure and anticipation. In a trice Mum carried out a tray bearing an oversized plate stacked with two pork chops together with lashings of steaming mashed potato, fried tomatoes and bubble and squeak. He smiled at her and then looked lovingly at the meal before drenching it all in brown sauce. A side plate of thickly buttered white bread was tucked in beside his elbow and he started to eat, twirling his knife and fork around while he gave his favourite talk — how to catch criminals.

'Course, this nutter's just the same as the rest of them. He's killing people and cutting them up just for the sheer hell of it. Trying to make us look stupid. Can't bear it that he's an outcast and not part of decent society, like you and me.'

He pushed half a chop into one side of his mouth and clamped it tightly between powerful teeth.

'Sick, that's what he is. The sort of bloke that would gladly give his right arm to join the police force but knows deep down that he's not good enough and would bottle it. Doesn't want to work hard for his living.'

One slice of bread was trawled around the tomatoes, soaking up all the excess juice.

'Wants it all on a plate.'

Dave's mum furrowed her already creased brow.

'I get worried about you going out with these people around. I don't see why you should have to go looking for him. You should get the others to do the donkey work for a change.'

Dave became suddenly very blasé and in his most patronising tone, shrugged an answer.

'I'm not looking for him. I'm simply looking to enable me to *find* him.' He speared a chop. 'Clues are the essence of a detective's art; surely even you know that.'

'Clues!' said Mum.' Who do you think you are? Sherlock Bleeding Holmes?'

***

Back at the police station, reporters started slouching around the special meeting room set aside by Dave for press conferences. Hitherto it had been used as the staff recreation room, but redesignation had deemed otherwise, and the table tennis tables, dart boards and newspaper racks had all been put into storage. There had been quite a call for press conferences since Dave joined the division, and now bored-looking men in drab and heavily creased, greasy clothes loitered around, idly laughing and chatting to each other about mutual acquaintances they equally disliked. They'd all been in the game for far too long to show any sign of enthusiasm about this particular job, and they'd certainly seen enough murder cases in their time not to get excited about this one. All the necessary telephone and fax points were within easy reach and the pecking order for prime position had been established for years. The TV crews kept themselves to themselves, away from the less glamorous hacks at events such as these. Instead, they were content with a lot of unnecessary shouting and making final superfluous changes to the lighting and camera positions.

Superintendent Haigh was still in Dave's office, looking despairingly at a typed sheet headed 'Murder

Investigation: Press Release'. Underneath the heading were the four points the detective chief inspector had sketched out in his car earlier that afternoon. He frowned as his eyes scanned the page.

'Dogs? What else are you going to say to them? For God's sake, they're expecting a little more than this, you know, Dave.'

'Don't worry, sir. I'll be explaining that this'll be the first of many conferences on this case. What I want to do today is start a relaunch. It's not the beginning of the end game, and it's not the end of the end game, but it's the end of the beginning of the end game for this nutter.' He paused and struck what he thought was a Churchillian scowl. 'It's the end of his game!' Dave winked. 'It should really give our lads a boost. This report I've put together will serve as a sort of rallying cry.' He smiled, excitedly. 'I want to get a crusade going.'

Superintendent Haigh reeled back in horror.

'A crusade!' he exclaimed, loud enough for his words to penetrate the press room. 'I hope you know what you're doing. Crusades are dangerous things; people get carried away in crusades and end up doing all sorts of crazy things. A crusade could bloody well crucify us!'

DCI Hicks smiled the smile of the wise and all-knowing.

'We're going to sail through it, Super. Fortune favours the knave.'

Watching the blissful smile spread over Hicks's face, Jim Haigh took an executive decision. On the basis that he'd rather face the music now, and not add to the strain on his stomach ulcer, he got up and walked over to the door.

'It's only twenty past four at the moment: I think we've got another ten minutes yet.'

'I know. We're going into the lion's den now, Hicks. If we catch them off their guard, they may have pity and decide to spare us.'

As the police representatives marched out into the press room, cigarettes were extinguished, camera lights were hurriedly turned on and all chatter ceased. The reporters readied their tape recorders, opened their notebooks, and prepared to receive the pearls of wisdom. A young PC handed out the typed sheets and Superintendent Haigh addressed the meeting.

'Good afternoon, ladies and gentlemen. This press conference has been called to let you know what the police are doing to catch the perpetrator of the recent murders that have occurred in this district over the past few weeks. It's intended to be the first of many, and will be coordinated by Detective Chief Inspector Hicks, whom I believe most of you are already familiar with.'

Dave beamed at the photographers and winked at a couple of press men he thought he recognised.

'I'm sure you're keen to find out what's been going on, so without further ado, I'll hand you over to DCI Hicks for the remainder of this session.'

40

The superintendent sat down quickly, pleased with himself that he had so far avoided any questions. He craned forward as if ignorant of the statement about to be issued by his junior officer.

'Right!' he thought, inwardly chuckling. 'We'll see how Sherlock bloody Holmes deals with this little lot!'

'Thank you, Superintendent Haigh,' began Hicks confidently. 'I see most of you have the document concerning the killings in front of you. As you're aware, at least six corpses have been found in this area of London over the past few weeks. I have reason to believe that they are victims of the same killer. I also believe that detection of clues to these murders depends as much on the vigilance of members of the public, as on the efforts of the police force. If you would examine the list in front of you, you'll notice that the discovery of the missing pieces, particularly the heads, are of crucial importance. We're desperate to complete these human jigsaws. It will help us not only to pinpoint the area of the crimes, but also to provide further details of the identity of the victims, and hence a motive for these despicable murders.'

He swayed slightly, taking in the moment.

'I appeal in the strongest possible terms to all good citizens of London to look out for this monster. He is amongst us, and someone must know him. That someone,' Dave said, lowering his voice and turning dramatically to face the cameras, 'must be found. If you know this man, do not protect him. He has killed many times before and may very well kill again. If you have any hints at all about his identity, please do not hesitate to contact your local police station. All information will be treated with the utmost confidence, and, unlike some other investigations undertaken by other forces in the country, every lead will be followed up.'

He turned once more to the main body of the audience.

'Please help us to do our job as effectively as we can. After all,' he said with a chuckle, 'we're not all Sherlock Holmes.'

Pausing, Dave glanced to one side to catch the expression on the super's face — glowing red, obviously with pride — and then looked back at the massed ranks of the press.

'Are there any questions?'

Reporters leapt up, knocking the carefully positioned television cameras out of place and making the proceedings appear even more frantic when broadcast on the news later.

'What makes you so sure that the killer is a man?' asked a woman journalist.

'Well, Miss,' Hicks beamed, 'we are convinced that a woman couldn't be involved in these killings, as there are certain specific characteristics which lead us to eradicate all women from our enquiries.'

He was making it up on the spot, but none of the other hacks took him up on it. As a matter of fact, he'd never even considered whether the nutter was anything but a man. He'd always been a 'he'.

'Are there any clues as to the causes of death, Detective Chief Inspector?' asked another reporter.

'Good question. Well, it appears that two of the six were definitely strangled, but the lack of a head or neck to examine means that we can't say for certain about the others. What I can say is that all of them have apparently been chopped up with the same sharp instrument, such as a carving knife, and the bodies all show signs of having been dismembered inside a building.'

He paused long enough for signs of puzzlement to cross the reporters' faces.

'They were all very clean when we got hold of them, you see.'

This news made the gathering rather contemplative, and even some of the more hard-bitten among the press felt uncharacteristically nauseous. The gory details, however, did nothing to wipe away Hicks's smile, which became broader. He even appeared to chuckle once or twice. Answering a final question, he pointed to the incident map showing where the parts had been found and finished off with a flourish.

'This has got to be a team effort between you the public, and us the police. Together we can make sure our streets are once again safe for ordinary, decent people. Remember, to get ahead in this investigation, we must get a head, or several of them. Thank you for listening.'

The police officers left by the side door which led into Hicks's office.

'Well, I thought that went quite well, Superintendent' Hicks said shaking with pleasure.

Jim Haigh furrowed his brow and lowered his voice. He decided to be curt and cut out platitudes.

'What I want to know, Dave, is this. What the bloody hell are we going to tell them tomorrow? If there's no progress to report, they'll soon come down on us like a ton of bricks. All I'm saying is that it's all your own fault if your career gets buried underneath the mess. I'm leaving the whole thing to you; it's your idea, remember.'

Dave said nothing. He knew it was a gamble and didn't need reminding. What he also knew was that all the greats had to take a gamble sometimes. He would stake it all on this case. Just let them see. He'd get his man all right. He glanced down at the list once more. Dogs: he just needed one to bark in the night.

CHAPTER THREE
YELLOW

At twenty-eight minutes past five, Clifton Gentle put the office telephone down and prepared to go home. Plucking his raincoat from the corner of the room, jangling the sole remaining wire coat hanger, he slipped out of the office and straight into the gents' lavatory. While washing his hands for the fifth time that afternoon, he pondered about what course the evening ahead would take. He peered at himself in the grimy mirror. Whenever, by accident, he came across a reflection of his own physiognomy, Clifton was appalled.

Peering back at him through a pair of square silver metal spectacle frames was a face featuring a big-lipped mouth under a thin nose. At school once, someone had cruelly said that his mouth resembled 'a latrine with teeth', but time and time again it was not his mouth that eyes lingered on, but his hair — thick brown and unruly, perpetually on the shaggy side no matter what the fashion. However, much he brushed or combed at it, Clifton's hair sat atop his head with a mind of its own, like a cat bristling with indignation. Back through dusty spectacle lenses stared 'mahogany eyes', as his mother described them. Dark brown mahogany eyes that served only to reinforce the false impression of a wooden nature. Now thirty-four years old, his skin for so long covered in a form of adolescent acne which had taken on an entirely unwanted and unusual longevity, now looked tired, flaccid and drawn.

Tired, Flaccid and Drawn; it sounded like the name of a ghastly '60s tribute band.

Clifton considered himself unattractive, but passable, if only in a dim orangey light. Living a life unlike others, he had no real need for a handsome face. He had his own Weltanschauung; his mantra, his own personal philosophy. On most days, either at quiet moments like this, in the staff toilet, or at home in his one decent armchair, he'd relax and mouth some lines from an early juvenile poem:

'I am the class-less, sex-less, face-less man of the land;

Dying as I have loved — by mine own hand.'

Wondering what to cook for his evening meal, he finally decided on shepherd's pie. He was usually very health conscious, not fanatical but just sensible, and ate a lot of brown rice, low-fat, non-red meat substitutes and artery-softening cholesterol-free vitamin drinks. Tonight, though, was different. He hankered after something old-fashioned and tasty to give him a warm feeling. Once again, unable to gain a seat on the Tube journey home, he was crushed up against damp, dull

46

people he didn't know and didn't want to know; breathing in the tepid vapours of their faded dreams, failures and lusts. The tightly pinched, mean, little faces all wore the same expression of distaste and mutual loathing. Distaste and Mutual Loathing; another rubbish double act.

Back in his flat, shaking rain off his drab overcoat, Clifton wiped his spectacles and looked around the living room suspiciously. Whenever he didn't have what might euphemistically be called 'having people over to stay', Clifton lived alone in what was once the two smallest rooms of a rather grand Edwardian house. Nowadays it was just an ordinary, shabby, old house divided into too many flats and he was still getting used to it after moving in a few weeks before. It contained a few sticks of furniture including an enormous cane-backed chair from the seemingly luxurious, but vulgar, 1970s. It was extremely uncomfortable, and Clifton rarely deigned to sit upon it. A large trunk covered in a colourful, but heavily worn woven tapestry affair was pushed up under the bay window and could have served as a window seat only no one would ever want to sit there in the draught. A small, undistinguished-looking dining table sat at the far end, occupying too much of what available space there was. Elsewhere there was a fairly well-stocked bookcase filled with poetry and upmarket fiction, as well as the universally ugly, large boxy television set and stereo record player. Clifton's taste in music was unexceptional and a number of seldom-played albums were propped up against the side.

Some unimaginative and slightly torn impressionist prints were dotted around the walls, and a great many dusty, neglected pots and vases, all empty, sat on top of ledges and shelves. Clifton detested them, but over the years he had built up quite a collection through having them gifted by people labouring under the misapprehension that he favoured ceramics. This in itself was probably due to the fact that the few visitors to the flat remembered seeing a great many of them about; yet another example of the diagnosis and symptom becoming confused.

To anyone stumbling into the flat for the first time, it looked like it was occupied, but without much thought or imagination. In short, it appeared to lack a sense of life.

Clifton had another glance around. Everything appeared to be just as it was that morning, with the exception of his sandwiches, which he'd already eaten. On the kitchen work surface, he had placed a small supermarket bag of minced lamb which he would cook later, along with a bag containing the pair of underpants he'd been wearing that morning which he'd changed before leaving work. He still felt a little confused about that. For the past three weeks or so Clifton had taken a fresh pair of grey Y-fronts to work every day and changed into them in the staff toilets shortly before coming home, and he didn't really know why. It was something to do with a vague sense of feeling 'dirty', but he couldn't understand how or why he'd got dirty in the first place. Clifton placed the small white plastic packet of mince on a plate and laid it next to the goldfish bowl, giving the occupants a scare by tapping on the rim. Passing the bathroom, he glanced down and noticed that the body of a young man was still lying in the bath. His skin was quite grey now and, judging by the smell, obviously engaging in a state of early putrefaction. Although the window was wide open and the evening breeze blew in uncompromisingly, an unpleasant odour could still be detected. Clifton peered down at the figure and sniffed.

'It's time for us to say goodbye, I'm afraid. I'm beginning to go off you, and you're beginning to go off.'

He'd killed the man a little more than a week ago, storing his body in the bath simply because he didn't have a clue where else to put it, a bit like coal in poverty-ridden homes during the Depression. Things hadn't been so easy in this new flat. There was no accessible garden, for one thing. What with too many people being squeezed into the converted dwellings and no suitable alternative dumping ground, disposal had become a nightmare. It had all been very different in his old place. It was true that there had been a lack of storage facilities, which was one of the reasons why he had moved, but at least Clifton knew all he had to do was wait until the people in the flat upstairs had gone off on one of their regular weekend trips, before nipping outside to chuck the bodies onto a well-built bonfire. In the gloom of the evening all he had to do then was make sure no one bothered to get interested in the conflagration until it didn't look quite so grisly. It was plain sailing in a nice solidly middle-class neighbourhood like that; a little sprinkling of charcoal soon turned the funeral pyre into a barbecue, and there were enough of those smouldering away in back gardens during weekends, so it didn't look out of the ordinary.

But here in London E8, alas, it was different. This wasn't typical BBQ land, and in any case not in March. What could he do?

The lease on the other place had not been renewed and he couldn't afford anything or anywhere better than this. Part of his reason for buying this new place, apart from the additional cupboard space, was that it might deter him from doing any more killings, but that hadn't quite worked out. It was like breaking your arm in an attempt to stop smoking when the craving was still there. Clifton's flat was the top one of three, and the lack of access to the garden meant he was now forced to use other methods of disposal. It was only the night before when a resolution to the whole affair at last presented itself while he was asleep. A little speculative perhaps, but this plan seemed to have more chance of success than any other.

'It's all a bit corny,' he thought, 'what with the idea coming in a dream.' But sometimes things *did* happen like that. Writing essays in English comprehension classes at school, after describing some thrilling and fantastical tale in vivid detail, he'd be faced with the necessity of devising an acceptable solution to his plot. Wracking his brains for a minute or two for something logical to say, he would have to concede and simply put down the time-honoured phrase 'and then I woke up and found that it was all a dream'. Well, perhaps this time it would work. After all, the simplest ideas are supposed to be the best.

Clifton decided to get on and cook supper before setting about his evening's work. It needed to get a bit darker before he could venture outside, and he required some sustenance before embarking on his task. The rain, exactly as forecast, was beginning to fall much harder, and now beat against the window with an insistent rhythm. People walking on their way home along the street outside hurried on their way a bit quicker, dodging the rapidly forming pools and soggy refuse that filled the pavement and dirtied their shoes. Clifton had always liked listening to the sound of rain falling, and with the comforting smell of the shepherd's pie wafting around the flat he felt curiously safe. The sound of the rain now incessantly drumming against the windowpanes made life somehow seem much more snug and secure. The central heating was turned up full, and the guest who'd overstayed his welcome would soon be paying up and be on his way.

Having eaten his evening meal and done the washing-up, Clifton took what he needed from the kitchen drawer and went into the bathroom. He emptied the bath, first pulling on his bright yellow TV-advertised *Sudzor* rubber gloves. As water emptied down the plughole, the flesh on the young man's body moved about perceptibly, and Clifton began to have some doubts about whether things would go as smoothly as he'd hoped.

Spreading black sacks across the bathroom floor, he started work with the electric carving knife given to him last Christmas and which up until now he had never found a use for. The thrifty side to his character cheered him up, knowing that at least it was being put to some use. The buzzing of the blade became harsher and more insistent while it worked through the skin on the top of the arm and bone. It wasn't at all how he'd dreamt it; no liquid spurted from the wound at all, in fact there was little evidence of any blood having ever been in the body in the first place. However, the knife made very little impression on the bones and Clifton soon became concerned not only about his progress, but also at his electricity consumption. When he could bear it no longer, the carver was replaced by an old bread knife with a coarse serrated edge. It was heavy work, and in no time at all he was perspiring heavily. Taking off his pullover, he changed into what his mother used to call 'gardening clothes' — things to wear when carrying out dirty jobs. He recognised the irony in that if he'd had a garden in the first place, he wouldn't need to be carrying out all this work.

When at last pieces of body began to come away from the trunk, Clifton wrapped them up in newspaper and stuffed them into a black plastic sack in which the local council rather autocratically insisted all rubbish be deposited before removal. The smell became most unpleasant, and Clifton took longer breaks while he sucked in tired, damp air through the bathroom window. Throughout the evening, he tried to think of nothing but the job in hand, cheering himself up with the prospect of being able to take a bath himself once the current occupant had left it.

After two hours had passed in this gruesome fashion, Clifton had only succeeded in removing both arms, each chopped in half at the elbow, as well as separating the head and partially taking off one of the feet. With his own arms and back aching, he desperately wanted to stop, but being deprived of full use of his bathroom was now becoming an obsession. It was getting more and more difficult to keep himself clean and he remembered what it was like when he was a child and his father had embarked on a decorating frenzy.

'Three days discomfort for ten years of joy,' he would say and would continue to repeat for the next twelve weeks that it invariably took him to finish a job. Dragging on into the small hours of the morning, Clifton's task became even more tedious and repetitive; attacking the flesh layer first, then having to change tools to deal with the bone and finally chopping it all up into manageable pieces. He couldn't even remember this one's name. When he used to cremate his victims, he had chatted to them to pass the time, but he didn't really feel like striking up a conversation with this one. He cursed the body for being so tough.

'If I'd known the trouble you would cause I wouldn't have picked you up in the first place,' he said petulantly. Sweat soaked through the back of his shirt as he grunted and groaned with the effort of reducing a man into his component parts. It wasn't nearly as much fun as he had hoped it would be.

At around five in the morning while it was still dark as hell outside Clifton at last set about disposing of all the pieces. He'd chopped up nearly half the body and black sacks were neatly stacked up beside the WC cistern. Strangely they seemed much bigger than the frame from which they'd been removed, even allowing for the extra bulk of paper and plastic. This man was no longer a man in shape or any other sense, but then to Clifton he'd ceased to be the moment they'd met. In fact, men as a whole stopped having that significance for him quite some time ago. Picking up a couple of the smaller bundles, he stuffed them into a Sainsbury's carrier bag, where they looked like the results of a very late-night shopping trip. Stepping out into the rain-soaked swirling night Clifton Gentle looked as innocent as any murderer could do.

***

It was just before Clifton's sixth birthday that things started to go a little awry. He'd been given a cute, little puppy dog, which his father with little imagination named Jack. Taking the dog out into the garden, the small boy decided to teach him some tricks. All Jack wanted to do, though, was charge up and down the well-attended lawn, trying out his wheezy bark. Very suddenly, and without any apparent thought, Clifton picked up a sharpened bamboo stick normally used for training runner beans and stuck one end straight into the puppy's eye.

'Stupid dog — look what that's brought you!' the boy shouted while the dog careered round and round, yelping and crying in pain. Growing angrier still he ran up to the dog, kicking him in the ribs with new bright blue sandals.

'Shut up! Stupid dog, do as you're told, shut up!' It wasn't until his mother ran out of the house, alerted by the dreadful sounds of dog agony, that Clifton even considered something might not be quite right. Later that evening he was mildly interrogated by his parents.

'Why did you do it, son?' his father asked. 'Did the puppy bite you?'

Clifton denied nothing.

'He annoyed me. I wanted him to do tricks like the dogs on telly, but he wouldn't, so I punished him.'

'But Clifton,' his mother rebuked gently, 'don't you understand he's only a dog? He doesn't know what we want him to do all the time. He hasn't got your intelligence.'

That really impressed Clifton. Not like him, but different. Stupid. Not like him. Different. He was sent to bed with a mild scolding after his tea.

'He's sorry for what he did, Sally. I'm sure we'll hear no more about it.'

'Oh, I do hope so. It was horrible, Tom. When I heard that awful noise I thought there was a maniac in the garden.'

***

Filling the carrier bags for the fifteenth and final time that evening, Clifton allowed himself a small sigh of relief at the apparent success of his scheme. All he had to do now was to be careful, avoiding any unnecessary risks while continuing to keep his head. Unlike his late friend.

All would be well. He had done what he had to do.

'I did him in my way,' he crooned in a poor singing voice, while trudging downstairs for the last time that night.

As expected, hardly anyone had been out and about in the rain that early in the morning and finding suitable dumping places for the packages hadn't been too difficult. He had stuffed most of them into rubbish bins which would be emptied without any great regard to their contents and otherwise just shoved them in nooks and crannies as he grew tired of carrying them.

'After all,' he thought later, 'it doesn't really matter that much if they are found.' As long as he made sure he wasn't seen he could never be linked with them, could he?

Lobbing the last package over a corrugated metal fence into an area of derelict land, Clifton trudged wearily back to his flat. He must have walked around and about for miles and was by now desperate for his bed, even if only for a short while. He also wanted that bath. Reluctant to throw away the carrier bag in which he'd transported many of the parts, he folded if up neatly and tucked it inside his coat pocket. A police car appeared at the end of the street and sped past with a disconsolate swish of wet tyres on the road, its occupants paying no particular heed to anything. Clifton wondered what he'd say if it had stopped, and he had been asked what he was doing there in the middle of the night. He'd need to be courteous and polite; not make anything up. Of course, he couldn't help making some things up. He'd better be careful what he said to them if and when they did ask.

'I've been out chucking away bits of a body of a man I murdered.' That sort of thing would really give the game away. He was beginning to feel confused again; he must think clearly. He'd puzzle it out when he wasn't so tired. At last, back indoors and recoiling at the state of the enamel, he decided not to take that bath after all. Instead, he had a good all-over body wash with a flannel. He glanced at his watch. Six a.m. It hardly seemed worth the trouble of going to bed at all, but he was totally exhausted. Crashing down into his cane-backed chair he decided to go to work later at around lunchtime, feigning a stomach ache. He'd blame it on something he'd eaten.

'It's taught me not to leave meat lying around for so long,' he said by way of explanation to his boss.

And over the next few weeks and months the bits of bodies left in the streets began to build up.

CHAPTER FOUR
ORANGE

Four months later Sammy Little was enjoying himself on top of the dump. It was situated behind one of the advertising hoardings and was regularly filled up by rubbish chucked over the fence by the feckless locals as well as being used as a halfway dumping ground by the local council's refuse men. It was the six-year-old's very own castle, and he was its undisputed king. Like a miser in one of his story books who spent most of his time running shiny golden sovereigns through his hands, Sammy loved nothing more than pitching up into the air the torn plastic carrier bags containing used syringes, tampons, baked bean tins and other discarded detritus, before watching as the riches tumbled back down to earth. This was surely paradise.

With countless long hours already spent examining the tip's contents, Sammy's young eyes fairly glassed over when he contemplated years of more intensive scrutiny. There was always a fresh stock of rubbish thrown on top every day, and who knows what might turn up? Perhaps, he thought, one day when he was grown up he might get a job in charge of a tip like this;

sorting through its contents and finding whatever treasure could be reclaimed. Perhaps, just perhaps, one day he might find something really brilliant, like the FA Cup, stolen by hooded villains, and then he'd be rewarded by being allowed to play football for England. Perhaps, perhaps, just maybe perhaps he would find a thing so wonderful and so valuable that he'd be the richest boy alive in the whole world for ever and ever.

'Are men...' began his small friend Joey, 'are men allowed to come up here and sort of look about as well?'

Joey Douvray was Sammy's best friend. A year and a half younger, yet displaying a far keener intelligence, the young Afro-Caribbean boy was almost Sammy's shadow. His mother allowed him to grow up even faster than all the other kids in the area. He needed to develop quicker though, without his father around, not that there was exactly an abundance of doting dads at large in the neighbourhood. Like many, his had been very much an un-immaculate conception.

Sammy looked down at him from the top of the pile.

'What do you mean, are men allowed? 'Course they are, they build this place, don't they?'

'Well, I just wondered because I see people wandering in here and leaving stuff and they look like they shouldn't.'

'I bet you never seen no one, stupid,' replied Sammy in the uncharitable language of the small. With a petulant sneer still on his face, the young boy resumed his inspection of a bundle of papers, some yellow and mouldering, others still dry and with the lettering preserved. He thought that the writing must be foreign, although he'd little idea what any writing said apart from things written at the side of the road like 'STOP'. He knew signs and symbols and stuff, like a big 'WC' for toilets and a big 'P' for parking, although he liked to think it meant that you could do a big poo where that 'P' was. He liked to think about that and laughed whenever he saw one. Looking at the writing soon became very boring though. He thought of shouting for Joey to come and see the foreign writing, but maybe Joey would say it wasn't foreign at all and start being a clever clogs, so he tossed the sheets into the wind and moved on to unexplored territory.

He looked back at Joey who was sitting on the big oil drum. It was one of the very few unchanging landmarks in the dump. Usually, things that had been left there got collected up and moved or were just covered up by more junk until they rotted away, but the oil drum was different — it was constant and gave the boys a sense of place in the confusion of an ever-altering world. Full of hardened concrete, it had a couple of rusting iron rods sticking out near the base which you could rest your feet on. Joey sat and swung his legs out in front of him. He looked over a thin shoulder at his friend who was standing transfixed on the top of the dump surveying the putrefying wonderland. It was complete and utter devastation.

Despite Mrs Thatcher's attempts to instil a rampant business culture across the United Kingdom, there were still pockets of anarchy still at large. Filth, decay and squalor were the order of the day on the dump; modern Britain at its best. Sammy himself was often hungry, dirty, unwanted, bruised and facing the prospect of his life not ever being very much different. He smiled.

'This is great!'

Suddenly the air brakes of a council refuse lorry hissed at the main gates and, swivelling around, Sammy watched it swing round the bend and head straight up the track to the dump.

'Joey, look, the dustmen are coming back. Quick, we've got to hide.'

For a moment Joey didn't appear to understand, but then vaulted off the oil drum and joined his friend behind a large mound of rotting household waste.

The two boys nervously looked out for any sign of the approaching bin men. Sometimes they'd go after trespassers and shoo them off, jealously guarding the place for themselves. The boys knew which ones to avoid. Usually, the younger ones couldn't care less, and just shouted at them to 'piss off'. Some of the older ones, though, took their duties more seriously and would occasionally give chase to anyone caught scavenging around the place.

'There's dangerous stuff in here,' they said to their grinning colleagues. 'People could get hurt in a place like this.'

The boys heard men's voices approaching. After the latest drop off from the enormous wagons, they were now checking around the piles of junk for whatever could be found of value. Gerry, the big Irish foreman had only the week before found a perfectly good transistor radio that someone had thrown out. Probably someone with more money than sense. Gerry had sense enough to scratch out a living, but, as for money, well…

Their haunches trembling, the two boys cowered down behind a large busted-open wooden box and hoped they'd soon be left alone. With their noses pressed so close to the ground, the rotten rubbish smell got stronger, and they knew that with the grime being pressed into their clothes, they'd be in for it from their mums when they got home. Well, there was trouble most days so they might as well get it for something they enjoyed doing.

The men's voices got fainter and then unexpectedly stopped. Sammy poked his head up over the top of the crate to see if the coast was clear, like a soldier in one of the films on children's TV.

'Gotcha, you little buggers,' said a large man dressed in combat- style overalls not more than twenty feet away. Joey tried to run around the other side of the pile, but more men appeared and started to close in. One of the older ones rushed towards him, panting while his shirt flapped around his expansive waistline.

'You know you're not supposed to be here. I could hand you over to the police for this.' The large man had hold of Sammy's arm and started to twist it sadistically.

'Please, mister,' he squealed in pain, 'let us go, we won't never do it again.'

The man laughed and called out to the others.

'Go on, Stevey, get the other little shit bag.' Joey watched as the other men stepped gingerly over the decaying morass of filth towards him. He took off to a chorus of 'Come back here, you little fucker.' Racing away from the pile on thin, short legs, he headed towards the wire mesh perimeter fence. Only one of the men followed him now, breathing heavily, and finding the footing awkward after the pints he'd sunk at lunchtime.

Joey looked up and saw that he not only had fifty yards to cover over bundles of rubbish bags and broken bottles, but he would also have to scale the sharp metal fence before he was safe. He was whimpering with fear, but it was only thirty yards away now. Then twenty. Now it was just ten and the chasing man had fallen down, cursing loudly.

Joey got to the fence and looked around for something on which to get a foothold. Spying a closed cardboard box, taped up and propped against the fence, he ran towards it. Putting his foot on the top, he tried to bunk up the mesh, getting a toe hold in the gap only for the flimsy box to give way, sending him sprawling onto the hard ground.

The man kept lumbering towards Joey, his arms outstretched like Frankenstein's monster. Making one last effort Joey looked around for anything that might help and picked up the box again when he suddenly saw something that had him screaming in horror and disgust. Poking out of the box and staring sightlessly back at him was a human head. Its mouth was open far enough to reveal some grey chipped teeth, and it seemed to be grimacing at the indignity of it all. The hair was still fairly smartly swept back over the forehead, seemingly out of place compared to the rest of the features, and it looked as though it had only just been combed for the occasion. Joey screamed and screamed, his lungs bursting with the effort, and when the pursuing dustman got to him, he screamed as well.

After everyone else had caught up and seen what was in the box the only mouth not screaming was that on the head itself.

***

The police radio in Dave Hicks's car lisped nasally into life.

'Nurgent call for DCI Hicksh — Nurgent call for DCI Hicksh.'

In his urgency, Dave struggled to pick the receiver up and held it in one immense paw as it almost slithered from his grasp, while steering the car awkwardly with the other.

'DCI Hicks to station control. I'm receiving you, please go ahead.'

'Thank you, Detective Chief Inspector — please proceed to Mitre Street; report of a body discovered in nopen ground. No further detailsh so far, sir, but I have requested a two-car back-up as well as presence of a nambulance.'

Dave was delighted. This was all part of his plan; this was one of the things that were meant to turn up and he knew that if he hoped hard enough, they would. While replacing the receiver, he wondered why the call had come directly through to him from Control and not from one of his own men. He made the connection again.

'Hicks to Control,' he barked. 'Can you tell me why I was radioed direct?' There was a silence and a crackle before the operator came back on air.

'Ninstructions direct from the superintendent. That you be kept directly ninformed of any further discoveries, sir.'

Dave was as pleased as Punch. Dropping the receiver down and making the nice 'ping' noise that he always liked, he roared off to the scene, casually breaking the speed limit along the way. If only he had one of those red lights that clamped onto the roof that he had seen in American cop shows on TV. He must get the boys at the station to fit one.

Arriving at Mitre Street, Dave noticed a small crowd outside the fried chicken takeaway, apparently waiting for a bus. Getting closer he saw that, without exception, they were avoiding the shelter and were instead pressing themselves against the wall, peering up into the air. A patrol car was already on hand, parked in front of a double decker bus.

'Detective Chief Inspector!' one of the patrolmen saluted Dave. 'One of the passengers over there reported seeing something suspicious on top of the shelter.'

'Show me the passenger. I want to ask a few questions first.'

A WPC led a white-haired old lady over and introduced her as a Mrs Christie.

'Good afternoon, Mrs Crippen, and may I first of all thank you for reporting this so promptly.' A little courtesy never goes amiss, he thought, and Dave usually laid it on with a heavy lead trowel. 'If only every member of the public were so watchful, we wouldn't have any crimes in the first place.'

'I never bloody did it, you great fool,' she said indignantly. No wonder people didn't like the police these days, accusing the first person that came along.

'All I did was look out of the bleeding bus window, minding me own bloody business, when I sees it on the top of this here shelter.'

Dave, unabashed, continued to smile serenely.

'And what exactly did you see? What did it look like to you?'

Mrs Christie became even crosser.

'Same as it bloody well looks like to anyone with a pair of eyes and some brains in their head,' she said, jabbing her finger in his face. 'Why don't you bloody well go and have a look for yourself instead of asking me the same old questions this silly girl has already?' With a jerk of her head, she indicated the young WPC smirking beside her. 'It's a bloody arm, all horrible and bloody.' Her voice was loud enough for the small crowd to hear, and they pressed excitedly forward. Dave turned to the WPC.

'Why didn't you say that you'd already questioned this lady?' The WPC started to answer but was cut short. 'Now do something useful. Get this crowd back and have a ladder brought along. I want to take a butcher's myself.'

A squeal of tyres announced the arrival of another patrol car and Dave organised the operation in a loud voice designed to specifically impress bystanders. In time a ladder was clumsily edged out of the door of the fried chicken shop, cracking a pane of glass, and Dave shakily began to climb up the rungs.

The crowd were buzzing with anticipation.

'It's probably some dog that wouldn't go into the fryer all in one go,' someone said. The manager, already upset at the damage done to the shop window, took exception and hit him. A scuffle broke out and bodies knocked against the ladder, jarring the bulky figure of Hicks halfway up.

'Shut up, the lot of you! If I fall off this ladder, you're all under arrest,' he bellowed.

'On what charge?' asked a man.

'Causing a fray,' said Dave, He had never quite understood what a 'fray' was, although he had charged people for it on enough occasions. 'Now, stand back while I get onto this roof.'

On top of the rickety corrugated metal shelter there were so many objects that he at first thought it was a false alarm and that there was no arm at all. (He could put that in his report later on; 'false alarm; no arm'). Several empty beer cans, one soiled training shoe, a ubiquitous traffic cone and several greasy orange cardboard cartons from the takeaway chicken place lay strewn all over the place, virtually covering every spare inch. Teetering precariously on the very edge of the roof, Dave began to work his way over nervously and very slowly to the middle; it began to buckle ominously, straining under the beleaguered man's great weight. At first he couldn't see anything of interest as cans and debris seemed to impede his every step. He kicked a few cartons out of his path, forming a delightful trompe l'oeil of late 1980s life. And then there it was.

Sticking out of a black plastic sack a hand and length of arm up to the forearm stretched out as though greedily reaching for a discarded chicken bone. It appeared to have been thrown onto the roof and broken free of the bag on impact. Dave wobbled and looked back at the police officers on the ground.

'There's an arm up here. Give me a hand.'

'Why, are you collecting the set?' shouted the man who had made the remark about the dog.

'Arrest that man,' barked Dave.

'On what charge?' asked the PC, squinting.

'Taking the piss,' he replied, climbing gingerly down the ladder. He was really beginning to dislike the nutter.

***

During the next week, the police station was inundated with reports of sightings of men carrying black plastic sacks through the streets of Hackney. Nearly all of them turned out to be dustmen. DCI Hicks had gone on television again to appeal for the public's help, but this time took the unprecedented step of releasing photographs of the recovered body parts in the hope that someone would recognise them. The dental records for the head found on the rubbish dump had so far proved elusive. And so, in living rooms all over the London Metropolitan area the large figure of a slightly jolly-looking policeman loomed even larger, with a blown-up image of a severed arm appearing as a dramatic and ghoulish backdrop behind him.

'Perhaps you've seen this before,' he said, tossing his head to one side indicating the monstrous limb, its fingers outstretched accusingly. 'Have you ever held a hand like this? Has one ever touched you? Have you shaken one like it?'

And then the head.

'Seen this chap around somewhere?' asked Dave. 'Shared a cigarette or a sandwich with him? Have a good look.' Dave paused and winked. 'Have you ever kissed him?' Stomachs heaved all the way from Watford to Welling and Superintendent Haigh wailed and held his own (unsevered) head in his own (unsevered) hands in abject misery.

CHAPTER FIVE
GREY

Clifton Gentle was a perfectly ordinary man. Yes, it was true that he was a killer — a resolute and determined butcher of several young men and well on his way to becoming an accomplished dissector of his victims' corpses, but he was an ordinary man just the same.

When he was a child, he acted as a child. He had normal childish pursuits, just like any other young boy. He was keen on animals, being particularly fond of bringing everyday creatures he found in the garden into the house. How he loved tracking down the small creeping things found under stones and decomposing plants and vegetation that small clumsy fingers could get hold of; the earwigs, spiders, woodlice, earthworms, and ants. Each one could be picked up with grimy fingers and brought into the kitchen to cavort and caper about on the shiny linoleum floor. His good mother didn't object too much, thinking it was all part of a normal, inquisitive phase that every small boy went through. However, she neglected to listen very closely to the childish babbling directed at his charges, and perhaps should have paid just a little bit more attention at times. If she had, then she would have heard her darling son exhibiting an altogether different kind of petulant prattling that bordered on a peculiar form of unusual hatred.

Clifton would try and line up the insects into a form of military parade line, imposing his will on the ranks and compelling them to scuttle backwards or forwards on his special command. The punishment for disobeying an order was a grisly kind of court martial.

'Move right now, all ants,' the boy breathed in his best sergeant major's voice copied from the World War II films his father watched on TV, picking out the ones that had failed and putting them into a matchbox, to be dispatched later on.

'I'm the chief here. The best there is. I'm special.'

The boy loved to repeat this, always mouthing the word 'special' with particular pleasure, as though it was an overripe plum. The ants, woodlice and the rest of the small creatures remained singularly unimpressed and trundled about on their own routes around the shiny vinyl floor, until they too were at last removed by short grubby fingers and squeezed a little too hard for their own good.

***

And, of course, Clifton had friends to play with. The neighbourhood his parents lived in was chock-full of young couples with small children and it wasn't difficult for him to skip outside and find a playmate in the streets. There were many boys of his own age interested in a bit of casual knockabout in jest and freedom. All he had to do was go out and find someone who liked what he did.

***

'Get out, Sticky.' The boys were advancing on Clifton, their jaws thrust out in pugilistic fashion.

'Yeah, get out of it, this is our place. We're building a den here'. Clifton stayed put. He wasn't going to be told what to do by the likes of these. He was in charge; he was a special one. The boys continued to stride across the fallen leaves and branches in the spinney wood towards Clifton.

'Get out of it, Sticky,' the bigger of the two repeated. 'Yeah, get out. Sticky, sticky, sticky. Ha, ha, ha, get out, stick insect!' But Clifton stood his ground.

'No, you get out. I'm taking this place over.'

The expressions of his tormentors' young faces became more serious. Tiny Jimmy Cagneys unused to challenge. Clifton walked over to the bigger of the two and struck his soft, downy cheek with a blow from a flattened palm. A fist, precociously expert, slammed into Clifton's stomach and he doubled up immediately. Kicks then rained in on his shins, while his hair, still a childish blond, received a fearful tugging. At last, the boys left him lying in the earth looking up at the mocking branches of the trees, bruised, bloodied and definitely bowed.

'Sticky, sticky!' the boys screamed into the canopy of leaves as they sauntered off. Clifton was now the insect — and out of his cocoon.

***

And, of course, it was natural for a sensitive only child to be dearly fond of his parents and other relations. He was taken to visit family members often, staying with them on occasion. And no one was more frequently visited than Clifton's grandfather.

***

The back of his neck grew redder and more painful.

'We'll soon get all of this muck off,' his grandfather said, scrubbing violently at the boy's neck with a coarse, wiry, flannel that he held in strong, gnarled fingers. A sharp, bony knee stuck in the small of Clifton's back, as the old man bent the young frame over the cold porcelain sink. An ancient, wheezing, geyser water heater spat occasional steaming droplets past Clifton's cheek, and he feared a scalding if the jet stream suddenly surged, as from time to time it invariably did. His back ached, but he knew it was no good to struggle; the man behind the knee was as tough and obdurate in body as in heart, so the scrubbing continued and even intensified when he resisted. At last, the iron grip began to loosen a little.

'Let's see what other dirt there is on you.'

Now for the real humiliation. Pulling the boy around against the sink so that his arms were pinned to his side, the old man bent over, and with the dexterity that comes with years of meting out torture, peered into his ears.

'Good God!' he shouted in mock alarm. 'Cabbages, spuds and, what's that… I can see a farmer sitting on his tractor ploughing the field!' And this was all supposed to be fun.

'It's going to need an all-out harvesting job to get this lot and no error!' he grinned. 'Now, let's choose which machinery we're going to use.' He picked up a coarse, stiff, rag lying beside the washbasin and fashioned one corner into pitchfork sharpness. Clifton closed his eyes and felt the probe burrow deep down inside his ears until he was sure the liquid running down his cheeks could no longer be just soapy water, but parts of his brains loosened by the buffeting. In a few moments, the old man was attacking his scalp as it was thrashed and flailed before being subjected to a scalding with unbearably hot water mixed with a generous squirt of washing-up liquid.

'We don't want you to catch any infectious, now do we boy?' the old man gamely chuckled, pushing Clifton's head perilously near to the drowning pool of water sitting at the bottom of the sink. It wasn't unknown for his nose to be submerged for up to a minute at a time. When at last this torment was over, and he was to be dried, it was grandfather who again took charge. Despite half-hearted and futile protests, the old man gathered up towels which in their texture resembled rough potato sacking. Clifton's head was continually pummelled and rubbed harshly by the gigantic harsh swathe of material that from time to time cloaked him in suffocating darkness. With an effort he shut his streaming bloodshot eyes and tried to imagine he was somewhere else, anywhere else. Certainly not at his grandfather's house, sent there to enjoy himself during the summer holidays.

***

And when, some years later, the dear old man finally departed this earth, did Clifton not mourn his passing?

***

Outside the small, terraced grey-brick house, a miserable huddle of black-clad mourners stood sentry-like resembling a group of tatty crows. Worse still, when in the dead man's house Clifton was approached by people he'd never seen before, while they spoke to him in friendly terms, they imagined fitting for such an occasion.

'It must be a shock for you to lose your dear old grandad,' one particularly shabby old aunt said to him. 'I know how fond of him you were.'

He let it pass. Everyone seemed so very ordinary in a contemptible sort of way. He thought that only his parents carried on in this manner. At length, the funeral cortège assembled and trailed off to the chapel, which turned out to lay in an even more broken down and melancholy setting than the dead man's house.

And then at last it came — the moment of truth. Clifton felt himself being led up the aisle by his father, now very lachrymose and strangely sweaty, to view the coffin in the damp chapel of rest. Clifton looked up at him and saw a man who looked like he was desperately trying to remember the words of a long-forgotten prayer.

'Take a last look at your grandad, Cliffy,' his father said. Clifton moved closer, and to his astonishment found that instead of confronting the expected closed coffin lid, half of it was folded back and his grandfather's dead face stared sightlessly back at him.

For an instant Clifton recoiled in genuine terror, and wanted to bolt away out of the place, but he managed to pluck up just enough courage, and he stepped back to the brink and peered into the faux-mahogany and ersatz-silk-lined casket. The ridiculous expression worn by the deceased was a shock and his first reaction was to laugh out loud, especially when he recalled the old man's features in life: stern, unbending and occasionally not a little stupid. That look was now replaced by one of gaiety and playfulness, as though somehow Grandad had transformed into a small boy himself and run away from home and peed in his pants for the sheer hell of it. Clifton was surprised to find none of the fear usually associated with the sight of his much-hated relative, and instead he enjoyed an enormous sense of relief. The old man couldn't do anything now — not to him, nor to anyone. The cleric broke into Clifton's reverie.

'And let us remind ourselves that our brother is now entering into a new life with the Almighty in Heaven. We bid his soul rest.'

Bollocks! That wasn't what Clifton saw lying in the coffin; there was no everlasting life for this one; death was final. He wouldn't be coming back. And that was just fine as far as he was concerned.

***

At home later that evening Clifton lay naked on his own bed, trying to recapture the expression his grandfather had worn in his final resting box, stifling some giggles as he did so. Once or twice, he thought he had it off pat, but wanted to be sure, so rigged up the long mirror from the bathroom at the side of his bed and peered at it out of the corner of an eye. The effect was good, but not quite perfect. Some minutes later, and this time after standing for a while in a cold shower and with his mother's cold cream liberally applied to his face, Clifton felt a tremendous surge of excitement when he saw his reflection. He had control over things that he'd never experienced before. He'd become dead himself, and it was wonderful. What he saw was recognisable, but different; a transformation from living dynamic energy to a frozen lifeless state. He immediately experienced an erection and, breaking the inertness, he masturbated joyously, allowing his bedspread to become wet and clammy.

The feeling of intense power experienced at release was unlike anything he'd known before. It was the way, the truth and the light, and it was wonderful. It was the meaning his life had lacked until now. From now on there was to be no going back. Not if Clifton could help it anyway.

***

Sex could be a prickly problem for nearly all young men, and it was no less so than for Clifton, that most ordinary of ordinary young men. Closeted away on his own, as he was most evenings, Clifton lay on his bed working on something a bit more expansive than his physics homework. A mirror, a tub of his mother's Nivea cold cream, and some dark eyeliner were all he needed to enhance the ensemble of death. Nearly naked, Clifton draped a plain white sheet around his slender and suitably cadaverous frame. Taking his glasses off to emphasise the blurred vision and with his eyes barely flickering, he studied the effects of death and early decay upon his features while lusting after his own dead body. Release, when it came — and it always came — was like a translation into another sphere of existence: perhaps Heaven, probably hell. Every now and again, just to make the entire procedure a bit more lifelike (or more appropriately a jot more death-like) Clifton would arrange to take a bath in water as cold as he could bear it. Emptying out ice cubes from the fridge, he slipped into the bathtub and lay for as long as he could stand it, and then, still wet, climbed onto the bed, hoping that he resembled a corpse fresh from the embalmer's tank. At times, moving his limbs to bring about release, Clifton thought he was sacrificing authenticity for the sake of personal pleasure, but that was the price to be paid. There must always be a price; Clifton already understood that. Lying on the damp sheets staring at his own reflection, he realised he'd truly attained power over life and death. He had only to move one muscle to be alive again, but by choosing to remain in his quiescent trance he could dwell in death for as long as he liked. He was playing at being God while shaking hands with the Devil.

***

All young men have childish and naïve fantasies, of course; otherwise, they wouldn't be young men, would they? And, of course, as Clifton grew up, he moved out of the fantasy stage. Nervously sitting at the bar of the *John Club*, he'd felt more scared than he could ever remember.

'Perhaps nothing will happen,' he thought, part-wistful, part in dread. He'd already drunk two pints of fizzy lager and had now started on a series of vodka and tonics. It had cost him quite a bit so far, this evening of sin spent alone. Only some of that cost could be measured in purely monetary terms. At least he'd be free from detection by his work colleagues. All the lads from his office were at the darts match and Clifton had slipped out of that one. A simple but trusted excuse had been enough to secure an exeat, for the evening. He glanced furtively around the club once more. There'd been some funny looks at first. The trouble was that he looked too ordinary. Though not harbouring pretensions to being the trendiest gay venue in town, the nightclub's policy was to encourage a clientele totally unfamiliar to Clifton. Leather jackets, bushy moustaches, upmarket haircuts and expansive gesturing featured prominently. The prancing men on the dance floor fascinated him as they jumped and gyrated without any signs of inhibition. Clifton wondered what they looked like outside; what jobs they did, who their friends were and what their wives and girlfriends thought. If only he felt confident enough to enter this sort of world and comparative degree of normality. He seemed to be an outcast from this life as well.

The rhythmic beat of Wham's 'Wake Me Up Before You Go-Go' was reverberating around the nightclub when all of a sudden something made Clifton aware that the man on his left who'd been sitting alone for quite a while seemed to be leaning across towards him.

'What happens now?' he thought.

He decided to turn around, smile at the man as if he were nonchalantly looking in his direction in any case, and then turn back to face the bar again. He gave himself a countdown of five seconds before he turned.

One… two… three… four… five. He turned round.

'Hallo, lover, how are you doing?'

Clifton was rooted to the spot. He had turned and was now staring a thin, young man with dishwater blond hair straight in the face.

'All right, thanks,' he faltered.

'I'm Tim,' the man said and held out his hand.

'Clifton,' he replied, taking hold of the proffered hand and shaking it as though it were a wet fish. He instantly regretted giving his real name.

'I've never been here before,' he blurted.

'Well, don't worry about that, lover, I won't tell your mother.'

A pause.

'This… this is very embarrassing,' he said, racking his brains and finding nothing to say. 'I'm not really sure whether I should be here at all; it's all very strange to me.'

'Just out of the convent, are we? Well, you'll be fine as long as you stick with me, pet; I'll make sure you won't get menaced. We've all been through it here.' He gestured round the room with a casual wave of his hand — 'and believe me it's no great shakes. Here, let's get you another drink; you look dead parched.' Tim leaned across to the barman.

'Another vodka and tonic for my friend, and a Gay Scotchman for me.' Tim winked at Clifton. 'That's a Drambuie on the rocks, just the way I love 'em.'

A tentative conversation began with Clifton asking questions rather than face an interrogation himself. In his small home town, the 'action' was limited to a couple of places with the *John Club* reputed to be the least intimidating. The various public toilet 'cottages' in the locality were itemised with relish by Tim who gave thumbnail sketches of the numerous characters and town celebrities who inhabited this particular area of bohemia, some of whom were in the club that night. Clifton looked a little downcast.

'Not bored with us already, are we?' asked Tim, flopping a swathe of curly blond hair out of his eyes.

'No, it's just that it all seems so easy for everyone else to live. To live like this.'

'Well, when did you first realise then?'

Clifton peered down at his drink and tried to think how to begin. The alcohol had made him a bit fuzzy around the edges and he was more confused than ever.

'I'm not sure that I have realised,' he said at last, reddening a little.

'Well, we can't have that now, can we?' Tim slid from his barstool. 'Let's see if I can put one or two points straight for you.'

***

Tim's flat was like nothing Clifton had ever seen before, and he'd done his fair share of browsing through interior design magazines in doctors' and dentists' waiting rooms. A large gilt-framed poster of Judy Garland hung over the double bed glimpsed through the open door in the hall, while saucy trinkets filled up every available shelf space and soft furnishings abounded. The overall colour scheme was fuchsia pink.

'Welcome to my Queen's Palace,' Tim hissed in a stage whisper when ushering him in. Clifton sat down heavily on the sofa, sinking deep into its inviting upholstery.

Tim swiftly surmised his record collection and put the needle down on an album already on the turntable, a much-loved copy of *Age of Consent* by Bronski Beat. The strains of 'Small Town Boy' started to fill the living room.

'What are you doing there, you great daft thing?' Tim said to Clifton as he beckoned him to the door. Tim then walked into the bedroom. When Clifton followed, he found the bed being plumped up. Tim walked round it towards him. Clifton stood stock still. His shirt was expertly unbuttoned and peeled off.

'Well, look at this!' Tim exclaimed, running his fingers over Clifton's pristine but rather skinny upper body and arms. 'I can see I'm in for a real treat here tonight.' Now clothed in just his underpants Clifton was pushed firmly onto the bed.

'I'm not sure what to do,' he said with ill-concealed hesitation.

'Just do anything you want, lover. I'll start and you can join in when you feel like it.'

Tim gripped Clifton's shoulders and moved him back onto the bed, or almost into it, as he sank deep down into the soft, spongy mattress and duvet. Straddling him, Tim ran his hands over his body.

'You're certainly all man, aren't you?' he said moving down the torso.

No single emotion ran through Clifton's mind and body. He tried to work out if he was enjoying it. Every time he made an effort to struggle free the unexpected strength of the other man's wiry arms pinned him back down on the bed. The effect of the alcohol hadn't had time to wear off and the room spun slowly on an axis centred on the Habitat paper lamp shade. Clifton felt his underpants being gently pulled off and skilful fingers caressing where he hadn't dare probe himself. He lay back on the bed, in a torpid, motionless state. He knew from experience that he could remain like this for as long as he liked. Amid the confusion that was one thing he was sure of. Drifting away into a languorous, dreamy reverie, Clifton found himself tantalisingly touched by fingers commanded by his body yet separate from it. He was dead again and knew heaven once more.

Tim's breath tickled his thighs, and a rich moistness overcame him. Heaving under the weight of the other man's body, Clifton squirmed. Try as he might, he couldn't keep his body as still as he wanted. The bucking motion at the base of the bed intruded into the secluded delight and, attempting to stop the rhythm, and he felt himself once more restrained by powerful limbs. Tim grunted as the full force of Clifton's resistance pushed his mouth out of position. He grabbed hold of the legs and sat up.

'Now it's my turn, before you lose interest' he said. The intrusion into his privacy annoyed Clifton. He had been forced to open his eyes and break the spell. He was alive again.

'Get off me!'

'Oh no, you don't get away from me that easily, lover. I want my share of this before you flounce out on your jolly little way. Come back here.'

Tim lunged at the retreating figure in an attempt to turn him over but met with some unexpected opposition. The initiative remained with Tim, however, and as he grappled, Clifton felt his own urges ripening to fruition.

Clifton looked at Tim's face, tight-lipped in combat and now appearing much older and pinched. Wrinkles creased up around the mouth while the eyes became more slitty and bloodshot. Disgust swept over him.

'Get off me, you fucking queer!'

He took hold of Tim's free arm and twisted it at an acute angle. The screams of pain broke the mood and Clifton managed to slip from beneath Tim and, still holding onto his arm, threw him against a bedside cabinet, sending a lamp in the shape of a Stetson-wearing cowboy crashing noisily to the floor.

'How dare you touch me,' Clifton bellowed. 'You're nothing; you don't deserve to be in the same room as me.' He picked up his clothes from the floor and started to dress.

'Where the hell do you think you're going? You're as bloody queer as I am. I can see it as clear as day, Lady Muck.'

Clifton reeled around and looked down at the weeping figure still sprawled on the carpet. Pulling on his shoes, he stepped across the room and kicked Tim straight in the mouth, instantly breaking a couple of teeth and knocking his head against the wall with a sickening thump. Standing over the body, he stamped on the exposed groin and Tim screamed out once more, only this time louder than before.

'Apologise to me,' hissed Clifton. Tim was in no position to disagree.

'I'm sorry, I'm sorry,' he repeated until at last Clifton lifted his foot from the tangled and bloodied mess and walked towards the door.

'No one tells me what I am!'

He was already too painfully aware of what he was.

When at last he heard the flat door slam, Tim dragged himself off the floor and pulled himself along the hallway to the bathroom. He examined his face in the mirror through badly swollen eyes. He tasted blood in his mouth, which now started dripping down his chest. Nausea washed over him. He rushed over to the toilet pan and vomited, sobbing in pain and humiliation.

The next man wouldn't be so lucky.

***

Clifton didn't remain a novice for long, though. No one ever expected the course of true love to run smoothly. Time itself determined when the great moment would come. And how.

***

He lay in his bed. From where his head rested on the damp pillow, he could see the curtain blowing softly open in the night breeze. The room was reassuringly warm and still, and in the darkness, Clifton had no idea what time it was. The ticking of his bedside alarm clock suddenly seemed to get louder, and he casually looked down at the expression on the face of the man beside him in the bed and smiled. Very lightly, he ran his forefinger across the man's lips, feeling the delicious warmth on the tip, making his heart beat a little faster. Here was another person, lying calmly and naked next to him; this was living.

Virginity was, at long last, a thing of the past as far as Clifton was concerned. The two had made love, slowly and with enormous care and affection. The man knew Clifton was nervous; he sensed it as soon as they held hands on the way back to the flat.

'Don't look so worried, it's going to be all right you know; I have done this sort of thing before, even if you haven't.' He paused, noticing the all too evident signs of apprehension portrayed in Clifton's manner. 'I won't do anything to hurt you, sweetheart.'

'I know you won't' Clifton replied.

Earlier in the evening they had drunk half a bottle of tepid white wine while listening to Madonna's *True Blue* album on Clifton's cassette player. Robert was very charming, and the two got on like a house on fire. It was clear there'd be no difficulty at all. It was going to be very casual: no problems, no complications. One hour later Clifton had finally consummated his contract with destiny, entering into both a new state as well as a new life. As well as being very skilful and gentle, Robert was also extremely communicative, not to say vocal. Throughout lovemaking he let Clifton know exactly how he felt and let him know what he wanted him to do. At first Clifton tried to block out the man's voice, but he soon learnt to accept it and then actually found himself enjoy listening to it. At the outset, as well as telling him what he liked doing, Robert also told him what he liked being done to him and, all things considered, it was a remarkably successful defloration. The combination of drink and music coalesced, and it seemed to Clifton, lying in a stupor of ecstasy, that the two men were actors in a film with a soundtrack powerfully directing their actions and emotions. When at last the cassette tape stopped and the machine turned itself off with a sharp mechanical clunking sound, Clifton sank back onto the pillow, falling into a languid slumber.

Upon waking and surveying the room, he studied the man lying next to him. The figure remained motionless. Robert's hair was still gelled and spiky on top, but a few lone strands waved ever so slightly in the caressing breeze. Slipping out of bed and standing by the open window Clifton relished the cool night air wafting across his naked chest.

Parting the curtains, he peered out into the garden. The bonfire was ready for lighting, built up quite high after his morning's weeding, and the borders were neat and tidy just as he liked them. It all seemed very restful in the shimmer of the moonlight. Smiling he went back to bed and got back in beside the body.

'Just one more time, darling.'

Picking up the man's legs, Clifton straddled the body and started stroking the finely muscled chest and stomach. He shook with pleasure and began rocking to and fro. The body moved with Clifton, swaying across the bed in an arc of pure abandon. Clifton soon came to release and lay on the already cooling frame, slowly drifting back into sleep.

The next morning Clifton covered up Robert's body with the sheets and pulled the duvet up to his chin, keeping the curtains drawn and went off to work.

Returning home that evening at the usual time, he pulled the body out of bed and took it into the bathroom before clumsily washing it. He took special care shampooing the hair to avoid getting any into those baby blue eyes, and then having dragged the body back onto the bed he re-dressed it. Noticing the bulging pockets of Robert's jacket , he discovered that they contained some keys and money as well as an A-Z of London. The keys and wallet went straight into the litter bin, while the money went to one side with the other bits and bobs.

There was a driving licence in the name of a Mr Robert Clements, Flat 7, 46 Meridian street, London, N1, a kidney donor card, credit and cheque cards, a book of first-class stamps and a couple of membership cards for gay clubs: the *Factory* and the *Rinx*. They went in the ashtray while he transferred the stamps to his own wallet. The A-Z guide went onto a bookshelf to be used later. He ignored the cash, leaving it uncounted on the side. After all, it was only money.

Clifton prepared his evening meal without hurry, got one set of cutlery out of the kitchen drawer and one plate out of the cupboard, and sat down in front of the

TV set with his vegetarian soufflé and mung bean salad. He watched the news and then a game show followed by a rather unimaginative detective drama. When the news finally came on again, he got up, took his dirty plate out to the kitchen, and did the washing-up. Back in the bedroom, Clifton bent down and kissed Robert full on the lips. The eyes still stared open, but the limbs had become quite pliant once rigor mortis had worn off. Clifton got more excited as the evening wore on. It was an evening to savour; just the two of them and a night of passion ahead.

Back in a trendy Upper Street bar in Islington, Robert's friends waited impatiently for him to arrive.

'I knew you should have rung him at work today to remind him,' one said rather petulantly.

'Found something or someone better to do with his time, more likely,' replied another.

The friends continued drinking before bumping into a couple of other friends and making the most of the evening.

'He'd forget his own funeral, that one.'

But the next day, phoning him at work, one of the friends, Simon, discovered not only that Robert wasn't there, but that he hadn't turned up the previous day either. Simon had no luck when ringing him at home. Other friends and acquaintances were contacted, but none had seen or heard from him. Finally, and with much trepidation, he rang the police and reported Robert as a missing person.

Simon accompanied a couple of constables later that evening as they gleefully smashed down the front door of Robert's flat and began the search. He watched their expressions change to disappointment when during the search it became clear that there was no dead body present. Everyone who knew Robert was interviewed. None knew, or said they knew where he was on Monday evening. Everything fitted into place: for the police it was the same old story — gay man disappears after casual sex. End of story. Probably dead but may just turn up later. Who gives a shit anyway? Probably better off dead anyway, the fucking queer bent bender.

Clifton kept Robert for just over a week until the weather suddenly turned for the better and Robert's body turned for the worse and an unpleasant odour started to fill the flat. It was clear that it would become increasingly awkward to keep him concealed.

While at work his behaviour aroused an unwelcome interest. Paul Craven, a chap from a neighbouring office, was the only one around his own age and certainly the only one who spoke directly about sex.

'Christ, I wish I was still single like you, Gentle,' he said in a lewd undertone one lunchtime. 'I'd give it to a couple of these new girls in "Enquiries". You want to get yourself in there, nice and tight, know what I mean.' Clifton told him that he found that sort of misogynism disgusting and increasingly tried to avoid him.

And then his boss started talking.

'You a bit on edge about anything, Clifton?' asked Mary Wilson.

'No, there's nothing the matter.'

'You sure? Only you seem a bit quieter even than usual. I might be able to help. I can be a pretty resourceful woman, you know.'

Clifton attempted a half-smile. 'Everything is fine. It's just that I've got a few things from home on my mind at the moment.'

Narrowing her eyes and adopting a look of pantomime confusion, Mary pouted at him alarmingly. 'Clifton, you're involved with someone, right?'

He looked back at his boss and this time gave her a full beaming smile.

'Yes,' he said, 'but we're not sure if it's going to work out.'

Needless to say, it didn't work out and eventually Robert had to go. He was just becoming far too smelly and before you knew it, love's first bloom wilted and faded to nothing. Nothing but bluebottles, anyway. That weekend, when the Rattenburys from the flat upstairs went away on one of their yuppie weekends in the country, Clifton was able to gain access to the garden in privacy and Robert became the first to end up on the bonfire.

He never wondered how he had come to kill Robert. He'd simply woken up in the morning and there he was, already dead before he even had to think about how to kill him. Life was like that sometimes.

***

Wide awake in his bed, alone, at five o'clock one morning, he tried composing a poem to express the way he felt about his life based on a troubling story he had read when a boy. It was called 'The Drawbridge'.

A drawbridge had been built between a castle on an island and the mainland. An infected man was kept at bay by the mainland inhabitants who provided him with food by leaving it at the gates of the castle each morning. They withdrew, allowing him to wind up the drawbridge. Although wanting to remain separate, the people retained their sense of honour and morality, according to the terms of a contract struck up with the infected man. One day, though, the man noticed the people had not come across the drawbridge with food; they'd completely forgotten. It was a long way to the other side and cry as loud as he might, the man couldn't get the people to hear him. Growing weaker by the day, the man decided to revenge himself upon the people when death finally struck. Tying himself down on top of the parapet, he waited for the end. When at last death came, so did the vultures and other birds to feed on his cadaver, and after feeding from the infected corpse, the birds flew back to the mainland, carrying the deadly virus to infect those who had forsaken the man in his hours of greatest need. At the end of each stanza appeared the line:

'The Drawbridge stayed up'.

For Clifton, that drawbridge always stayed up.

***

Over the years, Clifton's collection of photographic erotica had grown substantially. Mostly culled from newspapers, magazines and Sunday supplements as well as from the odd library book, the pictures depicted various scenes of men, both young and old, lying dead. It was really quite amazing how many such photographs had been published in the cause of promoting human knowledge. Their faces all seemed to portray a curious sense of peace and well-being. With no sign of any outward injury beyond the odd discoloration around the eyes, there was a complete lack of blood or disfigurement. The men depicted might just as well have been on the verge of waking from a deep, relaxing dream, about to stretch and remember their everyday worries and concerns. Shortly after Robert left, Clifton slipped his cassette of the soundtrack to the film *Top Gun* out of its case and put it on the tape machine while he took the photographs into his bathroom and set fire to them. As the flames blistered the enamel around the bath, and smoke started to swirl out of the open window the ashes begun resting on the bottles of shampoo and tubes of toothpaste.

Clifton started to sing along to the tape, realising that he knew all the words to the fifth track.

'Take my breath away' he said, to no one in particular.

CHAPTER SIX
GREEN

'And don't forget to hand over the special offer coupons before you pay at the till. They're on the sideboard with the list.'

Showing obvious distaste and with his mum's words still ringing in his ears, Dave hastily snatched up the tattered scraps of paper torn from the local freesheet newspapers and trudged miserably from the house. Mum was lying upstairs in bed with 'the flu'.

'Why me, Mum?' he'd pleaded at first. 'Can't you get someone else to go?' But after some maternal prompting tinged with a heavy dose of expert persuasion, the dutiful son eventually agreed to go to the supermarket and do the shopping for both their weekly groceries. Much to his chagrin, Dave noticed that the shopping list was written on both the front and back of the scrap of paper he had been given and was heavily annotated. ('Nice bit of Pork. nice Not measly ask Him if I will LIKE it.') Dave reluctantly clambered into his car and started off towards the shopping centre.

'Bloody waste of time,' he muttered.

Yes, the nutter was still out and about, yet here he was — the greatest detective in the country and what was he doing? Bleeding poncing around, trundling back and forth, fetching and carrying for an old woman when she could quite easily get up and do it herself. 'Flu,' she said. What was wrong with a simple cold, but of course it always had to be flu nowadays, didn't it? Dave's lower lip curled slowly but surely upwards, almost covering the top one completely by the time he met the first set of traffic lights just as they turned red.

There was a slight pang of remorse. Perhaps he was behaving a little uncharitably? It was true that Mum usually did all of his shopping and cleaning and laundry, so why shouldn't he step in just this once? Quite simply because he had much more important things to do. If he was an ordinary run-of-the-mill sort of chap, it might be different, but he had a tremendous responsibility. For the past three days he had appeared on a plethora of television and radio news programmes, telling the nation what he was doing in the hunt for the nutter, and now here he was setting out to get fillets of fish (not TOO bony), and jars of jam and pickle (big Not little Teeny ones) for his old mum. It just wasn't right. If the nutter knew what he was up to he'd laugh himself stupid. That's if he wasn't completely off his bleeding head already. None of the greats had to contend with this sort of thing; you couldn't very well imagine Sherlock Holmes nipping down to Tesco's for a packet of teabags, could you? Dave got to the shops and began to park in a spare space outside the greengrocers first of all, but a white minivan nipped in just as he was reversing. He wound down his window.

'What do you think you're doing?' he shouted at the emerging driver.

'Telling you to fuck off,' the driver replied and strolled into the shop. Hicks thought of arresting him for the profanity, but knew it wasn't worth the bother.

'I've got bigger fish to try,' he said to himself.

After a fifteen-minute search for a space in the expensive multi-storey car park he finally managed to squeeze into one situated beside a concrete pillar and succeeding in slightly scratching the side of one door and dislodging a bumper.

'I'll tell them it was done chasing someone,' thought Hicks, 'and get the boys in the station to get the repairs done in the machine shop.'

He retraced the route along the high street to the greengrocers. Mum had been most insistent about getting all the fruit and veg there.

'They don't have such nice stuff at the supermarket; best to get it all fresh at Hanratty's. He always has the best and he's such a lovely man.'

Once inside, behind a gaggle of old ladies, Hicks noticed that the man who'd stolen his parking space and sworn at him was serving customers. People referred to him as Mr Hanratty. Dave got into a muddle behind one woman, unsure of which type of oranges to get and subsequently lost his place in the queue, only to then forget to buy any at all when he was served at last. Fortunately, he hadn't been in the police service for years to no avail. Fixing evidence was second nature.

'Bugger it,' he thought, 'I'll get them in the supermarket — once the nylon netting's taken off, she'll never spot the difference.'

He was forced to take the shopping back to his car in stages as both flimsy plastic bags split open and leaked onions, tomatoes and, ironically, leeks along the pavement. The tomatoes were nearly all squashed anyway, having been stuffed by Mr Hanratty right at the bottom of the bag under five pounds of potatoes. As it was, Hicks had to stash one of the bags on the ground floor of the car park, right by the lift shaft, while he devoted all his attention to the most ruptured bag. It was the sort of thing they'd taught him on police training courses at Hendon called 'damage limitation'.

Arriving back at ground floor level after hurling the bag of bruised fruit into the boot of his car, he discovered that his hidden bag had since been uncovered and kicked open by some youths and its contents had been strewn about the place, with some resting in what looked suspiciously like a pool of urine. He heard voices calling out obscenities as he stooped to pick up whatever could be salvaged and thrust the remnants into his coat pockets. Walking around the corner and trudging gloomily up the few stairs into the supermarket itself, Dave was beckoned towards the antiseptic embrace by the Mecca of the Western World. Stepping forward gratefully, he was received within.

Whereas outside all seemed to be dirt, decay and filth, inside the supermarket it was always clean, fresh, bright and comfortably within the sell-by date. The neon lights and irradiated food saw to that. Inside the store there was no crime, no pestilence and no shortage of wealth. Life could be had cheaper, in greater variety and with less effort than ever before. That was the wonder of shopping the *U Like 2 Save* way. As the advertising slogan said, 'It's all served up on a plate!' or at least it would be if you could find everything and get it home.

Listening to the tinny muzak being played in speakers around the store, Dave couldn't help but feel happier. Taking hold of his trolley he trundled it around to the fruit and veg counter. Shopping here was less personal and accordingly so much more convenient, and he gleefully stocked up with what had been lost, chucking in a pineapple for good measure. At the next aisle he started dropping large tins of soup on top of the soft fruit. He smiled. There was a soothing smell of baking bread, and nice little old ladies swarmed all over the place. There was the odd man here and there, but he was mainly surrounded by twinkly crones pushing enormous wagons of goodies. Sometimes it was great to be alive.

Suddenly Dave felt a sharp pain in his ankle and exclaimed. 'Aaaaarrggh!'

He turned round to find an old hag craning her neck towards a shelf on her right, all the while continuing to push the wheels of her trolley into Dave's ankle. He removed his foot from the carnage.

'Excuse me, madam, but you've just pushed your trolley into my leg.'

She peered at him through filthy grime-covered spectacles.

'Pah!' she said and steered her mountain of food around the detective chief inspector and on towards a display of tinned ham. Dave decided to say nothing and bent down to rub his ankle gingerly.

'It's not worth the trouble,' he thought through gritted teeth.

Waiting for the white-haired menace to wheel her trolley into the next aisle, Dave inspected the note Mum had given him and moved off to find the tinned meats. Mum hadn't given specific instructions about any particular brand to buy, so he used his skills of deduction and decided to get the cheapest ones available. Reaching up he took down a tin of corned beef and looked for the price label but couldn't find one. He put the tin down and picked up another. This too carried no label, and he was on the point of reaching up for a third time when he was jabbed in the ribs.

'They're one pound forty-nine pee,' said a woman so tiny and wizened that at first Hicks couldn't see her. 'I see you looking, so I thought I'd come and tell you. One forty-nine; it says on the side here.' She indicated a price mark on the rail beneath the shelf. 'They don't have labels anymore; it's all done on the laser.'

Dave didn't have a clue what she was talking about, and his first reaction was to edge away.

'The tins have this funny mark on them,' the old woman persisted, 'and when they takes it from you at the checkout, they moves it over their X-ray beam, and it tells them how much it costs.'

Hicks still looked quizzical; the woman was obviously deranged. However, her voice only became louder and more insistent.

'Look, none of them have got labels on,' she expostulated, plucking tins from the shelves at random before thrusting them under Hicks's nose. Another trolley squeaked by, while its driver scrutinised what she thought were two suspicious furtive figures.

'Bloody shoplifters,' she muttered.

Hicks heard the comment, but ignored it, instead feeling honour bound to examine the tins proffered by the old biddy before agreeing that none of them appeared to have any price labels.

'See over there? That girl at the checkout is passing all the stuff over the laser beam. It's just like *Star Trek*,' she said.

Dave saw with astonishment that the old girl was indeed right. Remaining a little puzzled, he looked back at the mountain of corned beef tins.

'Can you tell me which of these is the best to get?'

'Chip-chop, that's what I get. Pass me one down from the top, will you?' Then she added in an undertone, 'That's where they put all the new stock. I don't want any of the ones that have gone rancid.'

Hicks again did as he was told, and the woman promptly scuttled off, leaving him once more alone in the aisle. He was beginning to feel irritated again, reinforcing his determination to let Mum continue to do all his shopping in the future. Pulling the list from his pocket an apple dropped out. It was the only one to have so far escaped a bruising. A lanky youth wearing a brown nylon jacket with *U Like 2 Save* emblazoned on the breast pocket approached him.

'You've dropped an apple, sir,' he said, offering the fruit to Hicks. 'You have to put them in one of the cellophane bags.'

Hicks eyed him with contempt.

'It's mine already. I bought it in the greengrocers in the high street.' He snatched the apple back from the boy, replacing it in his pocket.

'It looks like one of ours,' the boy persisted, keeping a trained eye on Dave's bulging pockets. 'Are you sure you bought it elsewhere, sir?'

Hicks exploded.

'Of course, I'm bleeding sure. I'm a policeman.' The boy stared some more, decided not to follow up the non sequitur and loped off.

'What the bleeding hell am I doing here?' wondered Hicks. 'Talking to senile old bags and spotty youths in a blasted shoppers' paradise. I should be out in the real world, a man's world, catching the nutter.' And then he saw little Alfie Skuse. Listlessly sweeping a virtually hairless broom over by the fish counter while he crammed a filched pork pie into his mean, little mouth Alfie cut a less than distinguished figure. Every now and then he stopped sweeping altogether and scratched at an armpit. Dave, head down, wheeled his trolley over to him.

'Hallo, Alfie, old son. What brings you out into the light?'

Alfie turned abruptly and attempted to squeeze out a thin smile.

'Oh, Detective Chief Inspector. Now of all the plods in the entire world, you're the last one I would have expected to see in here.' Dave momentarily grimaced.

'Well,' he said, 'I'm sort of... undercover. But more to the point, Alfie, what are *you* doing here? Not going straight at last, are we?'

'Oh, Detective Chief Inspector, now don't think the worst of me, will you? Course I'm going straight. Well, in a fashion anyway.'

'What do you mean by that?'

'Well, it sort of dawned on me, during my last brief spell inside, you know. I really appreciate what you done with helping reduce the sentence and that, and I thought, I'll really give it a go next time.'

'That's right enough, Alfie. And remember I could have got you off scot-free, but that would have been too easy for both of us.'

'Yeah,' said Alfie, his anorexic smile almost expiring. 'I kept saying to meself what's two years anyway when a great man's reputation is at stake.'

'Quite right,' responded Dave, nodding sagely.

'So anyway, I managed to get this poxy job and make up me money with enough Social Security benefits so I can afford to live in a mangey, little flat in Hackney and go to the pub once a week.' Dave looked disapproving. 'But not so I'm sponging off the state at all. Don't get me wrong, Detective Chief Inspector, after all I have to think of all the expense, I've put everyone to already, don't I? What with all those free, hot meals in the nick and everything.'

'Bleeding right,' said Dave, nodding earnestly.

'So, what I'm trying to say is this. You got anything else you need? Any eyes out for the prize? For a price, this time.'

'You? Are you asking to be my grass? Am I that green? Now don't be funny, Alfie.'

'Why not? If I done it before I could do it again. Remember I can go places you and your lot can't, especially now you're so famous and that. I see things you can't see and hear things you can't hear and if I got a little backhander every now and again, who knows what, I might see and hear a little more, if you get my drift. There's always got to be something you want.'

108

'Or someone,' said Dave a little dreamily.

'Come again?'

'Nothing. Nothing at all. But I tell you what, Alfie, why don't you give me a bell later on this week. I might be able to help you out with a little job after all.'

Fumbling in his pocket for some paper, he tore Mum's shopping list in half. 'Bread,' it said. 'Two Large Loafs White and brown with bits in.'

He scribbled down Alfie's telephone number, and reluctantly resumed his shopping expedition.

Standing at the delicatessen counter he greedily shoved a few lumps of 'EEC surplus' brie into his mouth from the runny pile of free samples and made a face. When at last the assistant behind the counter stopped pretending to clean the knives, Hicks asked for a pound of mature English Cheddar. He was most particular that he wanted English Cheddar. As it said on mum's note 'English. Not Foreign MUCK.' As he put it into his trolley, he noticed that he had instead been given some sourced from 'several countries in the European Community'.

'I wanted the English Cheddar,' he said to the assistant, who was now dealing with another customer. 'Excuse me?' There was no reply. 'Miss, you've given me the wrong cheese.'

'You'll have to wait your turn if you want something else. Can't you see I'm busy?'

At long last, Hicks was nearing the end of his ordeal. By then he had been required to help another old

lady by lifting down a jar of apricot jam from the top
shelf, only to discover that it was the last jar of its kind
and also featured on the now notorious list: 'Apricot
jam. One Jar. Absolutely NO OTHER KIND'. He took
a jar of grapefruit marmalade instead and was on the
point of trundling down the last aisle when he heard a
voice calling out to him.

'Excuse me, sir.'

He turned around to see the idiot boy in the
supermarket livery he'd spoken to earlier, hopping from
foot to foot next to a man dressed in a brown suit with
matching tie and wearing a ridiculous red trilby hat.

'Can I have a word, sir?'

'What about?' Hicks said abruptly.

The hat stepped forward.

'I'm the manager, sir, and Steve here says, that you
might be a little confused about where you bought some
apples. Would you mind emptying out your pockets for
me?' Hicks looked on helplessly as his morning turned
from bad to bleeding awful.

'Yes, I blinking well would mind,' he said, 'and I'd
like to scorch that rumour right away.' He fumbled
around in his jacket pocket before producing a very
official-looking badge. 'There, that's my Metropolitan
Police ID.'

He also fished out two bruised apples and a number
of tattered onions.

'And I bought these at the greengrocers in the high
street. When my bag split, I had to put them in my

pocket.' He decided to omit the bit about the others being trampled on and kicked into a yellow puddle. 'And this lad,' he continued, pointing to the boy, 'has been poking his nose in where it don't concern him.'

Turning around with the utmost dignity, he walked straight into a mountainous display of tampons. As he sprawled for a good yard or so along the highly polished surface of the supermarket floor, Detective Chief Inspector Dave Hicks screamed silently to himself. After the manager had helped him to his feet and put his things back into his trolley and pockets, Dave trudged wearily up to the checkout till with the grace of one already beyond despair.

'All this and I haven't even done a thing today about catching the bleeding nutter,' he thought, as the electronic whine of the cash registers crashed about his ears. 'He's out there, butchering people and making my life a misery. It's all his fault — this morning, every morning. He'll pay for it when I get hold of him.' The queue moved forward a little more. 'Oh, yes and when I've got him, I'll stick him in clink for ever. So, fast his feet won't touch the ground. I'll have him bang to rights all right. I'll have the bleeding nutter, just let him wait and see. Just let him wait and see.'

Alfie wandered up to the next counter and sloped off smirking, holding a pack of dried mung beans that lacked a barcode. The queue sighed in anticipation of a lengthy wait.

Dave's own queue inched forward again. The woman in front had already emptied the contents of her trolley onto the belt and Dave started to place his items behind hers. With a reaction so swift that Billy the Kid would have been jealous of it, the woman snatched the 'Next customer please' sign and slapped it down between the two sets of provisions, painfully pinning one of Dave's fingers in the same instant.

'I'm not paying for your stuff!' she spat.

In a few moments, the torture was almost over and all the items on the list were packed safely into shopping bags at the end of the belt.

'Fifty-nine pounds and ninety-four pence please,' said the cashier in a voice betraying the mundanity of modern life. 'And thank you for shopping the *U Like 2 Save* way.'

Dave Hicks grimaced and handed over the money in cash, forgetting to hand in the special offer coupons which mum had given him, and which remained in his breast pocket.

At the next queue, carefully placing the pack of now fully priced up mung beans into his own carrier bag, Clifton Gentle watched as a tubby man with a full beard, bright blue glasses and very red face rushed out of the supermarket while several provisions dropped out of a hole in the bottom of his torn *U Like to Save* shopping bag and rolled across the floor.

CHAPTER SEVEN
INDIGO

It was approaching six o'clock as the dusk started to ooze down around another dank late September Piccadilly evening. Stark neon lights began flickering on as the growing crowds started to assemble in search of any form of entertainment to cheer up an otherwise miserable and disappointing start to the weekend. Most people were generally milling about with nothing in particular to mill about for. The larger cinemas around Leicester Square leered through the thickly pigeon-infested trees, their slogans glinting on and off while unsubtly advertising the dubious charms of the various films on offer:

'DOUBLE TROUBLE' — So bad you'll need to forget it. Twice!

'CANDY BABY!' — The sweetest little thing on the block;

and 'LONE DOG' — THEY said he wouldn't dare return. What THEY said didn't matter anymore.

Jimmy Nichols blinked up at the signs. He wasn't really interested in films; it was artificial escapism and he needed something more tangible.

The smaller and shabbier 'exclusive' cinemas to the north of Shaftesbury Avenue were more to his taste anyway, although not for any cultural or aesthetic reasons. The clientele that Jimmy was interested in lurked around the sordid little porn film houses around 'Olde Soho'. They were a mixed bunch. There were older men, ugly men, desperate men, frustrated men, shy men, men who would, men who couldn't, men who wanted to be women, men who wanted men to be women, men who wanted men, and last, but not least, men who couldn't care just as long as it was nasty and cheap.

'Men' meant money to Jimmy, much as they seemed to for most people in London in the 1980s. Turning a fast buck might mean screwing some poor sucker for all he was worth just to make a few quid profit. For Jimmy, a fast buck was the reward for a fast fuck, and whatever screwing or sucking went on was restricted to the purely physical non-emotional kind.

He swept his long peroxide-dyed hair to one side, just enough to get it out of his eyes so he could get a better look at what there was out there. His style was simple and unoriginally classic; an unkempt, yet pretty vamp.

The old main drag hadn't quite begun to take its toll on his late teenage features just yet and he could still turn heads. It was true that his body wasn't as scrupulously clean as it could be, but then washing was restricted to whatever means one had at hand. A rich man living in elegance could hardly help but keep himself nicely sanitised and scrubbed. Likewise, a man in a modest lodging in London could also do quite nicely, while others in less well-served rooms managed as best they could.

It was quite a different proposition for Jimmy. Ablutions usually involved a furtive use of whatever facilities presented themselves. If he had managed to spend a few hours or maybe the whole night with a man in a hotel room, he might be able to sneak a shower or a quick rub-down before surreptitiously leaving. Otherwise, he was lucky to get to a cracked and stained sink in a deserted railway carriage in the sidings outside Victoria Station where he invariably slept. Because of the nature of his job and all the effort involved in an evening's work he'd end up getting even dirtier. The terms and conditions of his freelance occupation saw to that. 'Shit fun' and 'Water sports' could be pretty hard on anyone's hygiene regime.

This particular Friday evening a number of London's itinerant daily population had tried to take Tube trains out of town early, clambering, shoving and kicking their way aboard one of the hopelessly crammed carriages. Unlike normal evenings, tempers became frayed long before people even got home to their families. The bus strike had made things a little bit more fraught than usual; staff were taking one day's industrial action in protest against the beating-up of a driver by a passenger the week before. It affected almost everyone in London in some way or other, except for the man who had beaten up the driver in the first place since he'd taken the day off work to watch horse racing on television at home. Desperate to escape the city, men and women swarmed out of town by whatever means they could, into the suburbs and beyond, leaving London to those who wanted or still needed it.

Jimmy trailed along looking for a trick. He had exactly three quid on him. That was barely enough for a limp burger and flaccid fries from one of the cheap joints around the half-price theatre box office, let alone a financial footing upon which to base the rest of his life. He had just lost out on one bloke who was hanging around the telephone kiosks. The prospective john was coquettishly twirling his black briefcase when he first saw him and at first sight he looked like a small child with a new toy. However, before Jimmy could get to him, another grimy, pretty boy had gone over to chat him up and off they sauntered; the bloke, briefcase in hand, now looking like a slightly older more autistic brother. The symbiotic arrangement was held together by a bond of mutual distaste.

Jimmy glared as they moved off into the encroaching indigo dusk before looking around for whatever, or whoever, there was to be had. It was getting much darker now and somewhat easier for a bloke to approach and be approached. Despite the attention of the illuminated crowd and police within the Square, there was still some subfusc privacy to be had.

After almost an hour of casual approaches and studied glances, all to no avail, Jimmy decided to wander out of the area and towards its more immediate confines.

A breeze started to blow up and Jimmy shivered as it cut through the thin material of his fake silk blouson bomber jacket. He recognised that the summer had now ended and felt the cold wind more than most on account of having been up and about on the street since six that morning when he was obliged to vacate his train carriage. It was made worse since the jacket had to be unzipped to reveal his thin fishnet T-shirt underneath. It was supposed to make him look more alluring that way. Jimmy decided to look in on a pub or two to get warmed up a little. If there were any blokes to be had he could try his luck, otherwise he'd push off as there was no point in wasting any money on drink.

Walking halfway up Erith Street, he peered into the window of a pub he'd used with a fair amount of success in the past. The air in the street perpetually stank of cheap, cloying Chinese food, but it was more refined tonight, the steamy glutinous oriental goo transformed into something exotically delicious, and Jimmy felt an acute pang of hunger deep in his stomach. He glanced in through the window and saw a gathering of prospective blokes; quite a good gathering as well. It might have had something to do with the bus strike with people avoiding the rush, but it was the beginning of the weekend after all, and Londoners were still keen on enjoying a night out. Pushing open the door he was

117

instantly punched in the face by a muggy, smoky fug which bundled him in like an affectionate thug. Almost everyone in the pub was smoking heavily and the exhalations of stale air and fumes meant that it was quite an effort to see past a few yards, but it also helped to make him feel less obtrusive. Sidling up to one promising-looking bloke, he made the slightest of body contact and smiled at him, showing well-proportioned and surprisingly white teeth. The bloke, obviously on his own, smiled back.

'Hello,' said Jimmy, still smiling.

'Hello,' said the bloke, and Jimmy could tell that he was safe and that everything would be okay. He'd been wrong in the past, but so far not fatally.

'Do you want to buy me a drink and have a bit of a chat?' said Jimmy, moving a little closer and slightly lowering his voice.

Although it was overhasty and the line uttered too suddenly, Jimmy instinctively knew that this was already the make-or-break moment. The bloke seemed quite self-assured and without even looking over his shoulder, said that he did; what was it to be?

'Lager, thanks.'

'Two pints of lager, then,' Clifton Gentle said to the barman.

***

Two hours later they were both seemingly quite drunk. Jimmy felt that he hadn't genuinely got on so well with a bloke for ages. If ever. He'd spent his last precious three quid paying for part of one round, and the bloke had fortunately offered to buy all of the rest. This was a bit better than having to work for it, although that part of the employment contract would come later of course; it always did. Finally, they staggered out of the pub, strangely warmed by the chill of the beer. Jimmy felt woozy in the night air, leaning lightly against his newly found friend. Neither of them seemed ready for the evening to end just yet.

'Where do you live?' asked the bloke.

'Where I can, usually,' said Jimmy.

'You fancy another drink?'

Jimmy just shrugged his shoulders.

'If you want to keep spending money on me, I do,' he was tempted to say. It was all up to the bloke.

'All right. We'll go along to a little after-hours drinking club I know.'

Jimmy went along with the idea, after all the bloke had the money, and Jimmy had the mouth, or bum, or prick, or whatever it was that the bloke wanted. And anyway, for once he actually liked the bloke, so he was quite content for the two of them to use each other.

As they walked along the now empty streets, the bloke brushed his hand over Jimmy's hair in a confident, almost affectionate movement. Perhaps tonight, Jimmy thought, I've made a friend at last. A proper friend.

Rather than going into a West End drinking club and running the risk of being stranded with no emergency night buses running, the bloke suggested that they catch the Tube and head for a bar that he knew in North London near where he lived. Once inside he continued to prove good company and they sat snuggled up in a comfortingly dimly lit corner, ordering more drinks. The bloke leant closer to Jimmy and lightly kissed his cheek; the smell from his breath by now stale and beery. But that was okay, thought Jimmy; people were just people. He remembered what his sister used to say — 'Even the Queen has to take her knickers down when she goes to the bog. She's just the same as you and me, silly stuck-up cow!'

But that was before his parents threw him out and he ceased to be a legitimate person in the eyes of the world. As the bloke talked, Jimmy's eyes began to glaze over through his alcoholic blur.

Conversation continued to flow, mainly about the past. No mention was made of the present, or for that matter the future, just the past in all its glory, tarted up a bit after a seduction with time. Each seemed to be studying the paths that had led to this chance convergence. They were so different, yet so stunningly and mundanely similar. It seemed they were made for each other. At last, the bloke stood up, swaying a little, and announced that it was time to leave.

'While we're both able to stand,' he said.

Stepping out of the pub, they had the honour of a door being held open by a burly bouncer. Jimmy pondered at the change. Doors were usually slammed in his face. A light drizzle was still falling, but the bloke just took a long breath of fresh air and allowed the mist to settle on his face. He smiled.

'Come on, let's get a cab', he said, touching Jimmy very lightly and tenderly on his cheek. 'I'll see you're all right tonight.'

***

In the taxi, Clifton let his hand fall on the boy's knee and kept it there during the journey, taking care for this act of intimacy to remain out of sight of the driver. Opening the door to the communal hallway, Clifton found his mail still on the floor, with one envelope clearly showing signs of being trampled upon by a muddy shoe.

'My neighbours — they won't even pick up my post from the floor. They couldn't give a damn what went on in this house.' He stuck the bills in his pocket, together with another letter from his mother, and struggled with the key until at last he managed to open the door to his flat. He expertly and instinctively knocked on the light switch with the side of his head and pocketed the keys, looking back to see Jimmy still leaning against the landing wall.

'Come on in,' he said leading the crumpled youth into the living room. 'I won't bite.'

Tossing the unopened letters onto the top of the television set, he turned on the stereo record player, waiting for a second or two for the music to sweep over them, a bit too loudly. It was 'The Miracle of Love' by Eurythmics, full of soothing lyrics about the power that love had to take away life's inevitable pain. Clifton noticed that Jimmy was already half-asleep on the sofa. In the kitchen, kicking off his shoes and swaying to the music, barefoot on the cold linoleum floor, he opened the fridge door and called out.

'You hungry? I can make some cheese on toast or something.'

Not hearing an answer, Clifton slid back into the doorway. For the first time that evening he felt real desire stir inside. The boy lay sprawled out on the sofa, his neck at a crazy, vulnerable angle and his thin legs stretched out, the denim covering them taut and smooth, like a hermetic seal. Clifton moved over and knelt down beside him. He stroked the blond, wispy hair out of the boy's eyes and whispered softly in his ear.

'Let's go to bed.' The boy stirred and smiled.

'OK, but where's the loo?' he asked in an almost shy voice.

When he got to the bedroom Jimmy found a large, tidy double bed all made up and invitingly snug. He sat down on the edge and slipped off his shoes. Flopping down rather unceremoniously, he let his head sink into the fibre-filled synthetic non-allergenic pillow.

His eyes closed for a few moments, then opened a little while he registered the change in mood as the hall lights were turned off.

***

Clifton knew it was a real pity that the boy had to die and almost caught himself feeling sorry that Jimmy was going to be his thirteenth victim. Unlucky for some. Still, that was the way it had to be; everyone was just a number in one way or other, whether that be a National Insurance number, a number in the post office queue or on a list of murders. All the same, Jimmy looked so curiously innocent just lying there.

Kneeling down on the bed next to him, Clifton dropped the ball pein hammer noiselessly on the carpet while peering down into the smiling, peaceful face. A friendly face. Perhaps it would be best not to mess it up when he struck him; that was the least he could do.

The moment had arrived.

Jimmy was suddenly aware of something being wrapped around his neck.

'So that's his little game, is it?' he thought. 'A choker; that's how he gets off.'

With a lithe kick of his young frame, Jimmy suddenly twisted around and found himself straddling the bloke who gasped in surprise. Jimmy's free hands worked on Clifton's clothing until he was forced to let go of the tie and relax his grip. The rent boy was good at his job though and already had Clifton's genitals exposed and responding to touch. He started to move his head in for a closer inspection.

He worked rapidly and after it was all over, Clifton lay prone and outstretched on the covers feeling moist and sticky. He had the tie around his own neck now and it lay there, ridiculous against his otherwise naked body. It had been good. Too good. He wasn't queer, he knew that; it was just that he'd had too much to drink to be able to finish off the job. That must have been it. A wave of shameful self-reproach engulfed him. As if he would stoop so low to do anything with a cheap, little prostitute.

Jimmy could feel the bloke shifting about on the bed. Don't say he wanted it again. Usually once was enough for them after they'd had some drinks, but then perhaps this one was more desperate than most. Or perhaps he had deeper needs? A hand was placed on Jimmy's shoulder, and he felt his head being raised off the pillow. He could feel the silky tie once more being slipped around his neck. It looked like he'd have to really earn his money tonight. Jimmy opened his eyes once more and looked at the bloke. He seemed a bit different now, like a lot of them did; probably something to do with post-coital whatsit. Just as he was trying to see exactly how the bloke's expression had changed, a terrible tug on the tie jerked him into panic.

124

Then a fist slammed down onto his nose, squashing it halfway across his face. The tie was dropped momentarily while his groin was punched hard.

Jimmy tried to cry out, more in pain than in any attempt to raise help, but another thump in the crotch reduced his voice to a whimper as he tried to suck some air into his already screaming lungs. He saw the wooden handle of a hammer before it hit him again in the chest and then the man's hands came together around his throat and started to squeeze the life out of him.

He'd never liked rough games at school, but one of the few things he had been good at was a game called British Bulldog. The basics of this were that a gang of boys would rush down one length of the playground while another gang rushed the other way in an attempt to get past the first lot. The winner was the boy who had got through the wall the most unscathed. Despite his light frame Jimmy won quite often, not due to any inherent bull strength, but because he possessed a pair of sharp, painful knees which snapped into opponents' midriffs or chins and enabled him to get past bigger, stronger boys. With a lunge, his knee cracked into the small of the bloke's back, just beneath his kidneys. Jimmy heard him cry out and when he felt the squeeze of the tie loosen, he made contact with the other knee. Bounding off the bed he gave the bloke's jack-knifed body another kick and then grabbed his clothes and rushed in blind panic out of the flat and away from the house. He ran and he ran until the air stung his lungs, but he didn't stop running until his legs hurt more than anything else.

***

The time had come to end it all. Clifton had been caught out at last. That disgusting episode the night before had spelt the end. To have allowed that filthy boy to excite him like that was just too much. Well, he wouldn't have to think about it much longer. The moment had finally arrived. It was called the present. He climbed onto the dusty cane-backed chair. Socks dripped off his toes as though he'd just emerged from a swimming pool full of grey, woolly water. Bitter acrid tears ran down his face and he tried to focus on what he should do now.

Clifton Gentle's tears sprang from sadness, yet paradoxically they inconvenienced him in the current quest to end the misery which was his life. With blurred vision, it became extremely hard to see what he was supposed to be doing. Rocking on the balls of his feet, while attempting to tie the other end of a length of nylon twine from his neck to a cupboard handle two feet above his head demanded the utmost concentration. The wretched thing just would not take hold; the makeshift noose continually slipping out of its knot. He was bleary-eyed but persevered in this moment. His ultimate act.

Following some frantic scrabbling moments, Clifton finally found himself balancing, with the rickety squeaking chair swaying beneath him, but by then he'd worked himself up into a state of rage. In a perverse way his rage wasn't directed at himself — after all he didn't hate himself, but the very act of self-destruction. It was an anger directed not at his own personal failings, but at the need to commit suicide at all in the first place.

With one final lunge to end it all, Clifton hurled himself upwards, arms outstretched holding onto the jolly bright orange nylon garden twine. He missed and was sent crashing to the floor, the chair also giving way and falling at his side with one broken leg digging painfully into his ribs.

In the short moment of flight, the man intent upon his own death did a strange thing. He held out his arms and flailed about in search of support, of something to grab onto and break his fall; his fall from grace. What was he grasping for? As he should have realised, there was nothing to break this particular fall, and the suffering man landed heavily on the thinly carpeted floor. The farcical nature of this moment — a suicide attempting to save himself escaped Clifton's sense of the absurd and he lay in mild pain, glaring with indignation at the offending cupboard handle. In crimson rage he yanked the twine from his neck and wondered what to do next. He stood up, still shaking.

It is said that some suicides, finding that they don't even have the wherewithal to succeed in doing away with themselves, become even more morose and introspective and that their very personality deserts them so that they assume the attitude of the dead, but not dead. They are the ones who can be glimpsed sitting in hospital wards, with a few outward signs of physical damage; a bandaged wrist or head maybe, or perhaps a squashed nose and bloodied fingers. They exist, waiting for nothing much in particular to happen. Visitors arrive, quite regularly at first, and friends and loved ones to whom notes were addressed try to find out what drove them to do it. Employers come along not much later. They are the most difficult to deal with. The potential suicide has to decide whether he or she should laugh it all off and convince the boss to keep them on or try to blame it all on the company and demand some form of redress, while pointing an accusing finger and behaving hysterically. This was more effective if they made a scene and loud enough noise for a nurse to be called and act as witness to the charade. For their part, the employers had to navigate a fine balance between an apparent show of concern while discreetly making surreptitious enquiries as to whether the patient/employee was worth the effort as well as weighing up the number of HR forms they would have to fill in. These hospital visitors leave unpleasantly antiseptic wards believing that they've found the answer as to why poor Bill or Marjory or Duane did it, yet they trudge back to their homes, offices and factories looking much like the people they have left behind; all squashed hope and damaged effrontery.

Within a few days, weeks or even just hours if things are really all that miserable, the visits begin to trail off and are instead replaced by jolly cards and pedestrian letters crammed with talk of meals enjoyed, films watched, fields of daffodils glimpsed or accompanied by photographs of young baby Bryan. Dreaded communications from employers arrive by the hospital bedside or on the hall mat, stiff both in prose and sentiment, informing the intended suicide victim of his or her employment rights, or simply stating that 'unless a return to work is not effected by Monday the 27th, then he or she should look elsewhere for wages/salary/succour.* *(delete where appropriate.)'

And what of the intended suicide themselves? He or she simply sits and stares and goes through the motions for a while, pondering on failure, becoming an office joke. The person who even fouled up their own suicide. (Probably couldn't organise a piss-up at a brewery, ha, ha, ha!)

Some get better, some get worse. It is often quite difficult to fathom which are which. Sociological studies of attempted suicides digested, popularised and regurgitated for the Sunday supplements reveal that the act of destruction has the potential to be the one great watershed in a person's life; that so many people gain an inner strength and conviction leading to eventual personal success and happiness that it seems like a good enough reason for everyone to attempt suicide. Well, at least once in their lives.

For others — well they simply fall back on the old maxim that if at first you don't succeed, then try, try again. Inevitably, as time goes by, this group attains less statistical significance. These people are the martyrs and examples for other more timorous souls to emulate.

The third major group, as itemised in the surveys, consist of the grey ones — neither one thing nor the other. They may revert in time to the lifestyle they led before 'all that unpleasantness began'. They may well live on quite safely and comfortably for another ten, twenty, or even sixty years, before confessing on deathbeds that they wish they'd succeeded on that damp dismal dawn in September oh so long ago, and that they've simply been biding their time ever since. They smile a thin, watery smile at the outraged assembly of family and care home workers, and slip away into the night on a pillow, if not a prayer.

On the other hand, it's not unknown for some to actually finish what they started years ago and go on to kill themselves after what had appeared to all intents and purposes to have been useful, happy and fulfilling lives, leaving behind spouses, sons, daughters and friends more bemused than upset.

If Clifton had known of this study, and it *was* the sort of quasi-scientific reading that he liked, he would not have been able to categorise himself. He was just a normal thirty-four-year-old man. But he could be far more than that if only he used his imagination. He was the extraordinary nestling amongst the ordinary, the jewel in the pigsty, the Mardi Gras amid the mundane. Clifton sat for some moments, pondering over the main aspects of his life and weighing up his available options. As the dawn light started to invade his flat his attention was arrested by a lone gull circling and wheeling around outside the window. He could hear it calling, eerily screaming a discordant screech. Clifton knew one thing for certain; that things could simply not go on as they had up until now. There was no life at all in a half-completed life. If it were true that he had been put on this earth for a reason — and he believed that to be so — then he must search for that reason, no matter what the consequences.

He stood up and walked over to the window. The gull had been joined by others and was spinning through the grey dull sky in pure abandon, catching the upswings of the wind, revelling in its gift of flight. Clifton wondered what they were actually doing. Looking for food? Mating? He wasn't sure and tried to find a clue by seeing what they were looking at. Attempting to focus on the birds' tiny, cheerless eyes, he watched their forms swoop and swoon around the greasy rooftops, broken television aerials and ravaged tops of trees, but seeing nothing he was just about to turn around and draw the curtains when suddenly… it all became clear. The birds were doing it for fun, for their own amusement! They were free to do what they wished. Well, he thought, if them, then, why not me?

Why not?

Clifton turned and pulled the drab curtains together before switching on the stark central light when he noticed the length of orange twine cast aside on the carpet; the instrument of his intended destruction. He bent down and put it away in a kitchen drawer. He felt so refreshed he could hardly recall the events of the last few hours. A sanguine wave of rosy warmth overcame his body as though he'd just been swathed in a cloak of warm, rich velvet. The luxury of the moment was almost too much, and he felt in serious danger of toppling over, steadying himself like a drunkard against the wall. He had to fulfil some sort of destiny.

Now, destiny is a heavy burden to carry, and Clifton had carried his too awkwardly and for far too long already. He needed to create a little life again. He sat down and remained quite still. A thrill of illicit pleasure flooded through him. He remembered his grandfather's body as it balanced between this world and the next, or at least between this world and the dampness of its final resting place. The sheer folly of death captured on his lined face made Clifton smile. Settling back, Clifton too became dead, and like an inverted Mary Shelley he constructed a monster of false death. Images of lust clambered over Clifton's imagination as he slowly came to release. It was the first time Clifton hadn't needed to see his body in its trance-like state before gaining full satisfaction. Mind over matter, he thought to himself.

'I don't mind, and you don't matter.'

He laughed out loud. That had been what he'd say at school to younger children who were frightened on their first day. That had to be right. To assuage any guilt, he felt about his special gifts, he'd need to fulfil the promise that he had only yet half-delivered. He must allow others to experience the ecstasy and rapture of being dead through life. He must do that to realise his true potential. Singing out with relief and exhilaration, he knew that, like the gull he could be free from the torment of this dull uneventful outer life; he could combine his two lives as one and by that means maybe attain fidelity with destiny. Clifton had achieved something of worth from his intended suicide after all. He'd learned that there was no real difference between life and death.

He thought that the most likely scenario was that Jimmy would go straight to the police and report the attack. There wasn't much point in trying to hide, so Clifton decided to stay put and see what happened. Seeing what happened next was the way that he had led his life up until then and seemed as good a strategy as ever. He could always deny it of course, it was his word against that of a drunken male prostitute.

And if things worked out differently, perhaps he could start living with a more positive attitude. He knew that while Jimmy was still out there he would always be in danger, so he might as well try and finish the job which meant that one day, he would have to make sure that Jimmy was finished off. For good.

CHAPTER EIGHT
CERISE

Sitting at home two weeks later, and still trying extremely hard not to become too obsessed about Jimmy, Clifton wrote a nice, chatty, lying letter to his mother and got carried away. As the pen dashed across the page at a furious rate, a wondrous tale unfolded full of days spent with friends, imminent promotion at work, the ease and comfort of travelling around London and the delightful manners of the people he came in contact with. It was a tragedy that Clifton found he could only write about his life by fictionalising it. With a couple of human limbs in the bathtub still waiting for disposal, he was forced to write of an everyday world of which he knew nothing. After a distressing amount of inaccurate detail, he at last signed off in the usual way — 'With all my thoughts of my parents on this day, your loving son, Clifton.' This was followed by twenty upper case 'X's and seven 'O's; the 'X's being kisses, and the 'O's hugs.

Sighing the craven sigh of a charlatan, Clifton flung down his pen. He wanted to write some more, but in his heart, he knew that he just couldn't face it. There was once a time when he fancied himself as a gifted writer, an intellectual man of letters, but that was before all the killing started in earnest. Killers weren't meant to be poets. Nowadays, he reserved moments of lyrical creation to periods when, as his former English teacher had put it, 'the good lady Muse decides to flutter down from the ether and settle upon my undeserving brow with her fevered embrace'. Fortunately, this was not one of those occasions.

And so, Clifton continued to sit patiently, fidgeting a little, while he waited for a subject to suggest itself. Another minute passed. And then another. None of the topics he came up with seemed particularly suitable. His imagination kept going back to the severed limbs resting in his bathroom; an arm jointed at the top and a leg up to the knee. At least it was an original idea. He'd killed this one three days after Jimmy had got away. Expecting to be picked up by the police the very next day, he was surprised when they didn't come knocking on his door. He decided to get another one in quick before they arrived later on that week.

But they never came. He knew that something was up but wasn't sure what on earth it could be. The rent boy would be bound to turn up sooner or later, either with the police in tow or demanding to be paid off for his silence. He'd deal with him then if he didn't bump into him sooner.

And there was now another temporary guest that needed attention. This one, a particularly big and baggy, old queen was loitering with intent in a dirty, little public convenience near Clapton station, and was despatched with indecent haste. Clifton realised his mistake when it came to disposing of the monster; fat men meant not only more heavy lifting, but more mass and bulk to get rid of.

Clifton considered composing a sonnet or possibly an ode on the beauty of the silent scene in the bathroom, but after a moment's thought, he came to the conclusion that the scene was neither beautiful nor silent. The recent, uncharacteristically warm October weather had resulted in a lot of insects hatching out and the body in the bath had now attracted a large number of flies and as a consequence the flat was filled with an almost constant and irritating buzzing sound.

He turned on the television. A woman newscaster read something about the release of the 'Guildford Four' who had been found to have been wrongfully convicted of IRA bombings, as well as a piece about the rapid increase in the divorce rate. Neither of these developments interested Clifton, but it was swiftly followed by a photograph on the screen of that policeman who was working on his case. Even though Clifton had seen the man before he looked strangely more familiar. The detective's image loomed onto the screen, surrounded by microphones. Clifton thought he looked a bit cocky, stroking his clipped beard with an overly thoughtful look before answering questions in a fairly pompous manner. Sat next to him was another older policeman and this one was hunched deep down in his chair and appeared to be perspiring heavily under the glare of the hot lights. The bearded one did most of the talking, while the other one looked a bit miserable. Clifton sat down on the sofa and turned up the volume.

'Detective Chief Inspector Hicks, how many men do you believe this man to have killed?' asked a reporter holding a BBC-branded microphone.

'That's a difficult question to answer exactly,' he replied, 'but from the number of bodily limbs, torsos and organs recovered so far, we think that the total would not exceed nine.'

Clifton snorted. 'Thirteen' he muttered.

There was another barrage of shouted questions.

'And do you still have no idea about the murderer's identity?' asked the man from ITN.

'Oh no, on the contrary,' said Hicks. 'We have a very good idea what sort of man we are looking for.'

Dave Hicks looked deep into the television lens, and for a second Clifton felt extremely uncomfortable, as though he was somehow being personally scrutinised.

'Undoubtedly this creature is a man unlike others. He'll have no friends; he'll have a worthless job and a worthless life, living alone in squalor as part of an underclass in order to carry out these horrendous crimes. Cutting up his victims and mucking about with them without a care in the world isn't what normal people do. He can be best described as...' Dave paused for effect '...useless scum.'

The large head craned forward to the camera, now almost leaning into living rooms all over the country.

'Ladies and gentlemen, this man is an evil monster, but we will catch him. The British police force is the cleverest in the world and filth like him are no match for us. Believe me when I say that he can't keep away from us for long. I'll get hold of this vile, worthless creature, and when I do, I can assure you that I'll not let him go.'

The hairs stood up on the back of Clifton's neck and he felt his temper rising. He wanted to protest, but before he could even open his mouth, the abuse continued.

'And I would like to take this opportunity of appealing once again to anyone who happens to know anything to get in touch with me. I don't appeal to the murderer to give himself up, because I don't believe he has any compassion or normal decent human feelings to appeal to. This man is a sick monster, no better than a diseased animal. An idiot. Please help us to get him off the streets and banged up where he belongs. Thank you and good night.'

Hicks disappeared from the screen, to be replaced by the newsreader looking suitably stern. Clifton leaped up and turned off the set.

'Bloody idiot!' he shouted. 'Who the bloody hell does he think he's dealing with?' The bit about 'mucking about' with the bodies really upset him. It made him sound like some kind of pervert. The image of the burly man with bright blue spectacles and a full beard once more steamed up in front of his eyes, being practically burnt onto the screen while Clifton's rage developed with greater intensity.

'Useless scum? Idiot, idiot, idiot!' he screamed before slumping back down on the sofa. 'I'll show him who the idiot is.'

Clifton returned to his writing pad. Perhaps that was the way to get back at the fat policeman. He had wanted to put something down on paper for posterity and perhaps this was his opportunity. Once again, his thoughts turned to the grisly limbs lying on the enamel and he smiled. He'd always fancied himself as a writer, only this time it wouldn't be poetry but something a bit more action packed..

***

At the police station three young cadets on full-time letter-opening duty sat reading through letters from assorted misguided correspondents. The mountain of mail had grown quite significantly since the first television broadcast and showed no signs of abating. The letters read much the same; a lot signed 'Jack', or 'The Ripper', and one or two from prize lunatics supplying their full name and address.

'… So, I did it all, you see, to get my own back at society.

Yours Sincerely,

Edward Bundy,

107 West Street,

London

E17 3NR'

During the first few days of their new assignment, cadets Oldfield, Abberline and Slipper diligently read each and every one of the letters, categorising each according to a system devised by Dave Hicks called 'The Three Cs'. They were 'Crank', 'Criminal' or 'Clue'. Letters placed in the 'Crank' pile covered all those which contained a useless and nonsensical tirade against the Establishment penned in the main by outpatients from mental institutions. The Thatcher government's disingenuously named 'care in the community' scheme meant that there were more of those in circulation than ever before.

'Criminal' letters mentioned information which, although not directly connected with the North London murders, could throw some light on other cases of misadventure. Dave had decreed that these should be referred onto other officers working on their investigations, but most of them ended up being thrown away by the cadets who considered they already had enough to do.

'Clue' was the most important of the three categories. It was also the shortest pile. It comprised of those letters where the contents were considered to warrant further investigation. So far, the cadets had put only four letters onto this pile; mentioning places and modus operandi which matched what the police already knew. There was a hint of malice in all four. However, the cadets' diligence didn't last long. Perhaps Dave should have personally stressed how important this apparently menial job was or maybe he should have changed the rotas around to avoid boredom. Then again, he could have used more experienced officers and not gone for the budget option of employing rookies to do the job, but whatever the reason, the cadets' disaffection with this tedious task meant that the letters were barely perused at all and an ever-increasing proportion of them were chucked straight into the 'Crank' bin. And this was where Clifton Gentle's letter was dumped only a few short hours after it had been delivered and read.

It consisted, as many of them did, of sentences made up of words and letters snipped from magazines and newspapers. It read:

'HICKS — ConsiDer this — A Man called Flo0d will Tell you

ALL You need to KnOw — after all HE is Number 13 and theE LAteSt,

BUT is Quite ArmLesS.

RegaRDs,

Mr?'

Clifton felt quite pleased with himself. It had taken quite a bit of hunting around for all the appropriate letters. He'd written, giving Hicks the name of the last victim who was found without any limbs. Only the murderer would know this. It would show that blunderbuss that even with a head start he couldn't catch him. He was also pleased that he put the record straight on the number of killings, including those despatched and burnt of which Hicks obviously knew nothing.

For the next few days Clifton scrutinised news reports with even greater interest than usual, expecting to see his handiwork displayed on the TV screen or in the newspapers. He'd be bound to get top billing in the case now instead of that idiot policeman with his foolish theories. At last, there'd be a real focal point; the murderer himself as the organ grinder, and not that monkey detective.

But nothing happened. The only news consisted of that tubby policeman repeating the same vile lies about him.

'We're too clever by half for him. I can assure everyone watching that the days of freedom for this beast are numbered. He's not got too much up top, that's pretty clear and it can only be a matter of time before we put an end to his foul perverted cravings.'

This enraged Clifton beyond belief. 'Not got much up top!' He was special, not just any old murderer; he had a Mind and a Mission. And the 'pervert' tag again; that was going too far. Staring at the screen with utter contempt he started with a jolt as he became increasingly worried. Why hadn't they mentioned the letter? They must have found it; the details were so clear and would have stared out at anyone reading it. Unless, of course, it was a trick; something they were keeping back to fool him. Something to lure him into making a mistake. Perhaps Jimmy had been in contact with them after all and was luring him into a trap? What had happened to that blasted letter?

It wasn't fair that only the police could comment on the killings. Clifton must have his say; it was becoming all too one-sided. Whatever happened to freedom of speech in this country? There it was again; that voice stabbing away at him from the television screen as Hicks continued.

'There's no way on earth he'll get away from us — these crimes will not go unpunished. We've got him cornered, and as long as the great British public keep their wits about them, we'll have this creature inside where he'll have plenty of time to try to turn himself into a human being. If that's at all possible.'

This was absolutely monstrous. Clifton had never had to listen to such outrageous lies in all his life. What was all this about crime? He'd show them a crime if they wanted one so badly. How about this for starters: a so-called detective who couldn't even follow up a clue when he was served one on a plate.

***

Jacqui Lane voraciously slit open the mail dumped on her desk by the super-keen post boy flashing a smile that was not reciprocated. Jacqui had been the first woman crime reporter to be employed by a major national paper three years ago and she was still the only one in Fleet

Street. And not only was she good, but she was also sexy. Slickly determined, she used her charms to ample effect when dealing with policemen, judges and male members of juries who she approached. With her raven-black glossy shoulder-length hair, gorgeous red lips and long stockinged legs she, like DCI Hicks, always got her man, or at least his attention. It wasn't that she didn't see herself as a feminist, but that the best way of promoting the interest of her sex — and her career — was by promoting her own sexuality. This particular morning, she was trying to think of a new angle about the 'North London Murders', which she preferred to call them. Mulling over a possible story based upon the concept of the murderer-making a 'cry for help', she casually tore open the dozen or so letters personally addressed to her.

One in particular stood out. There was some very tortured script on the envelope, with the letters remarkably angular, as though someone was attempting to conceal their handwriting. Probably another love letter from a wet dream merchant who'd seen a photo of her wickedly gorgeous body in the paper.

The thought didn't upset her. Even the tiniest of ego boosts helped set her mood for the day. A Polaroid photograph fell out and before she picked it up, she read the accompanying letter with a growing sense of apprehension.

'Dear Miss Lane,

I enclose a photograph of human body parts that I cut from the corpse of a young man called Nigel Flood. I have already sent a letter detailing this to the police, but they appear to have ignored it.

Perhaps you would be so kind as to bring the photo to their attention, as it seems that they need all the help they can get.'

It was signed by a 'Mr?'

Excitedly focussing her dagger-like eyes on the snapshot, Jacqui saw what did in fact look remarkably like an arm and part of a human leg, lying curled up on the bottom of a white enamel bathtub. She stared at the picture, unable to believe her luck. Snatching the letter and photo from her desk, Jacqui stalked into the editor's office, taking just a few seconds to touch up her lips with her vivid cerise shaded lipstick.

'Good morning, my darling, and what can I do you for?' her editor asked lasciviously.

She handed him the letter.

'Read that, Charles. I want to lead with this in tomorrow's first edition. I'm sure it's genuine.'

Charles Manson skimmed through the letter before scrutinising the photograph.

'When did you get this?' he asked.

'Just now. I opened it up with the morning mail.'

'This is dynamite, Jacqui. Contact that chap in charge of this investigation and get him down here immediately. I think we're going to run this as an exclusive. We will retain picture rights until tomorrow morning, and I want you to get some sort of medical opinion on these limbs; probable cause of death, how they were dismembered, was it the work of a doctor or an amateur, that sort of thing. And try to find out anything about this Flood man while you're at it.' He glanced up at Jacqui, still standing wide-eyed in the middle of the office floor.

'I've already started that, Charles,' she lied. Manson's eyes glazed over in lust and wonder.

'Well, go and finish it,' he snapped.

As she turned to leave the office, her pert bottom came into view and Charles experienced a rush of blood as the curves twitched beneath the tight skirt. He made a play for it, but she was too quick, and instead blew him a kiss, as she slipped out of the office. Charlie Manson heaved a sigh of intense frustration.

'Outrageous!' he moaned. 'My God, she's absolutely bloody outrageous.'

***

Dave Hicks was sitting in his office, tugging away at his spruced-up beard and humming the theme from *Z Cars*, when the telephone rang. He didn't want to pick up the receiver immediately and instead opened a drawer to turn on a tape recorder connected to the phone.

The tape was his own idea. He knew the killer would try and contact him sometime, especially if he

146

kept up the abuse on television and in the press. Or at least, Dave thought that he knew.

As he had said to the superintendent, 'We've got nothing else to go on, so we might as well give it a try.' The look of resigned discomfort on Superintendent Jim Haigh's face said it all but was misinterpreted by Dave as adulation.

He let the phone ring one more time. Perhaps it was that grass Alfie Skuse with a lead or even the killer himself. He could get a recording of his voice which he could broadcast across the country as a way of identifying him. It could be the vital breakthrough. He picked up the receiver.

'DCI Hicks,' he barked. 'Who's calling?' It was a woman's voice.

'Jacqui Lane from the *Herald Review*. Detective Chief Inspector, could you come over to our offices right away? I've been sent something through the post that I think is from the murderer. Your murderer.'

Hicks kept up the gruff voice. 'What sort of something, Miss Crane?'

'Er, that's Lane,' she said. 'I'd rather not discuss it on the phone you understand, but it really is awfully important.' She had put on her little girl lost voice. It worked.

'Right. I'm coming straight over. And don't move a muscle until I get there, Miss.'

Dave had by now managed to secure a driver to ferry him about. He justified the request on the grounds that a successful resolution of the case depended on a solution being 'thought out', and by being driven around by someone else he would have more time for thought. To the mortification of the lads at the station, his request was immediately granted. So here he was, sitting in the back seat of a swish unmarked ebony black Daimler, flicking a few papers which had slipped out of his shiny new briefcase, a recent present from Mum. Dave skimmed over the details of his intended speech for the afternoon press conference. Extra insults, a bit more stonewalling together with a new note of aggression in his voice. Mum herself had suggested the latter.

'You look like you're trying to find a stray cat, not a murderer,' she'd said to him while hoovering his living room the evening before. 'Why don't you act a bit angrier and show some emotion? People respond to that.'

Arriving at the newspaper offices, he was ushered up to the editor's suite, and introduced to Charles Manson and Jacqui Lane. He was in no mood to be trifled with.

'Right, I'm here. You have my undevoted attention, now what do you want me to see?'

They looked a little affronted. Perhaps he was just overdoing it a little with the aggression.

'I mean, I'm a very busy man. What is it you'd like me to take a butcher's at?'

'It's this, Detective Chief Inspector,' said Manson, sliding the package over. 'It came in the morning post, addressed to Miss Lane.'

Dave examined the envelope with painstaking care before even opening it up.

'Ah,' he said, eventually getting round to reading the letter inside. 'It looks like we're getting closer to Chummy.'

The editor and Jacqui looked at each other quizzically.

'Chummy?' she asked, arching her eyebrows.

Dave smiled to himself. His beady little eyes seemed to sparkle behind the enormous blue frames of his glasses, and he relished the moment for a second or two before replying. Respect, pure respect for a professional. They all had it and knew how to use it: Holmes, Poirot, Marlowe and now… Hicks from Hackney. He carried on the pause for a little too long, almost prompting Jacqui Lane to ask her question again.

'Chummy is my little name for the nutter, Miss Lane, my pet name if you will. Although when I catch him, I won't be leaving out a saucer of milk.'

Charles Manson saw he was going to have to do something to move the interview along in the right direction.

'Detective Chief Inspector Hicks, we've taken the opportunity of carrying out your eminently sensible advice in doing what we can to assist the police in this matter and have already sought a medical opinion concerning the condition of the body. We intend to publish the findings of the examination in tomorrow morning's edition of the paper. If you'd agree to delay announcing the disclosure clue, we'll make sure that we inform the public with the full details. With the benefit of your considerable experience in these matters, would you agree that the public can only take in a certain amount of information at one time?'

'Well, speaking from experience, I would.'

'And so, you have no objections to us retaining ownership of the photograph until, say tomorrow at noon?'

Dave readily agreed. They could do whatever they liked with the snap. It was all coming together nicely. After he had left the office the newspaper people laughed uproariously.

'I never thought it would be as easy as that, Jacqui. What did you say to him on the phone to make him so tame? I've never come across such a compliant policeman in my entire career.'

Seizing on the chance to impress, she lied convincingly.

'Oh, you know the sort of thing, Charles. One or two things I've picked up since working in this business. A little bit of flattery and a lot of sizzle.'

Whatever it was, it was hers, and it was going to be the biggest newspaper scoop of the year so far. As her editor made another lunge for her behind, Jacqui beat a less hasty retreat, allowing him to grope her for a tantalisingly few moments. After all, he'd been very good for her career so far, and it was the least she could do. They were almost family.

***

Clifton left for work earlier than usual that morning. Arriving at the news kiosk, his eyes fixed immediately on the front page of the *Herald Review*. It featured a photograph of his bathroom, and beside it a copy of his note sent to that tarty woman reporter. This cheered him up momentarily, but after reading through the story he became less pleased.

'Printed with the full endorsement of DCI Hicks… our own medical evidence points to an evil, warped mind behind the series of incredible crimes… detection by crime reporter Jacqui Lane… unknown whereabouts of Mr Nigel Flood… last seen alive on his way to a pub in East London… full confidence in methods of DCI Hicks… efficiency of modern police force… forensic evidence to be revealed at today's press conference by DCI Hicks… DCI Hicks… DCI Hicks… DCI Hicks…'

Damn DCI Hicks!

They'd let him get away with it, the fools! The letter and photograph seemed to have backfired, and it made him feel curiously uneasy. What were these 'other' leads? It must be that bloody rent boy, Jimmy. But then *he* must know where Clifton lived, so why didn't he lead the police straight to him? There wasn't even any mention of the first letter sent to the police. His mind was alive with questions that he wanted to put directly to Hicks. No one called him names and got away with it!

**

The press conference at noon the next day was like a showdown in the old Wild West. All the reporters began loudly voicing criticism of the recent developments and smarted at the granting of an exclusive to the '*Herald Review*'. Throughout the proceedings Jacqui Lane sat impassively, running a smooth, tanned hand through her silky long jet-black hair. Smiling occasionally whenever her name was mentioned, she resembled a particularly glamorous movie star. She even had the regulation perfect white teeth while her gorgeous cerise lipstick and figure to die for dared others to doubt her role as the current queen of crime journalists.

Sadly, Superintendent Haigh got a pasting from the majority of the press boys, and he almost choked while defending Hicks's tactics. What was worse for him, the strategy appeared to be paying off. How loathsome was the prospect of admitting that the blessed, little jumped-up fatso might have been right all along?

Dave all the while swelled up throughout the conference with the importance of it all, while he remained uncharacteristically taciturn. He knew it didn't matter if there was criticism now. He could take it. They'd all taken it in the past; it was natural that unorthodox schemes would be too much for other mere mortals to understand. It shouldn't be too long before things became very different. And the prize would be his. That showed real genius as well as courage; not minding if he at looked like an utter prat if it worked out in the end.

At last, the anger subsided sufficiently for Dave to address the meeting. The Metropolitan Police were well and truly on their way to catching their man. The photograph of the body parts in the bathroom was invaluable and at this moment copies were being made widely available to the public, together with all the forensic evidence.

'There's no doubt in my mind that this photograph is genuine and that the dismembered corpse recently detected is that of a Mr Nigel Flood. We have our clues — we'll soon have our man.' He flourished Clifton's letter like Neville Chamberlain holding the Munich Agreement after stepping off the plane in 1938. 'This will lead us to him. I've instructed my officers to start searching through magazines and publications to discover where the various words and letters came from. When we have that information, we'll know what he reads and what his interests are and that will be an enormous advantage. The police and press are working on this hand in hand. We'll put all the pieces together in our time.'

153

He stood up, waved at the journalists and swept away, like a boxing champion after a prize bout. Superintendent Jim Haigh, knocked out by the effort of restraining his temper, could do nothing but smile thinly and follow sheepishly out from the ring, with his white towel slung between his legs.

***

Watching television at home Clifton became even more incensed. Initially he'd been cheered up by the openly antagonistic tone of the other reporters, but he now felt cheated. The whole thing might be too much to bear; his patience had been sorely tried. All this and Jimmy still to contend with. But he just had to carry on. After all, this had become his life; his mission and there was only one course of action open to him.

***

'But if we do that we'll end up with crap on our faces!'

Dave was again having to justify his plan to the chief. He was also getting the better of the argument. Mum's advice about being a bit more forthright was certainly paying dividends. He was getting real respect at last.

'If we ignore the killer himself and just concentrate solely on the murders themselves, we'll never hear another dicky-word from him. All my sources say the same thing. I've got to keep up the pressure this way.'

Jim Haigh was fed up.

'And by "sources", I suppose you mean my old nark that little weasel Alfie Skuse?'

Dave just smirked back at him. All the time he kept trying to argue cogently and dispassionately, but he returned time and again to the injustice of it all; the sheer bloody unfairness of not only having a lunatic butchering people on his manor, but to have Hicks of all people put in charge of stopping it! The monstrous, fat fool was having a whale of a time enjoying himself at his expense. Meanwhile here he was — a really decent good old-time copper who'd served his time and should now have been in the position of looking forward to a spot of hard-earned and well-remunerated remission.

Just under a year until retirement. But there was no stopping the big blue whale. Haigh finally crumpled, floundering against the tide. He was the one who was beached, but at least there was no one else at hand to witness the wet manner in which he submerged. How had it come to this? Losing an argument to someone who couldn't even express it properly in the English language? The door opened and an officer handed Dave a sheet of paper.

'Oops!' he said. 'Looks like another bit of body's been found. I had a feeling that something else would turn up.' He looked back at his superior officer with an

'I told you so' smirk. 'Would you care to come and have a butcher's, sir?'

'No, I would not,' Haigh replied testily. 'I don't suppose there's anything I'd be able to help you with.'

To his disgust, Hicks gave a cheery nod of his massive head. That was the last straw.

Stalking out of the office, Jim Haigh set off for the relative peace and quiet of his own offices; just the constant pestering from his superiors and the Home Office wanting to know what was going on every fifteen minutes. But at least it got him away from Hicks. Soft, comfy seats, kindly old tea ladies and polite subordinate officers who smiled and said 'Good afternoon, Superintendent Haigh' as though they almost meant it. That's where he was off to.

***

Emerging from the back of the Daimler, its door being dutifully opened by his driver, Hicks arrived at the crime scene. He sprang into action, giving instructions to search the immediate area and rope off the entire patch of waste ground to stop members of the public from trampling everywhere and spoiling the nice new site. He was truly in his element.

'As happy as a pig in shit,' as one of the constables on duty observed.

Indeed, Dave was in the very best of moods.

'I'm afraid the super won't be able to lend us the fruits of his considerable wisdom this morning,' he remarked to a couple of detectives. 'He's gone back to headquarters in a bit of a hurry. I can't imagine why!' The detectives laughed the hollow laugh of sycophants. Dave had always been adept at hurling these barbs and, like small pieces of jagged metal secreted in jars of baby food by would-be blackmailers, they always left their mark.

The search went on for the best part of the afternoon, and Dave even decided to forego the pleasure of appearing in front of the second press conference of the day. With nearly all of the photographers at the crime scene anyway, there wasn't really much point. Precious little came of the search, though, and by teatime it had got far too cold and dark anyway, so the operation was all but closed up. An arm and a leg. That was the sum total of the day's work. They had been stumbled upon by a couple of teenagers while climbing through a fence behind a giant advertising hoarding displaying an 'AIDS' awareness poster.

They spotted the grisly remains a few yards into the waste area, and reported the discovery immediately from a heavily vandalised, but still operating, telephone box along the road. There were times during the next few hours though when they wished that they hadn't. Interrogation after interrogation followed, carried out on Dave's express orders, while they were held in the self-styled 'Incident Wagon'. Quite clearly most of the policemen believed the kids' story, but it wasn't enough for Dave, who wanted to know exactly what they were up to. There were enough used condoms scattered around to have made that quite obvious, but Dave wanted everything checked and then double-checked. Eventually, after the crying got on his nerves, the teenagers were allowed to go home. Dave thanked them most earnestly for their assistance.

'And don't let it happen again!' he cheerily called after them as they disappeared through the hole in the fence. The medical boys took the arm and leg away for tests, but said it was a good bet that they were the same ones in the photograph sent to Jacqui Lane. Dave looked pleased with himself; Chummy was evidently getting a bit impatient. Dispensing with his personal driver, Dave climbed into the Daimler and picked up the car phone.

'Alfie!' he boomed. 'It's me, DCI Hicks. What have you got for me?'

Alfie Skuse was smoking an increasingly reedy-looking roll-up whilst skimming through the local paper and continued to flick listlessly through it during the course of the conversation.

'One or two little titbits I've heard on the grapevine, Detective Chief Inspector. Why, what do you reckon they're worth?'

'Your neck probably, Alfie. What is it?'

Alfie stared at the Classified Ads in the newspaper. 'It might well be to your advantage to take a look at the

Cortina Estates,' he said glibly. 'Reg numbers with a P in them.'

'Right, right,' said Dave, scribbling away. 'What else?'

'Oh, not much else at the moment,' Alfie said, flipping towards the back pages. 'Just that the Sunday park football scene might prove interesting if you know what I mean. Sort of a spot the ball thing.'

'Very good work, Alfie. Now tell me something else, won't you?'

'What?'

'You have been very careful, haven't you? No one has any inkling as to our relationship. In a vocational work-wise situation, I mean.'

'Course not. No one knows nothing at all.'

Hanging up the phone on Alfie, Dave immediately dialled Mum to tell her to get tea ready before setting off for home. For once he didn't bother to listen to the news programmes on the car radio, and instead inserted a somewhat reluctant cassette tape. A country and western tune rattled out of the tinny speakers and Dave sang inaccurately along as the music howled away over the creases in the tape.

''Cause I'll make me your wifey to be,' he growled.

Indoors, Mum had set out an enormous plate piled high with pork and lamb chops, kidneys, sausages, mushrooms, bubble and squeak and mashed potatoes, while three thick slices of bread and butter jostled with each other on a side plate. Everything was dripping in butter, glistening golden and inviting, looking like the sun rising just before it suffered a fatal cardiac arrest. The mashed potatoes had been made with double cream and Mum started dishing them up the moment she heard Dave's car approach. She always knew when it was Dave because the squeal of brakes had more authority, the slam of the car door carried more weight, and there was invariably much jangling of keys as he strode towards the door.

'Hello, Mum,' he boomed from the hallway, 'that smells good.'

'Come on in and eat it up before it gets cold. You need it more than ever with all this business going on.'

'Not long to go now, though. I've had a few more breaks.'

Mum clattered around the kitchen, putting the final touches to the gargantuan 'afters', and made an 'I'm interested' noise.

'Another bit of body turned up today. I'm well and truly on to him.' He speared half of one of the chops with his fork before shovelling it deep into his mouth.

'Mwohnt bhe long befohre I put the cuffhs on him.'

Mum emerged from the kitchen, sitting at the table to admire her boy eating his good dinner.

'I knew you'd be hungry,' she said in triumph. Watching the whiskered jaws moving up and down in steady rhythm, she had to stop herself from becoming mesmerised. She had always encouraged a good appetite and Dave had never disappointed. 'I've got you a pudding and custard when you finish with that.'

Dave smiled and nodded while some of the food made a brave attempt to escape through his open mouth.

'Thwanksh, Mum,' he said, inadvertently spitting some potato over the back of his hand. It took Dave just under six minutes and thirty seconds to finish off the meal, and he then slumped back in his chair, allowing Mum to whisk the plate off to the sink and let him rest for a short while before commencing his assault on the pudding. Dave had read once that Napoleon took no more than four minutes over any meal, and he strove to keep up with the Imperial table manners. He himself usually took longer than four, but then the Frenchman had only been a little bloke, and Dave was more substantial and probably needed more grub than a midget. Still, he was able to sit back and feel pleased that he had done quite well in the time it took to polish it off. He always thought more productively about cases after a big meal.

There were enough limbs and heads down at the morgue now to start assembling whole people. All you needed was something to link them all together; something to tie up the loose ends.

'Do you want some skin?' said Mum.

'Eh?'

'This here, on the custard.'

Mum proceeded to pour thick yellow goo on top of the red pie.

161

'Er, later please, Mum. On a separate plate.' That was how Dave's father had liked his custard skin. Yet, he had been different in so many ways from his son. He hadn't bequeathed much to his son, just his table manners, but never mind. That's what mums were for; to improve their sons into images of themselves.

After she'd eaten her own meal at a more leisurely pace, Mum brought out a steaming pudding to Dave, who was hunched over in an attitude of acute anticipation, with his spoon gripped upright in a large hand.

'Cherry pie and custard!' Mum announced grandly while presenting an enormous portion in front of him.

Mum also had a second plateful. 'I shouldn't have any of this myself, it's for you really,' she said as the man mountain scooped heaps of scalding stodge inside his slavering mouth.

Dave was a surprisingly silent eater; the spoon seemed hardly to touch the bowl as it dredged the goodness out and into his sticky mouth in one rapid, fluent motion.

'So, you've got a better idea of what this bloke looks like?' Mum asked.

There was a longish pause. Dave didn't quite know what to say, but he knew that it wouldn't be easy to put Mum off the scent.

'Well, not exactly.'

'But I thought you said you were on to him. What are these new clues you were talking about on the telly?'

Some more custard found its way down into the abyss.

'Oh, this and that,' he said in a slightly less forthright tone.

'What do you mean "this and that"? Her eyes stared keenly.

What so commonly occurs in police interrogations occurred now; when the chips are down and he has found himself in a tight corner, the suspect will often lose his composure and panic. He will contradict himself, display a hitherto unseen nervousness and perhaps get aggressive. On the very few occasions when Dave's emotions did give way to anxiety, he found himself resorting to rudeness.

'You don't know everything you know, Mum.'

'Well, I know that if you say something on the telly about knowing who the murderer is, you're supposed to tell the truth. If I was in your shoes, I'd be a bit more careful about what I said, my boy.'

'I'm the detective in charge of this investigation, Mum, and I know more about this case and policing than you ever will. You don't understand the way things are done in a murder investigation, and I strongly suggest that you keep your nose out of it.'

A swift, sharp slap across his bearded cheeks sent tears rushing to Dave's eyes and he abruptly stood up from the table, the empty bowl crashing onto the floor and breaking in sticky pieces.

'Don't you ever think you're not too old for a slap, young man! You're still my son, no matter who they think you are on the telly, so don't you ever say anything like that to me again, do you hear?'

He stood in front of her, smarting with remorse and pain. His podgy hands trembled with fear.

'I'm sorry, Mum. I shouldn't have spoken to you like that. It won't happen again. I promise.'

He stood gently swaying in front of her for a second or two on the balls of his feet until neither of them could take it any longer and they fell sobbing into each other's arms. They were all they had in the world. They had to get on.

CHAPTER NINE
LILAC

The water gurgled down the plughole and Hilary West (neé Ellis) hauled herself gingerly up out of the bath. Her leg was in plaster, following a road traffic accident with a police car which was in hot pursuit of another vehicle. She had been crossing the road outside work in the rain, just as the car turned too sharply out of a side road and bumped her into the gutter, causing a shoe to be lost forever in the process. The record breaking recent extraordinary downpours of rain had left the country in a state of damp depression. Meanwhile, in Berlin there were seismic events as the Cold War appeared to be coming to an end and the Wall was being torn down. There was a lot of international tension, and a world war wasn't out of the question. Life might never be the same again, and yet she couldn't even go to the shops!

Clifton, however, had been wonderful. Hilary had only met him a week before the accident while, of all things, waiting for a number thirty-nine bus. They were the only two people at the bus stop, in the middle of the first torrential rainstorm that swept in during late

September. The bus seemed to have made up its mind that it wouldn't ever bother to turn up when Clifton gallantly offered to share the protection of his umbrella. Hilary was at first unsure and declined, but he looked so hurt and sincere that she immediately changed her mind and the two started chatting.

'I moved in over there last year,' said Clifton, pointing to the oxblood facade of a house just across the street. 'It's surprising that I've never seen you before.'

'Well, you know what it's like living in London. You can live next door to someone for twenty years and never even know their name.'

'As long as that? I'd never realised.'

They arranged to have the odd cup of coffee every now and again, and soon became real friends. Somehow, Hilary never felt that Clifton was a threat in the same way she did with some men.

He wasn't the sort to challenge her lifestyle or fashion sense or say any of the things her other female friends would, and she particularly appreciated his lack of interest in her love life. Being separated from her husband she found that most of her long-standing friends still saw her as half of a couple and had long since stopped recognising her as a woman in her own right.

'I do so hope Hilary will find herself someone soon,' her best friend Valerie complained. 'It's just too awful for words trying to balance numbers with her in dinner parties.'

In reality, of course, her friends were more afraid of their own loneliness than that of Hilary herself, not that there was anything to be afraid of anyway. The transformation since those early days of complete and utter despair was strangely soothing. If she compared the calm she experienced now, to the days of her disastrously tempestuous marriage she was grateful to be living the uncomplicated single life again. And now, just as she'd managed to lug the plaster cast onto the bathroom mat, there was a ring on her doorbell.

'Blast!'

There simply wouldn't be time to get to the door on her one good leg before whoever it was had given up and gone away. Frantically she tussled with a dressing gown before flinging it to the ground and hopping as fast as she could to the door with her crutch swinging against the frame and chipping off some more paint. Pulling the door open she saw Clifton, who grinned and held out a big bunch of vibrantly coloured lilies.

'I thought you might need a lift, so I brought you these.'

Hilary smiled, balancing awkwardly on one foot while she gave him a customary peck on the cheek.

'A lilac lily lift! Thanks very much, you're far too sweet. Come on in, my hero,' she said.

Clifton followed her into the flat, tenderly supporting her by the elbow.

'How have you been?' Hilary asked, while noticing that he looked none too happy.

'Oh, pretty good,' he said unconvincingly.

Hilary could see that his eyes betrayed signs of sleeplessness. Although never particularly tanned, she thought that his face looked even more pallid than usual. Clifton sank, while Hilary swayed, onto the large paisley patterned beanbags that lay on the living room floor; one of the last vestiges of an almost forgotten student past.

Clifton realised that Hilary was still clutching the flowers, so heaved himself up and put them into a vase and made coffee, sipping at it as he went over the account of his day. After about five minutes of fairly pedestrian narrative, he realised the tedium of his tale and stopped.

'And what about you? Have you seen anyone recently?

'Not a soul. And it's been wonderful! No, I mean, I like to see you; well, I mean it's always good to see you when you pop round, it's just that...'

'That's all right, I know what you mean. I'm not likely to take offence and cut off your supplies. I know I'm sensitive, but I'm not paranoid.'

They both laughed.

'I know what you mean, though. It's good to be alone sometimes. I was an only child and learnt to treasure my solitude and take comfort in it as well as sometimes resenting it at times.'

'It's so good not having to bother about any of the usual everyday things, like what to wear and having to go to work. It's been great; they keep on about me not going back until I'm really ready and feel up to it. As if I'd struggle to get back to the daily grind. No, I'll make sure that I will only go back when I'm fully recovered.'

'When do you think that will that be?' Clifton asked.

'In about three years, with a bit of luck!'

They both laughed again. Hilary looked at her discarded dressing gown lying on the floor.

'I'm sorry I'm not dressed yet. I haven't bothered today. I was heaving myself out of the bath when you called, and it just didn't seem worth it knowing that I'd only have to fight to get all my things off again before bedtime.'

Clifton's brow furrowed.

'I didn't make you get out of the bath to answer the door, did I? Oh God, I should have rung before coming over; you could have slipped and hurt yourself.'

Hilary smiled. 'It really doesn't matter. And I'd have had to rush to answer the phone, in any case.'

An awkward silence fell. There hadn't been many silences during their brief friendship, but all of a sudden Hilary felt awkward. She was always a bit embarrassed and slightly clumsy at the best of times although she detected that was one of the things that Clifton secretly liked about her. She wanted to ask what the matter was, but knew he'd say the same as always: There was nothing wrong; nothing wrong at all. She searched desperately for scraps of conversation, anything, anything at all to end the dreadful enveloping silence.

'Has there been anything else about those awful murders? I haven't heard the news today.'

She watched as the spell of silence was magically lifted.

'No, nothing today, although I'm sure that bloody fool of a policeman will be on the television again tonight expanding his ridiculously enormous ego as wide across the screen as his fat body. God, that man sickens me!'

Hilary was taken aback by this sudden outburst but was at least thankful that they were talking again.

'I didn't notice his big ego, at least not on my little black and white telly. He's only doing his job though, surely?'

'What — wasting everyone's time and getting on their nerves? I bet he never catches anyone. It's been going on for ages anyway, and they're still nowhere near him. After all, the bits of body they turn up were chucked away weeks ago in some cases. He's just wasting everybody's time.'

Hilary wasn't particularly keen to pursue the matter and decided it might be for the best if she dropped it.

'Have you heard from your mother recently?' she asked a little too hastily.

Clifton ignored her.

'What really gets me is the way Hicks harks on about how clever he is, when the entire world can see that he's nothing special. He's as thick as two short planks but won't admit it.'

'Who is Hicks?' asked Hilary, thinking that he must be a friend of Clifton's mother.

'That bloody policeman — the detective on the case! You must have heard his name; he mentions it himself every night. I'm sick of his name; I'm sick of him.'

'I'm sorry, Clifton, I shouldn't have brought it up. Do you think we can have another cup of coffee, this one seems to have gone a bit, err... tepid?'

Clifton busied himself in the kitchen. 'Is there anything else you need for the time being, Hilly?' he called out, opening cupboards and peering in. He seemed to be getting very worked up.

'Not for the moment. I've got enough food to last a week with the stuff you brought the other day, thanks. Anyway, I'm not eating much at the moment; I don't seem to have the appetite.'

'All the more reason to eat, then.'

Hilary laughed. 'Yes, I suppose I ought to make the most of it, but I'm being a bit too responsible about the whole eating malarkey. I don't want to end up like a pig when I emerge from my sty.'

Clifton came back into the living room with one mug of coffee.

'Aren't you having one?'

'No, I can't stay long. I've got a few things to do this evening.'

Hilary thanked him for coming round and Clifton told her not to get up then let himself out of the flat.

If anyone had watched the figure leaving the house, they would have seen an unassuming looking man in his early thirties cross the road and walk purposefully up the street to a large, drab Edwardian house. He looked just like anyone else on the street on his way home to an evening spent watching telly or playing with the kids.

Clifton absent-mindedly kicked at a stone and watched it bump off the wheel hub of a car, making a loud clang. He looked around a little guiltily but noted with relief that there were no observers, this was at least one thing he didn't have to worry about.

Once at home, Clifton went into the bathroom. For once there wasn't a dead body in there, so he decided to have a bath himself. Scrubbing at the enamel first with *Dettol* and then some cream cleaner, he gave it a good rinse with more hot water before finally filling it. Pouring in some bubble bath, he swirled it around to produce a few tiny lacklustre bubbles. He tipped in some more, making a mental note not to waste any more of his money on the stuff in future. He'd hoped that a hot bath, the first he'd been able to take in over a fortnight, would help soothe away tensions that had built up. It would be just like the adverts claimed on the television. It was a shock to realise just how uncontrollable his anger had become over that blessed idiot, Hicks. He'd almost broken down and admitted the whole bloody thing to Hilary. He must make sure that he controlled himself and kept his emotions in check in future. What he needed was concentration, so things didn't get out of hand. The business with Jimmy still unnerved him, and it was just as irritating to wonder why nothing had happened so far.

As he lay back in the water, feeling the chill breeze blow in through the ill-fitting window, he realised what a truly hopeless situation he'd got himself into. Of course, he couldn't be expected to control his temper entirely when he heard about the case; after all, it was a lack of control of sorts that led him to commit these acts of destruction in the first place. What could he expect? He became morose and felt like doing… well, what did he feel like doing?

All of a sudden, he couldn't bring himself to do anything at all; not even to get out and pull the draughty window closed or turn the tap on with his foot to get some more hot water in the bath. He just couldn't be bothered. So, he lay there in the rapidly cooling water. He was truly dead now and didn't even feel that old sexual thrill when he tried to recreate that old familiar feeling. It was almost as if there was no life force at all within him; no desires, no opinions, no nothing: just a floating dead weight of disappointment. He shut his eyes; pretty much the only movement he felt capable of. The very notion of getting out of the bath and having to get dried and dressed, filled him with absolute terror. All the actions that would have to take place before he could even attempt a semblance of normality seemed far too arduous to undertake. And so, he continued to lie in the lukewarm water, drifting further and further away from reality into the narcotic of his tortured imagination. He might just stay there for ever, getting colder and colder while staring up at the spots on the ceiling. They were probably fly spots which had been collecting there for the past year, or whenever it was that anyone had last bothered to get up on a pair of steps with a mop and bucket and clear the dust and muck and cobwebs off. He remembered visiting the flat for the very first time and being shown, or rather dragged, around by the admiring former owners keen to sell it to him for a sum over the odds.

The hygienic aspects of Mr and Mrs Rosenberg's lives were brought to Clifton's attention in no uncertain terms. He was shown the back of the lavatory cistern and behind the self-cleaning oven as evidence of dirt and dust-free zones. He was led into the cupboard under the stairs with a torch pushed into his hand and implored to 'Seek, seek!' for any sign of human waste or hygienic negligence. He could find none. The old couple told him that every April they cleared the flat out thoroughly, sometimes even going so far as to physically remove all the furniture to a storage warehouse. Then, with pink rubber gloves pulled onto their fingers and snapped up to their wrists, they would force each other into nooks and crannies in their search for filth. Clifton could picture them even now as they rammed, squeezed and pressed themselves into corners of cupboards of fixed

Formica units on the never-ending quest for hairballs. They teetered and perched atop ladders waving at cobwebs with feathery cane-handled dusters; risking life, limb and lucidity swiping at fly spots with an orange synthetic sponge. But not anymore.

Clifton thought of the other word for the fly spots; vomit spots. The common house fly vomits up its food in order to digest it more completely. In so doing, it produces pretty little opaque dots, not much bigger than the full stops on a printed page. These little milky dots are themselves licked by the short pink tongues of small children, who call them 'window sweets'. This practice is nothing if not character-forming. To eat something that has been forced up through the digestive tracts of a vile and universally detested insect is to smile, breathe, shout and indeed participate in the whole carnival that makes up life on earth.

Clifton Gentle thought all this and more in the thirty seconds it took for his eyes to flicker across the bathroom ceiling and down onto the window. He closed his eyes once more and thought about the day's events. The poetry of the moment flew through his mind. Accepting man's admittedly primitive intelligence, it seemed to him that people must have been put on this planet to justify God's very existence through whatever means they could. To leave a lasting impression on the world, be it through word, deed, thought, physical beauty or ugliness; this, surely was the meaning of everything. He tried to think of his life as the opportunity to scream in a void for a short time; to touch others, to change their own lives in whichever way he could. As a terribly scarred and deformed face might linger in one's memory for decades, so would his life. To linger. To creep softly over the imaginations and fears of a million men. In that way humanity in all its bleak self-congratulation could be judge and jury in the case of Clifton Gentle vs The World. Perhaps they might find that he was unworthy of membership of the human race itself. But then, like Groucho Marx, he would not want to belong to any club that would have him as a member.

So many people rarely consider their lives in the context of the whole history of the universe, but Clifton did so on every possible occasion. And he was doing it now because he felt compelled to do it. He had to escape from the rotten poetry again. Macabre verses stretched across Clifton's tortured mass of brains. Images of the most horrific mutilations twisted around inside his imagination like a wounded eel, writhing around in agony on a wet slippery grass bank. His mind, like the eel, waited for an end to this torment — a mind that wanted to scream, but was unable to do anything about it. He knew that he had to wait for Peace to fall upon him once again. And after a few more oppressive moments some peace did arrive, and with the calm at last the pain left him.

He lay still in the bath, which was by now freezing cold, calmly breathing through his nose; his mouth clamped shut by the rigidity of his jaw, set in a contortion as he fought in vain against being physically sick. The room leered at him now; the fly spots mocking and laughing like the children that licked at them, while the tiles around the sink seemed to be enjoying a good joke at his expense. A trail of saliva oozed out of Clifton's mouth, preceding the torrent of vomit that spewed out onto his chest and into the bath water. He soiled himself. When it was all over, he knew that the sign had arrived at last. It had been a cathartic reaction and he now had to do something to prevent the state of torpor from recurring. It had to be stopped from happening next time, because there always was a next time. There had always been a next time.

At last, Clifton Gentle knew what it was that he had to do to justify not only his, but God's and the Devil's own existence. He had to become a member of the human race again. He had to kill again and keep on killing.

***

The next morning Jimmy woke up next to a stinking pile of urine- sodden rags under which a derelict homeless man was coughing himself awake. He felt his own damp clothes; moisture having seeped in through his rudimentary bedcovers and he hoped that it was just the morning dew and not something worse. A dreadful moan from another bundle lying nearby in the drab morning light made him shiver. As for the cold, he was mostly impervious to that now. A rat which had been standing on the other man's stomach felt the movement and scuttled off without much concern for its own plight. Jimmy blinked and stared about around him, recognising where he was. Filth, degradation and depravity. He was home again.

The night before had been spent in the usual fashion, sucking another punter's tired old penis for a long enough time until a thin weak trail of slime had oozed somewhat reluctantly into an already used condom. All the while Jimmy thought about other things. Any other things. Things like the way the dim thirty-watt light bulb swayed above the old bloke's head as he puffed and blew, about whether he was going to get paid for this evening's work after all or just end up with getting a fist to his jaw, but most of all he thought about a time when he might not have to live this way. It was trite to say that he had drifted into it, but that was the way things had happened. He was just a piece of scum on the surface that could only stay afloat by sticking to the grime that was around. He had always believed that one day things would change, despite making no efforts himself to achieve that improvement.

With a shudder that made him grasp the thin jacket closer to his wiry body he also thought about that night and the maniac who tried to kill him. That night had really frightened him. Ever since coming round and finding the lunatic standing over him, he had not been able to really feel at ease. He had been more careful recently, not going with just any old bloke; they had to be ones that looked decent. Or decent enough, anyway. Why should anyone want to kill him? Why should anyone want to kill *anyone*? Life was bad enough already without it being shorter.

He knew he had to find out more about the madman. It might even be a way out of this mess. It was worth a try, anyway. If only he could remember where that awful house was. When he shot out of it terrified that evening, he was so drunk and in a state of panic that after running scared for a mile or, so he wasn't sure where it was. He only had to remember, and he would find it. He just had to. Perhaps it would be a way of getting out of this life for good. It would mean getting out of life one way or the other, anyway.

CHAPTER TEN
PINK

Dave was lovely and warm in his own bed. He kept his eyes shut tight as he half-dreamt, half-wished for an enormous breakfast to be brought sizzling and singing to him. He pictured the sexy little, black-skirted French chambermaid giggling as she peeked through the door and coquettishly perched on the side of his bed while popping laden forkfuls of food into his open mouth. She pouted whenever his lips parted to receive the delicious back bacon, eggs, kidney, sausages, large field mushrooms and double fried slice. After eating it all up, she would pour him another cup of sweet black coffee, dab the crumbs off his beard and, with a tinkle of laughter and a wink from a naughty eye, swiftly slip into bed beside him. As she stretched out her legs in the bed, Dave would feel the sheer of her stockings slipping around inside the sheets. When she brushed against him, he felt the heat of her naked upper thigh brush tantalisingly against his hairy, muscular legs. Her warm, soft, yielding body thrilled him while he blew strands of her silky long black hair out of his mouth. Pushing against his chest, she wriggled out of her white cotton blouse, tight skirt and stockings, and begged him to remove the rest of her underclothes while she sat astride him, panting heavily.

Grunting and pulling off his own thick stripy winceyette pyjamas, Dave started masturbating before catching the semen in an ancient yellowing hanky used specifically for the purpose which he kept in his bedside drawer. He groaned, peeked out of one eye and lay, safe, secure and sweaty, in bed. Alone.

He had never been very successful with women. There was no real reason why. He was no misogynist; it was just that he had developed a bachelor life without gaining any idea about how to communicate, empathise or make himself attractive to women. During his late teens, his worries about girls had upset him, just as they did for many other boys lacking the necessary wherewithal, but he was now pretty much in control of the whole disappointment thing. True, he did not relish the prospect of sexual deprivation, as his early morning weekend fantasies showed, but at least he'd got used to the whole idea of chastity.

It was always nice to dream, though, and Dave thought long and hard about that particular chambermaid. Christine, she was called, or sometimes, Léa. It was all based on a film he had watched five years ago when he attended a policeman's night out. Taking pride of place were a few 'blue' films seized with great relish by the vice squad, and which were due to appear in court as evidence the following month. Dave had sat along with the others, laughing a bit too loudly, and calling out as the soft porn flicks romped on to a makeshift screen. But when the narrative started to develop more expansively, he fell silent and watched mouth agape, as his trousers filled out even more than his girth demanded. Most of the other lads were a bit disappointed with the films, but Dave was left sitting in awe and quite shocked by it all.

Of course, he never told Mum where he had been or what he'd seen, but the memory had often come flooding back. He would never talk about 'that sort of stuff' with anyone. Sex was to remain a forbidden mystery; just one of the things that distinguished him from the common mass and what made him special. That was why he and he alone was capable of catching this nutter; he had 'Inner Discipline', something he had read about in a self-help pamphlet when trying to understand and justify his celibacy.

Lying back in his comfy, sweaty, pungent bed for a final five minutes more deep thought, Dave then got up, farted long and loudly, and prepared for the weekend. It was time for him to recharge his batteries and take some time out so that he could focus on catching the nutter next week. 'A bit of Ahh and Ahh,' he thought he had heard it called.

For the last couple of years, he had been interested in scuba diving, spending what little available leisure time he had practising in swimming pools across North London. It was just the kind of glamorous pastime he thought he ought to be involved in and had managed to get himself elected secretary of the North London Scuba Diving Association (NLSDA). Dave loved acronyms and had desperately tried to come up with something catchy — something like SODA or SUDS, but he could not get the words round in the right order, so NLSDA it had to be. This particular Saturday he was due to conduct a workshop for new recruits on the different methods of changing compressed air cylinders underwater, following it up with a practical demonstration in a swimming pool hired specifically for the purpose. He'd already prepared his discourse, including a few good scuba jokes ('why do scuba divers dive off the boat backwards? Because, if they dived forwards, they'd fall in the boat, ha ha'), and set about packing up his gear when there was a ring on the front doorbell. Plodding heavily down the corridor, Dave could make out the outline of a man through the pane of frosted glass. He appeared to be wearing a uniform. Dave got excited. It looked like police business.

'Morning, sir, parcel for delivery. Could you sign here for receipt please?' The postman proffered a pad with a pen attached to a thick piece of string. Dave signed and waited for the parcel. It must be the new breathing masks he had placed a mail order for from Aqualung Ltd, which was a stroke of luck. He could take them with him and use them as part of the practice today.

The postman walked back to his van and started struggling with an enormous package, tied together thoroughly with more string.

'You couldn't give me a hand with this, could you, sir?' he called out.

Dave walked out to the postman and helped heave the parcel from the back of the van into the doorway of the ground floor flat. The postman wheezed, nodded, and then staggered away cursing under his breath. Dave hauled the package into the hallway. It was a lot heavier than he had imagined. Presumably, there were lots of manuals enclosed as well as the masks. Pulling off the string Dave could see that there was a lot of plastic wrapping inside. Because of the amount of packaging, he couldn't manoeuvre very well in the confines of the hall, so he tugged the parcel into the kitchen. The light was better there as well. Dave detected a chemical smell and became intrigued. Taking a small kitchen knife from a drawer, he cut open the tape which covered the box. Ripping it open, he reached in and pulled out a smaller parcel covered in white plastic *U Like 2 Save* supermarket carrier bags. He turned it onto the table and emptied out the contents.

With a ponderous thud a human head, severed at the neck, rolled across the kitchen table, and came to rest with its eyes fixed straight above Dave to the top cupboard where he kept his breakfast cereal. It appeared to be covered in a film of glutinous wax and smelt very strongly of formaldehyde. Dave was surprised.

Surprised, but not shocked. As he constantly reminded people, a policeman has to be prepared for any eventuality. Taking the remainder of the contents out of the box and subjecting them to a cursory examination, he identified them as being part of a torso and a leg. There was an envelope in the bottom of the box, again wrapped up in plastic. He could see that it was addressed to 'Mr Hicks'.

'Not calling me by my proper rank, is he?' Dave muttered to himself. He opened up a drawer and put on his forensic examination gloves. The smell from the remains grew stronger now they were exposed to the open air. The letter was in the same careful handwriting as on the box.

'So, you think you know me better than I do, do you? Well, let's see how very clever you are. This is part of the body of a man I killed under the very noses of the police last week — Tuesday the first to be precise. His name is up to you to discover, but I can tell you that he was captured in Hackney, just round the corner from the police station itself. You will be hearing from me again in the near future, I can assure you.'

Dave grunted and read on.

'I heard you boasting on the television about me and how stupid I am. Well, let me tell you this, Hicks; compared with you I am the greatest intellect the world has ever seen. You couldn't even get near to catching me if I fell through your letter box like my friend here. I'm going to show you up so people will realise what a fool you are. After all, if we haven't got a decent police force capable of keeping the streets safe, we might as well live-in anarchy. I will keep on killing until you are removed from office and someone more suitable replaces you.'

It was signed, "Yours in disgust, Mr?"

Dave was a little taken aback, but on the whole very well pleased with the entire business. Chummy was falling into line. The nutter was walking right into the trap he had set. He was so close to him now; he could almost smell him. With a twitch of his nostrils, Dave reached over and opened a window. He smiled a broad smile of self-congratulation before calming down. He must not allow himself to get cocky. They always kept their cool, the pros.

'Don't count your eggs before they're smashed,' he muttered.

Taking a closer look at the head he could see it belonged to a middle-aged man, although the waxy covering put on to preserve it made the features quite difficult to distinguish. It had dark brown hair, a little balding on the crown, and looked quite startlingly ugly. Dave had seen enough corpses and faces of dead men in his time not to be put off by a lack of beauty though and instead saw only a typical police description of the deceased: 'A middle-aged man, balding, no distinguishing features'. That was it; end of excitement.

He picked up the phone and rang the station. After requesting the presence of a full forensic team and a couple of junior detectives, he sat down in his living room and sighed.

'Bang goes my scuba diving for today,' he said. 'Murder can be a messy business.'

***

After he had sent the parcel Clifton began to cheer up. It was comforting to summon up the image of the bleary-eyed, fat detective opening it up before screaming in uncontrollable terror. Clifton's main concern was whether the package would be delivered on Saturday morning, when he was confident that Hicks should be at home. If it wasn't, it might be returned to the depot until the smell obliged a postal employee to open it up. His whole plan had relied on it being Hicks himself who opened up the package and for that to work it had to be delivered on Saturday morning. He had been most insistent about that at the post office, asking the man behind the counter more than once whether or not it would get there on time.

'Why don't you deliver it yourself if you're so keen?' the man had replied. 'After all, it's not very far away.'

That was typical of what was wrong with this country; no idea of courtesy and customer service. Everyone was just after whatever they could get. He realised nothing else could be done without causing a scene. He had done his best, and Hicks would see it sooner or later. But if only it would get there on time!

Dave Hicks was not the only recipient of mail that Saturday morning. Clifton's parents had written to him asking whether he would be spending Christmas with them. In a long rambling letter, they explained that although it had only turned November they needed to know because otherwise they would go to stay with his aunt and uncle in Epping. They went on to say that they usually preferred to stay at home for the festive season, but they had not seen as much of the rest of the family as they should lately and thought it might be nice to get away, especially since they'd been invited and everything.

'Remember though, Son,' the letter continued, 'if you want to come here for the Break You are more than Welcome, and we can always go Up to see Uncle and Aunt later On in the New Year.' They always used capital letters in abundance in their correspondence, scattering them as freely as they did the salt and pepper on their mashed potato.

'You're also very welcome to invite a special Friend.'

Clifton read dismissively. He had no intention of wasting his time staying with his parents over Christmas. And as for the idea of a 'special Friend?' He felt a shiver of disgust as he brought to mind the people he'd been intimate with lately. They were literally a bunch of stiffs.

Tossing the letter to one side he pondered what on earth he was going to do with himself on this Saturday. He'd nothing urgent to do, all the shopping having been done the evening before. Hilary didn't need anything else for the weekend and he wasn't due to see her until the next day and he had no one else to care about so that was that.

There was literally nothing to do. With a shudder he anticipated the Monday morning questions at work about what he'd 'got up to' over the weekend. If all he did was spend his time tracking someone down before killing them, he would be hard pushed to say anything at all. Paul from the office was asking more and more searching questions, and Clifton was almost sure that he suspected something was up. Whatever he said, he mustn't even hint at the package sent to Hicks. He ought to do something, anything that was normal, so he could talk about it convincingly. Something normal.

Sometimes, very rarely, he had gone to the cinema to see some arty film or other, usually on his own and arriving after the cinema was already quite full so as not to draw attention to himself. Sometimes he might go out for a dull drink or a meal with a work colleague, but usually he did nothing whatsoever of note. Perhaps he ought to go for a walk or mope around in a few tatty bookshops in the Charing Cross Road or browse at the trinkets along the shops near the Seven Dials. He had done that a few times before, but he never bought anything. His life was a fraud. It was more a living death than anything else. Today, for example, there was absolutely nothing at all to do until it got dark, when he planned to lure another man to his death. But what on earth could he do to fill his spare time until then? Even if Hicks had received the parcel in the post, it would not be reported until the evening news at the earliest, and he'd wasted enough time in the past waiting forlornly for news items about the case, only to be ultimately disappointed. He was not going to do that again.

He looked out of the window. It was starting to rain. More showers. He turned on the radio, but it was just the religious morning service on one station or programmes featuring various types of music that he detested on all the others. He switched on the television set instead. The news was still full of events in Berlin while there were renewed arguments in the Conservative Party following the fallout from Michael Heseltine's continuing attacks on Thatcher's leadership style. That little toady who was her press secretary, Bernard Ingham, had apparently given a message of 'Put up or shut up' and the BBC journalists commented that something was going to break. It was apparently going to be a seminal moment in Britain's relationship with Europe. This was followed by the sports report. Clifton groaned. He got up and turned the knob on the set to find that all there was available was a diet of Australian soap opera, sport, puppets and… sport to entertain the great British public on a Saturday morning. No wonder people resorted to violence and the streets weren't safe. He turned it off and peered out of the window into the street again, but there was nothing interesting going on.

What about buying a newspaper or magazine? The idea perked him up. Perhaps there might be an amusing article about him in it? Pulling on his blue fleecy-lined anorak, Clifton ventured out into the wind and rain. He was an intelligent man; of course, he could make his own amusement. He had even pointed out how intelligent he was when he wrote to that congenital idiot Hicks. He would surely be able come up with something to pass the time until the evening, no trouble. The library, for example. He would go and mooch about in there, maybe taking a browse through the records and tapes for hire and even take something out so he could record it at home on his cassette recorder. He had meant to join for a long time anyway. When he thought about it there were literally hundreds of things he could find to do. If he had any spare time later on, he might just pop in to say hello to Hilary in advance of tomorrow; take her round the papers to read and have a laugh. She probably wanted a laugh.

As he strode through the puddles forming on the pavement, Clifton became a little more cheerful. He even dropped a fifty pence piece into a plastic bucket held up by some kids standing next to their grotesque Guy Fawkes dummy. They were soaked to the skin in the hazy mist of fine rain. The Guy looked pretty hopeless as well, which is what prompted him to fish in his pocket for some spare change. Made primarily out of some ragged pyjamas, it was stuffed a little too full of newspaper and bits of cloth, some of which were beginning to swell up with moisture and stick out of the neck. Its head was quite horrible. The kids had stuck the head of an old, battered teddy bear on the torso, and pinned it in place with some rusting safety pins. It hung awkwardly to one side, giving the impression of having had its neck broken. A strip of red cloth had been stuck on its mouth to form a tongue, and this lolled out like a piece of raw liver.

After he'd bought his newspaper, Clifton realised with dismay that the rain was getting heavier and the paper itself was getting soggy. Deciding not to go back home straight away and risk a soaking himself, he hurried inside a small, cheap department store to take a look around at all the things he didn't want and wouldn't care to buy. The other customers plodded along on their own safe, secure, boring paths. The regular routine was sacrosanct: some chatted with each other, and others tried to avoid eye contact. Yet more marched lifelessly like zombies through the store with the same lack of purpose and desperation as Clifton Gentle. This wasn't all there was to life was there? Surely there had to be something else that he could do? Things couldn't be as drab and lifeless as this. Could they?

***

Still wearing his carpet slippers, Dave Hicks met the other policemen and forensic experts at the front door. They seemed unsure how to approach or address him: as victim or boss?

'Good morning, Detective Chief Inspector,' said Detective Sergeant Chas Bravo as he was led reluctantly into the kitchen to view the grisly remains. 'Would you like me to keep a watch outside in case the press turn up?'

'No need,' said Hicks. 'I've already telephoned them.'

The junior detective seemed shocked. 'Are you sure that's wise, sir?'

Dave smiled and nodded. They had not got a clue what to do in this sort of situation, these younger blokes. They just didn't understand what he was up to. It was a good job the super had entrusted the entire investigation to him, and not to some of these daft plods.

'Just do as I say and you might learn how to catch criminals, Chris. Not using our contacts within the media has always been one of my big bears.'

Chas Bravo just managed to swallow his pride, together with the bile that was rising in his throat. How dare that idiotic tub of lard talk to him like that, he thought. He was sure that he had got his name wrong on purpose. Big bears indeed! And fancy ringing the press; they would be swarming all over the place in a matter of minutes, getting in the way, spoiling the crime scene and interfering by asking daft questions. Well, at least he had the satisfaction of having a nose around Hicks's house, with his knick-knacks and that mess sitting on the kitchen table. The fat slob wouldn't be eating off that again in a hurry.

'Anyone feel hungry?' asked Dave, who had not yet had his breakfast and was beginning to feel a bit peckish, what with the excitement and everything. 'I'm going to put some bacon under the grill if anyone's interested.' The others watched queasily as the DCI opened up an extremely well-stocked fridge to extract a monster 'family' pack of streaky rashers. He peeled a few from the slab of meat and tossed them under the flames on the eye-level grill. Just then a woman's voice broke through from the hall.

'Oh, my David, David! Where is he? Is he all right?' Mum, panicking at the sight of an influx of police cars early in the morning, had hurried over the road to check that her boy was safe. Hicks called out to her from the kitchen.

'It's all right, Mum, I'm in here.' He glanced down at the horror which was still sitting on the kitchen table. 'But you'd better not come in; there's something you wouldn't like.'

The other policemen winked at each other. 'So, his old mum was still looking after the great fat lump, is she?' thought DS Bravo. Wait until the boys down the station hear about the big mummy's boy.

Mrs Hicks tore further into the flat and appeared at the kitchen doorway.

'What is it, Davey, are you hurt? Has someone had a go at you?' She was breathing heavily after the dash across the road and was dressed in a bright baby-pink nylon dressing gown with matching fluffy slippers. Her thin, pale, varicose-veined legs stuck out the bottom. Everyone looked appalled, although each for differing reasons.

'Oh, my God, thank heavens you're safe,' she said, advancing further. 'I thought you'd been done in by the killer. I thought he'd got his own back for all those nasty things you said on the telly.' She flung her arms around Dave's neck and sobbed heavy sobs of relief. Dave tried to shrug her off, but the grip was too determined and Mum too full of emotion to realise the embarrassment she was causing.

'Come on, Mum, can't you see I've got work to do with these gentlemen?'

'What sort of work?' she asked, disentangling herself. For the first time she noticed the others standing around with soppy grins on their faces.

'Oh, I'm sorry for barging in on you all. I'm Dave's mum. Glad to meet you. It's good to meet some of his work chums — I'm always asking him to bring some of you back for tea some time.'

They murmured greetings; DS Bravo in particular relishing the moment of Hicks's acute embarrassment, though baulking at being described as one of Hicks's chums. Dave tried once more to rescue the situation.

'Come on, Mum. Now you've met everyone, perhaps you should go back and get dressed. I don't want you to catch a cold.' He put a giant paw on her arm and attempted to steer her away from the table. And then she saw the head.

With a terrible scream and with her dressing gown falling open to reveal ancient, lined breasts, she pointed towards the lump of dead flesh on the table. The acrid smell of suddenly burning bacon did nothing to improve the ambience and she fell to the floor in a dead faint. The policemen rushed to help her, fetching water, pillows and a blanket. Hicks went deathly white himself and looked like he was about to cry. In a few moments Mum came round, but was shaking visibly with fright, while an ambulance was called.

'You can never be too careful in cases of shock, sir,' DS Bravo said as he radioed for aid. At that precise moment, the press arrived en masse. With no one to stop them they entered the house and started swarming all over the place, noting both the parts of a cadaver laid out on the kitchen table, as well as the prone body of a half-naked elderly woman being lifted off the floor on her way into a waiting ambulance.

Hicks was by now over the fright himself and his emotions turned swiftly from anxiety to anger. The nutter had gone too far this time. Sending this thing through the post was one thing, but involving Mum was another, especially with the media all over the gaff. He would bloody well make sure that Chummy would pay for this. He would pay for this with his life. Dave would make sure of that.

CHAPTER ELEVEN
VIOLET

Whhhheeeeeeeeeeeeeeeeeeeeeeeeeeeeezzzzzzzzzzzzz!

Another rocket flew up into the night sky, exploding in a bouquet of brilliant red and green flashes; it's wooden stick unobserved and unwanted, falling silently back to earth only to end up entangled on a television aerial on someone's roof where it interfered with their reception for the next few months. It was Guy Fawkes Night outside, characterised by all the incumbent screams, whizzes and bangs that always made Bonfire Night such fabulous, organised hooliganism. Over the next few hours, hundreds of people across North London would be injured and admitted to local Accident & Emergency hospital wards; burnt, bleeding and begging for doctors to save their sight, limbs, reputations or new designer trainers from a bloody end. In much the same way as the original conspirators of 1604 had suffered the inevitable consequences of their actions, fate would call in its dues this night. November the fifth always had its victims.

All afternoon Clifton had killed time until he could kill it no more, impatiently waiting until he could go out and kill a man. He had tried thinking of something he could usefully do with his day; anything at all. In the end he had visited the local library, enrolling at long last with the record and tape section and taking almost an hour to choose albums that didn't appear to be too scratched. Back home he lay listlessly on the unattractive sofa, listening to one all the way through a couple of times; Julee Cruise's 'Floating into the Night' which had been used as the soundtrack to a TV show he'd enjoyed, *Twin Peaks*. He then decided to go back out again since it had stopped raining. With the words of the theme tune 'Falling' in his mind he wandered around.

The music washed over him with a hint of languid menace.

He still couldn't see anything he wanted amongst the oh-so-normal bric-a-brac that surrounded him but did take an interest in a few knives in the kitchen section of Whiteway's, the department store, while he dragged himself around the high street shops like a reluctant schoolboy. All he really felt like doing was stalking men down before killing them. Death was the only interest he had in life anymore. His only hobby, if you like. He needed to show the world what an idiot that prat Hicks really was. It seemed he was the only one who could really see it. Even Hilary had defended the great jelly.

He had finally popped in to see her, but she was still hopping about on her crutches and making conversation wasn't easy. He did not stay long. After all, there wasn't much to say; he'd done nothing, and she could do nothing. To make matters worse, she had invited her ex-husband round in the evening for a meal to discuss 'arrangements' and was getting progressively more nervous about the whole thing. Naturally, Clifton had nothing in the way of useful advice to offer and could only help out by offering to peel potatoes and lay the table. He imagined her getting tipsy and capitulating later on before getting tearful and suggesting that she and her ex get back together again. That would just be typical of her.

Eventually he decided to go home and watch the last hour of an old black and white weepy film on the telly, although he didn't weep, but just became increasingly aware of the welcome darkness settling outside. Around six o'clock, just after listening to some more news about the impending challenge to Thatcher's leadership of the Tory party he got wrapped up and set off for the bonfire display on Hackney Marshes. He was determined to get someone quite early on in the evening if at all possible so he could get back and see the late evening film on Channel Four, *The Hitcher*, a thriller which he'd made a note of watching. He was also determined to pick up someone fairly attractive this time; at least it would give him something aesthetically pleasing to look at while he cut up the body. He was sick of studying buck teeth, prominent ears, knobbly legs and fat bellies. It might also help if he could get the thing over and done with while there was still a good crowd watching the display. He wouldn't be easily spotted chatting to someone casually, and the two could slip away back to his flat before any nosey parkers knew what was going on. There had been nothing but talk in the papers, especially the trashy local free sheets, about the need for vigilance and to look out for anyone out of the ordinary, and Clifton had discerned that people were noticeably more inquisitive than they had been. Paul Craven, the nasty piece of work at the office had been particularly meddlesome, jokingly asking Clifton some alarming questions about his whereabouts on the Friday evening that he had done the last one in. It made Clifton's head spin, and not for the first time he wondered if Jimmy had been in contact with him, before dismissing the idea as ludicrous. All that was probably Hicks's fault as well.

Arriving at the marshes from Lea Bridge Road, Clifton found several smaller bonfires were already alight. In the faint orangey glow, a one-legged man hopped along on crutches in the midst of the festivities as boys threw bangers at him with impunity. Clifton smiled, considering whether he should try to murder him on the grounds that a one-legged man would involve a little less disposal. After walking a short way, he soon spied a likely quarry; a youth standing a little apart from the others, who stole a furtive glance in Clifton's direction. Clifton walked over and started off the usual chat.

'Do you know when they're going to start the display?' he asked.

The youth looked at Clifton, a little apprehensively. 'Around seven thirty, I think,' he said.

A Midlands accent: that was good, it gave Clifton his next line on a plate.

'You're not from round here?'

'No, I'm a student. At the Poly — PCL.' He left his answer floating in the air, as bald as a coot.

'PCL?' asked Clifton. Christ, how he hated people who used acronyms.

'Polytechnic of Central London.'

'Oh, I see,' said Clifton. He started to stamp his feet on the sodden ground.

'How do you fancy going for a quick drink before the fireworks?'

There wasn't a moment's hesitation. 'Yeah, great. Where do you suggest? I've only lived in this area since the beginning of term.'

'Oh, I know a good place that's not too far, come on.'

'Ace, it's getting a bit cold standing here now.'

The two figures moved through the thickening crowd across the marshes. Clifton was taking no chances and, despite the gloom, kept his head burrowed deep down inside the fleecy lining of his anorak. The boy said his name was Gavin, and then started prattling on about nothing much that Clifton wanted to hear.

When they came in sight of a pub, Clifton suggested that they give it a miss.

'It could be a bit rough tonight. Bonfire Night always brings out the rowdier elements. I tell you what, why don't we go back to my place for a drink? It's cosier, and we'll have much more chance for a chat and to get to know each other.'

The boy agreed a little too enthusiastically and kept blathering on.

'I'll have you quiet for good in a while,' thought Clifton.

It was becoming a bit too easy luring them back. He might not even have to give away any drink this time, which would cut down on expenses.

They got to Clifton's flat at about the time that the firecrackers started going off. A thick fog of smoke from individual bonfires was beginning to drift over the street and all the lights in neighbouring windows were extinguished. His neighbours were either all out, or tucked up in bed, too frightened to venture out into that most naughty of nights.

Hal Roberts and Tim Evans smirked to themselves as they convened underneath a street light across the street. They had spotted that wimp Gavin earlier on when he first arrived at the marshes and were delighted with their coup. They had always thought that he seemed to be a right nance the way he declined to help out the student hall of residence football team and complained about the noise the common room toga party had made. So, this was why.

Andrew called out at Gavin from behind a Nissan Micra while the smoke from the bonfires helped obscure them from view.

'Oi, poofter face!'

Both boys roared with laughter, beer cans splashing precious lager over themselves in the process. Peering above the bonnet, they saw Gavin and the older one looking about.

'Find someone your own age, you old wank!' Tim shouted again. More hilarity.

Clifton put a hand on the boy's querulous shoulder, steering him round the corner and out of sight. 'This way,' he said, literally leading the boy up the garden path. Mounting the stairs inside the flat the boy wheezed and stalled, before being pushed through the front door and into the living room.

Turning on the light, Clifton displayed the executioner's room in all its charm and beauty. It looked just a little too neat and tidy. To fill up some of his spare time Clifton had given the place a very early spring clean and the whole place had almost taken on the look of a museum. Like a veritable chamber of horrors, it was all technically correct, but, like an exhibit, looked curiously artificial. The boy blinked and again appeared a trifle nervous, although more out of excitement, rather than fear. He took from his jeans pocket a small blue canister.

'My inhaler,' he gasped apologetically, 'for my asthma.' He took a hurried embarrassed puff before reaching out for Clifton's hand.

'I'm glad I met you,' he said. 'You're the first person I've met who isn't a student since I've been in London. At home I always found it easy to, you know, meet people like me, but it's different in London.'

He tried to pull Clifton towards him. It was difficult imagining what sort of people the boy had befriended.

'I'd just like to say that I hope we can be friends. You know, like... real friends.'

This was all making Clifton feel quite nauseous, especially after the near miss with the youths.

'Let's have a drink, eh? There's plenty of time for that later on,' he said. 'After all, it's early yet.'

The boy let go of his hand and frowned.

'You do... you do like me, don't you? I mean, I'm not making a mistake, am I?' Clifton didn't reply but went off to busy himself in the kitchen. It was always a source of the greatest amusement to him, the trite things they came out with just before they met their end. He must get around to writing them all down before there were too many to remember. In the kitchen he took a couple of largish tumblers from a cabinet and called out to the boy.

'What do you fancy?'

The least he could do now was offer some of his precious drink.

'What do you have?' Gavin replied.

With that the boy signed his own death warrant. Whatever sympathy Clifton may have felt was dashed. He couldn't bear it when people answered one question with another.

'Beer, whisky, gin, vodka, wine and port,' he said briskly, adding rather camply, 'but I'm not going to let you have any port in case people talk.'

The boy laughed and said he would like a beer. Clifton poured a can of lager into a glass. Gavin was now sitting on the sofa, still in his coat which had bunched up and looked even more graceless.

'I'm just going to the bedroom for a minute,' Clifton said to the boy, 'so why don't you get comfy. We'll probably stay here for a little while now.'

He stepped out into the hall and deftly removed the ball pein hammer he had secreted in his back pocket while rummaging about in the kitchen drawers. Quickly unscrewing the lid off the meter box and taking hold of the main fuse lever, he turned it, plunging the flat into complete darkness.

'Hey, what's happened?' Gavin said, his voice tinged with the tiniest of doubts.

'Oh, it's probably only the fuses; they're always going. You stay there, I'll change the wire. There's some in the kitchen cupboard.'

Poor stupid trusting Gavin never stood a chance. Even if he had been aware of Clifton creeping up, he wouldn't have been able to do much about it.

Clifton stood in the darkness, watching the jumpy little figure squirm about in his chair.

Whhhheeeeeeeeeeeeezzzzzzzzzzzzzzzzzzzzzzzzzzz zzz!

Inside the flat it was even darker and more hostile than outside in the screaming street. Occasionally the room was illuminated by the violet sparks from passing rockets, but it was dark enough. Gavin's grotesque asthmatic wheezing sounded a little like a firework, Clifton thought, although it was a bit more like a damp squib. He moved closer, sliding across the carpet.

Riiinnnggg!

And then again, only longer.

Rrrriiiiiiiiiiiiinnnnnnnnnnnnnnngggggggg!

Hal and Tim fell against each other, screaming with laughter at the thought of poor little tossy Gavin frightened to death by the doorbell. They were pleased with themselves for finding the right flat. It was the light going out that gave the game away. Hal sang through the letter box.

'Gavin is a poofter; Gavin is a poofter.'

They banged their beer cans against the door and shouted up at the darkened window.

'Come on out and play, Gavin. You can bring your Vaseline and your boyfriend, you little bender.'

Inside the flat a mood of intense misery engulfed both occupants.

'What are we going to do?' panicked Gavin.

Clifton ignored him. He was glad he wouldn't be able to kill him now, it just wasn't worth the bother. He would just sit there in the dark, making out the lines of panic spreading ever wider over the callow boy's creamy-white craven face while more bangs and crashes went off in the street and the two adolescent oiks outside on the step eventually got tired and went home.

After all the anticipation that had led up to this moment Clifton knew that death wasn't going to happen tonight. What a waste. There just had to be more to life than this.

***

Dave had had a bad day. As soon as the ambulance had drawn up to take away his delirious mum, the press arrived in the curvaceous shape of Jacqui Lane accompanied by a ratty-looking photographer called Vince. The photo Vince took of Mum weeping as she was being lifted into the ambulance was syndicated at great profit to other newspapers and appeared on the evening TV news as well as on covers of every single one of the next day's Sunday papers. Dave himself was unusually terse when interviewed by reporters about the whole bizarre incident and appeared to show uncharacteristic signs of strain.

'I'll get the bastard for this,' he spat with venom, while reporters scribbled furiously to catch every quotable word. 'He's made a big mistake now. I'll have him and I'll bite him hard when I have him. He'll never get away with this. What he's done to me, and my mum has taken the bees by the knees.'

The story took pride of place on the *Sunday Herald Review* front page, together with photographs of the human remains in the box. Dave had raised no objections when the pictures were taken, but by the time he'd given serious thought to the idea that his kitchen was going to be the feature for some grisly 'Room of My Own' it was too late. Jacqui had the whole thing wrapped up an hour after she had left Hackney.

'I want to put photographs of the body and Mrs Hicks underneath this headline,' she said to Kenny Pitchfork, the bloated, bleary-eyed Sunday editor, handing him a mock-up of the front cover under a huge banner headline:

'THE CEREAL KILLER'

'I don't get it,' Kenny said, blinking.

'Look at the words on the box, darling.'

Emblazoned in bold print on the side of the cardboard box sitting beside the bits of body were the words *Fluff Puffs*.

'It's a pun, you see — serial cereal killer. You must get it now, sweetie?'

The editor started to grin and nodded. At last, the case had got its moniker.

Later that evening, on his way back from hospital, Dave stopped to pick up the early editions of the Sunday papers from a news-stand on the Seven Sisters Road. He could hardly believe his eyes as the vast array of front-page photos of Mum assaulted his senses. Most annoying of all, though, was the headline in the *Sunday Herald Review*. This was the end of his dreams for the case to be known as 'The Hicks Murder Case'.

The Cereal Killer! What sort of a name was that to give the case? At first, he felt like giving up, but recalled Mum's last words when he left her in the hospital.

'Get him for me, son. I almost died when I saw that thing on the table. I thought I was for it; it was horrible. Get him for me, Davey. Just go and get him so he can't do this to anyone else's mum ever again.'

'He'll not hurt you again, Mum,' he sobbed, blinking through tearstained eyes as he drove home in the car, 'and he's not going to hurt me again, neither.'

The streets were still full of swirling smoke from various back garden bonfires when Dave parked outside his flat. He didn't like the idea of staying in his own place all that much and decided to spend the night back at Mum's in his old boyhood bedroom. That way he could keep an eye on the place while she was away. The doctors said she might be allowed home on Monday. He settled down and reluctantly started to read the various reports in the papers as the last of the fireworks fizzled away in back gardens. The more he read, the more he cheered up. Without exception the reports were sympathetic about what had happened to him and Mum.

'This monster must be stopped. Our honest cops and their families must be allowed to go about their everyday lives without fear,' asserted one paper.

'Only one question now remains — when will this maniac be put behind bars? This paper cannot predict the date. Only one thing is for sure. It will be handcuffs belonging to DCI Hicks that will finally ensnare him,' said another.

'PROTECT OUR BRAVE POLICE' shouted a third, over a large flattering picture of Dave looking brave and resolute.

As the gloom lifted, Dave felt a funny feeling, such as St Paul night have experienced on the road to Damascus. It was the inkling, just the smallest inkling, of an idea for a plan that was so implausible that it just might just come off. But when it did, it would surely place Dave's name among the greats.

***

Leaning uncomfortably against railings outside Highgate Tube station while lone firecrackers continued to disturb sleep, Jimmy drew a pale hand across his brow and wiped off some of the night sweat collected earlier servicing one of the local middle-aged married men on Golders Hill. After his trawl around the area, he had put in a search around the smoke-filled streets that made up Muswell Hill borders. Pacing along the nice safe middle-class avenues that divided those living in real respectability from those making up bedsitter land, Jimmy hoped to see something familiar. The only thing that rang a bell was a street sign that read 'Cranleigh Gardens'. There was nothing else, but he had to make sure just the same. All this stuff about the latest developments in the case seemed pretty weird. Even Laurence, the nervous man from Golders Hill had talked about it while his cock was being sucked, adding that he had stayed in specially to watch the early evening TV news.

Although he'd been searching regularly, Jimmy hadn't even got close enough to sniff the killer. It had been difficult, though, what with not bringing in as much money as usual through being pickier about who he went with, as well as finding the time and strength to wander around North London. Just trying to remember places drunkenly glimpsed on that awful night was harder than he could have imagined. His clothes looked noticeably threadbare now, while definite lines of care were traced around his eyes, already panda-like from lack of any meaningful sleep. But he had to go on; he just had to; it would be worth it in the end. Ironically, this could be the break he was looking for. Funny it coming from being half-strangled, but that was how things were sometimes, not just only in books and films. Perhaps he should even consider going to the police to talk about what happened that night.

Hang about! Could you imagine a meeting between him and that fat, old git who was leading the hunt? He'd more than likely charge him with an offence himself. But he had to do something. Things were hotting up, and unless he got to the killer before the detectives, he would have got nothing out of it. If there was one thing that Jimmy believed in amongst all the bitterness and crap that made up his young life, it was that you must try and profit from all your experiences, no matter what they may be. His mum, the old bat, had taught him that and sometimes you had to listen to what your mum said.

And then suddenly, just around a crumbling corner wall opposite an abandoned shopping *U Like 2 Save* shopping trolley, he saw exactly what he was looking for. There it was, as innocent as a condom in a cassock. At last, this looked like the right street and the right house. Jimmy had found where the monster lived. And he would exact his revenge no matter where that took him.

PART TWO
AFTER AND
AFTERWARDS

CHAPTER TWELVE
TURQUOISE

Dave Hicks stepped confidently out of the car; its rear passenger door reluctantly held open by the latest unfortunate police driver assigned to the detective chief inspector. He was the fourth such pressed volunteer for the 'Monkey Run' as Dave's operation had been uncharitably termed inside the force and was already seeking a transfer.

Raising himself to his full height, and without a word of acknowledgement to the driver, Dave strode off in the direction of 'out there; out there where the clues lie'.

The particular 'out there' for today was an area of scrubland by the side of a railway line near Clapton railway station. It was here that the greater part of a foot and calf as well as a portion of human arm had been discovered by schoolboys who had gathered for an illicit smoke the evening before. With his usual customer relations hat firmly perched on his head, Dave had them locked up in the cells all night for trespassing. And now it was the turn for the great super-sleuth himself to see what could be unearthed from the incalculable amount of detail and man-made waste that lay all around. Trains rumbled past on their habitual late-running schedules along the adjacent track and supplied eerie whistles while they slowed down near to the scene.

Passengers, their waxy early-morning faces leering up against the smeared windows, wondered what was going on and got excited by the glimpse of police tape sealing off the latest crime scene. They would need to watch out for the news later on to see if it had anything to do with the Cereal Killer murders. They could then tell friends, family or work colleagues in offices, on building sites or shops what it was they had seen, proud of their own personal, albeit fleeting, involvement in the murder case of the decade. During that telling they would watch out for signs of respect, or jealousy or fear, because everyone was interested in some of the rubbed-off glamour. Equally, everyone was guilty now.

In fact, as far as Dave was concerned, everyone *was* guilty. Everyone, except of course him. If the current scraps of bodily material now under examination turned out to be new and not just some more missing bits of a previous victim, the body count would have reached at least nineteen. That was a record. If people wanted to stop it, they could. The trouble was people just couldn't care less. As long as it wasn't them or anyone they knew, who was being carved up it didn't matter. People were nasty, brutish and short-minded.

But Dave instinctively knew that someone *did* know who the killer was. It just wasn't possible in this day and age to knock off so many people in the bursting heart of a modern capital city and get away without someone noticing something. Not even Alfie Skuse. The miserable little good for nothing toerag had added insult to injury by disappearing as well. Somewhere out there a big, fat clue was waiting for him. That had always been the beauty of this case; you never knew what would turn up next.

Margaret Thatcher, who had been increasingly beleaguered since the poll tax riots a few months earlier, was now engaging in open warfare with several senior members of her party. The Labour Party had moved into a huge virtually unassailable lead in the opinion polls and change was certainly in the air. Not only that, but the first anniversary of the discovery of the first body was due in just two days' time, and it was becoming imperative for the police to come up with something big. Dave knew that he had to circumvent the inevitable articles already prepared by newspaper editors anticipating the milestone. They were looking forward to printing something different from photos of Paul 'Gazza' Gascoigne doing daft things in the run up to the World Cup in Italy, and a couple of special pull-out Cereal Killer supplements had already been prepared by the Sunday papers. Meanwhile Jacqui Lane had got herself booked onto a TV special, appearing alongside a number of eminent criminologists as well as a couple of the victims' families.

Superintendent Jim Haigh, terrified of having to hear any further philosophical statements from Hicks about the general malaise in twentieth-century civilisation had also agreed to appear on the programme himself. He was under intense pressure to get rid of the popular image fostered by satirists that he was just an organ grinder's monkey, dancing away to the tune of that blessed idiot. He must control himself, or he would soon be as remote from real life as Hicks undoubtedly was himself.

It was all taking its toll. Dave had heard rumours that control of the case might again be challenged high up in New Scotland Yard itself and there was talk of ministerial involvement to give the impression that things were going to be shaken up. There was a new man in charge at the top after the recent musical chairs played out in Whitehall and this time there was a genuine chance that he would be taken off the case altogether, or almost as bad, get saddled with someone else micromanaging the case. Someone like the dreaded DCI Boyson from the frighteningly no-nonsense South Yorkshire force, for instance. That force laid claim to have the necessary expertise even though they had badly botched the Yorkshire Ripper case and a bunch of interlopers would be bound to make Dave's life a misery. Christ, could he imagine having to scrape and bow to someone else, and a bloody northerner at that!

All this formed a dismal, shabby backdrop as Dave tried to muster up all of the natural pluck and blind confidence that he still retained at his disposal as he swung off into the steaming killing grounds of North London. The rookie constables, already searching in the knee-deep piles of decaying refuse and vegetative matter alongside the perimeter fence, looked up when they heard the familiar voice booming out across the crisp morning air.

'Good morning, gentlemen. And what do we all think we are here for?' The detective in charge looked a little uneasy.

'Morning, sir. I've taken the liberty of commencing the search already.'

Hicks looked straight through him, his bright blue glasses forming a delicious contrast in the grim, early light.

'But what exactly are you searching for, Detective Sergeant?' he barked.

The men shuffled their feet and looked sideways at each other. They recognised that tone of voice. It meant someone was headed for a dressing-down.

'Items of significance, Detective Chief Inspector; any indication as to the identity of the person or persons who dumped the remains.'

Hicks marched forwards until he drew level.

'I don't think so,' he said. 'We are not looking for any of that, my lad. We are looking for clues. Always clues. Clues that will tell us not only who did it, but also why it was done, and how and when and where. Clues will tell us the whole story and the whole story is what we need. And when we have the whole story, we will know the best means of catching the person or persons who did it. And that will provide justice. Clues are the essentials for justice. And justice is what we are here for. That's right, isn't it, Sarge?'

Hicks smiled. He had always wanted to give that particular little speech and had kept it in his head for as long as he could remember. It was the sort of speech that demanded awe and respect, carrying the unmistakable voice of authority and experience symptomatic of the professionalism that a true master of the arts of detection could bring to an investigation. Dave had learnt it word for word from the Alfred Hitchcock detective comic he'd read religiously since the age of eight.

Impulsively charging into the undergrowth, like a shy rhino suddenly desperate for a pee in the savannah, Dave began looking for those elusive clues in earnest. After a somewhat gloomy and cold spring, summer had hit North London with a vengeance. It had not rained for ages and the dry ground resembled a peculiar kind of desert with instead of sand a substantial amount of plastic and other rubbish being blown all over the place like confetti. He decided to head straight down to the railway track itself; breaking through the blue and white tape Detective Sergeant Bamber had set up. Almost immediately he appeared to find something. Waving frantically for an evidence bag to be brought, Dave picked up a pair of ancient, soiled men's underpants with a stick and then with a flourish, dropped them into the bag with aplomb. He knew they most likely had nothing to do with the case, but he had just noticed a press photographer's car pull up on the bank opposite and the driver emerge with cameras at the ready and didn't want to disappoint.

Within five minutes though, Dave *did* come across something which really interested him. He gathered everyone around to inspect it, arranged for police photos to be taken, and explained to anyone within earshot that he considered it to be possibly the most important clue yet discovered during the entire investigation.

He beamed broadly for all to see, especially the telephoto lens on the other side of the tracks. Later on, that afternoon, at the hastily convened press conference, he resembled a favourite uncle, slapping reporters on the back and doing a lot of waving at the assembled masses like the winning captain of a sports team.

Staring from the television screen into pubs and living rooms all over the country came the familiar, round, bearded face announcing that 'a very significant piece of information has been personally found near the site of the latest discovery'.

'Because of this find, I have an important announcement to make,' Dave proclaimed, leaning in close towards the camera lens. 'I can now promise you that the murderer will be in police custody within two weeks from today. Start the clock! The countdown begins now, ladies and gentlemen. I can confidently predict that we will catch this nutter within fourteen days from today. This is going to be the deadline to end the Line of the dead. Oh, yes, this is definite; it's a dead cert. It's going to be as easy as falling off the back of a boat.'

***

Watching that TV broadcast while unpacking his suitcase was a tanned Clifton Gentle. He had just arrived home after a fantastically relaxing holiday in the Greek islands with Hilary, and it had been simply wonderful. The sun had soothed and massaged both of them back into a feeling of general contentment, while laughter had blotted out all thoughts of grim, grimy London and the daily grind of life in the capital. Hilary had proved to be the perfect holiday companion, going along with Clifton's itinerary of a mixture of sunbathing and sightseeing, without complaint and now she was fully mobile the two of them had revelled in their freedom.

On the last evening, clearly under the effects of far too much ouzo, they had sworn to remain friends for life, come what may. The holiday had been sheer paradise and the warm deep turquoise Aegean Sea had helped to wash away most of the memories of his old life. All thoughts of murder and killing lone men had vanished forever from Clifton's mind.

Over the past six months, since his failure to kill Gavin the student on Bonfire Night, Clifton had turned his life around, getting interested in normal everyday things and had even managed to get a temporary promotion at work as reward for the extra hard work he was putting in. He had enrolled in a modern language class in the local college and enjoyed the company of other mature students, even venturing to go out to the pub with them afterwards. There seemed to be a real meaning to life after all and it was good.

And now this. At first, Clifton found it amusing. He had read the courtesy newspaper supplied by the airline on the flight home and was pleased to detect a more critical change in tone about the way the investigation had been handled. There was speculation about imminent departures in personnel leading the case which made him chuckle. For a moment Clifton began to imagine that he had won the battle already. All that rubbish Hicks had come out with just showed that the man was cracking up. The ravings of a condemned man on the brink of a massive public humiliation. But the more he read, the more the words didn't seem to quite fit the story. What was this new discovery? He had successfully weaned himself off killing and had promised himself to only kill twice more since the Guy Fawkes Night fiasco, with the last and final victim being as long ago as February; a funny little weasel-faced man called Alfie.

He had felt better after that and was now fully committed to getting on with the task of living his life rather than ending that of others. Anyway, for the last couple of weeks he hadn't even been in the country and certainly hadn't scattered any more body parts. As far as he was concerned, they had all been recovered by now or were in such a state or physical location that they were impossible to find.

Film showing the 'discovery' on the railway embankment came onto the screen, showing Hicks excitedly rummaging about in the undergrowth and shouting instructions. What on earth did it all mean? Clifton's mind turned mental somersaults as he tried to remember whether he had ever been on that particular site before. It certainty didn't look familiar, but there had been so many dumping grounds, that it was difficult to be absolutely certain. He knew that he had dropped off a head by a railway bank once, but that particular one had already been found. He had left some clothes bundled up in a black plastic sack once underneath a railway bridge, but that wasn't anywhere near any body parts. It just didn't seem to make any sense. It must be a trick; another stupid and desperate game being played by that fat fool.

After unpacking his holiday things and putting his T-shirts, shorts and beachwear into the washing machine, Clifton went to bed convinced that it was all a psychological trick. But the next morning, closely examining the newspaper on his way to work, Clifton read the details concerning the foot and arm found at the scene. If it was a trick by Hicks, then it was an uncharacteristically very clever one, and moreover one that held a fiendishly concealed twist. He read on. According to the report, Hicks had himself come across something while searching the area. At this stage he wasn't revealing exactly what it was but felt sufficiently confident that he promised that he would find and catch 'the nutter' within the next fourteen days.

This was simply appalling. What in God's name was going on? Perhaps his holiday with Hilary had come too late and he really had lost his mind? He knew that he had undergone a period of temporary bewilderment over the past year or so, but he was definitely back in the real world now. Perhaps he ought to give himself up before he truly toppled over the edge?

By the time he had got to his office, the grey concrete building shrouded in a heat haze, Clifton was thoroughly miserable and morose; all the benefits from his holiday in the sun now completely dissipated.

***

'Now what made you go and say something stupid like that, Davey? You know they're bound to find out sooner or later. Fourteen days! What am I going to do with you now? You always used to do what I said.'

Mum pursed her lips and stared long and hard at her son who was spread out on the ottoman like a sultan home from a spot of despotism. He seemed so out of reach nowadays, and nothing she did or said got through to him.

227

'David!' she said again, this time a little louder. 'What are you going to do?

At last, it seemed that her frantic cries were about to be answered as Dave opened one eye for a second before giving her a wink that was almost lascivious. He knew exactly what he was going to do. While Mum continued bleating on, the mind of the great detective wandered. What treasures lay in store for him; true recognition for the most audacious confidence trick ever attempted during a criminal investigation. Ordinary people like Mum lacked that certain something, that vital spark of originality possessed by all the greats: nerve, intuition, following a hunch, call it what you will. What mattered was that Dave had it. And he knew how to use it. He had laid the most cunning of all traps, and he had waited for just this moment in time to do it. Just when it seemed that all was lost.

Because there *wasn't* any clue of unbounded significance, just as there wasn't any breakthrough. What there was though was belief. He wasn't sure that it would work. No, not sure, just 'one hundred and ten per cent certain'. It was going to work because it had to work. There was nothing else but for it to work.

Dave's mind nimbly turned over the delicious intricacies of his stratagem, while his body continued to languish lumpishly, on the sofa. Mum gave up berating him and went out to brew up one last pot of tea in an attempt to bring her poor boy back to his senses. When she came back into the living room he was still lying

228

there, apparently lifeless. There was nothing else to do now but wait: wait for the nutter to respond to his challenge. The gauntlet had been thrown down.

As Dave had said to Superintendent Haigh, aghast at the news that his DCI had no surprise clue to offer the investigation after all, 'It'll be like waving a red herring before a bull.'

CHAPTER THIRTEEN
PURPLE

'I've just met the most wonderful man in the world.'

Clifton sat like a lump of unrisen dough in Hilary's armchair, trying not to spill any more coffee than he had done already. He attempted a smile but found it even more difficult than usual while Hilary continued to gush.

'He's kind, really good-looking, and guess what? He wears a tie when we go out together. I can't believe it. I mean, no one I've been out with before has bothered to make much of an effort to look nice, but Peter — that's his name, it's great, isn't it? — Peter actually wore a suit the first time we went out together properly.'

Clifton wondered what it might mean to go out together 'improperly', but continued smiling his vacant, insipid smile, painfully aware that he was expected to say something encouraging in response. After sagely nodding away like an all-seeing guru in a retreat for new age hippies, he struggled to construct a response.

'That's really very heartening,' he said. It wasn't much, but it was the best he could manage, and although it was said with very little   semblance of sincerity, Hilary didn't appear to notice anyway.

'I know I said I was never going to get into this sort of situation again, not after my rubbish marriage, but this feels so very different. When that bastard left me for his silly, little tart, I felt absolutely wretched, but now it feels like I am being born all over again. Peter's had his share of problems as well, and we've discussed our previous experiences at great length, but can you imagine it, Clifton? I'm in love with someone who feels the same way about me!' Hilary beamed at Clifton; her sparkling, clear, bright blue eyes didn't look the same as the usual muddy grey he thought she had. Perhaps it was the new lick of make-up, or the full-on all-teeth smile or maybe even the bubbling voice with its new-found range of pitch and emotion replacing her normal flat tones, but Clifton found that he was suddenly unable to recognise his friend. He certainly was not able to share in her joy.

'I suppose you're going to make plans to move in together?' he asked at last, cutting through his desire to be physically sick.

Hilary was brought up short, her smile fading a little.

'Oh, Clifton, you're not jealous, are you?' she pouted.

He grimaced. How he loathed the constraints normality thrust upon him.

'Why, what's he like at sucking cock?' he wanted to ask but didn't.

'Of course not, Hilary. I just want to be sure you're not doing anything silly and letting things run away too fast.'

'I don't think I am,' she said a little defensively, 'and neither Peter nor I are silly young things any longer. We won't rush into anything without considering it responsibly. We're both adults.'

This hit the nail on the head. Why should he, a killer of well over twenty complete strangers, feel qualified to pontificate about normal loving human relationships? After all, murdering wasn't exactly a qualification for one-to-one personal counselling. He decided instead to try to be nice.

'When will I be allowed to meet him?'

'Soon, I should think. As a matter of fact, he's due to ring any minute to make arrangements for this evening. If you want, I could suggest we all go out together. Make it a threesome.'

Clifton panicked. He didn't want to venture this far into apparent normality; an evening out with a happy couple, with him as a dirty great big green gooseberry. He wanted to blow a raspberry instead. The strange events of the last few days and the odd turn that the investigation had taken had certainly left him feeling very vulnerable.

'Er, no I don't think that would be a good idea quite so soon. Anyway, you probably want to spend some time on your own until you know each other better.'

He held his breath and then relaxed as Hilary again smiled her brand new, soppy, giggly schoolgirl's smile.

'You're probably right,' she simpered.

Clifton got up from the too-spongey armchair and walked over to the window to stare out at the same old, soulless street. He looked furtively at his watch and then turned back to face Hilary who was still beaming.

'Well, I suppose I ought to be on my way. I'll call you in a day or so and you can tell me how things are going.'

He shuddered at the prospect and added it to his growing list of worries. Trudging despairingly back to his flat through pavements strewn with growing piles of litter and bleached dog faeces, Clifton remembered how hot it was. The sun beat down like the Devil himself. It hadn't rained for ages and temperatures had not dropped below seventy-five degrees Fahrenheit for the past four weeks. It was all very well in Greece where it was meant to be hot, but Clifton didn't like hot weather in England; it was always far too humid and muggy. He felt like a walking sponge what with the sweat trickling down his neck while the growing stench of the filth in the streets made him feel decidedly queasy. The forecast for the foreseeable future was the same and the nightly news pictures of emptying reservoirs and singed parks had even started to compete with the Cereal Killer for prominence. Needless to say, the misery was felt hardest in the capital. Standpipes had been introduced in parts of South London already, and Hackney was rumoured to be next. Everywhere you looked there were glowing, shiny sunburned purple faces.

Clifton counted up all his troubles and concerns. Firstly, the small point about whether or not he really had lost his mind. Had he really killed the last victim the police had found or not? If he had and not remembered, that was bad enough. But if, on the other hand, he hadn't, then it was almost worse. It might mean that there was another killer out and about. And not only that, but one who was killing and disposing of body parts in the same manner that Clifton did and using his own methods and trademark. Was he pinching his copyright? Clifton could not avoid harbouring a suspicion that it was someone he knew. Maybe it was even that little bastard rent boy Jimmy or, he considered with a shudder, maybe even Hicks himself. It wasn't beyond that maniac policeman to try something as desperate as that. The more Clifton tried to fathom it out the more upsetting it became.

There was also the 'clue' which Hicks had sprung on the world, along with his fanatical claim that 'the nutter', as he irritatingly continued to call him, would be caught within fourteen days. Well, that was four days ago now and there were only ten left. If he could hang on for ten more days, he might just see Hicks off for good. His superiors would have to act then after all the

234

publicity. It was a shame that his commander, Superintendent Haigh, didn't look up to much, as he obviously couldn't control his subordinate. The way he had collapsed in a dead faint when questioned by that slaggy presenter on television the night before wasn't exactly indicative of a man in control. He would have to be replaced as well. Perhaps the police would finally recognise Clifton's skill and put a real professional in charge of the case.

The 'Cereal Killings' case. That name really made him nauseous; what a bloody stupid thing to call it. That was probably Hicks's fault as well.

And next on the list — Jimmy. He must still be out there somewhere and was capable of leading the police straight to him. The one thing Clifton just could not work out was why he hadn't yet turned up. Perhaps he was too frightened or was already working covertly with Hicks. He had surely contacted the police already? Even if he hadn't it would be better if he was eliminated, and not only from police enquiries, but from his entire existence on earth. *He* would have to be polished off for good if only for Clifton's own peace of mind.

While he was at it, he might as well finish off that annoying office creep Paul Craven as well. Clifton felt sure that he suspected something. That was the trouble; you just didn't know what people were thinking anymore. Worst of all, he couldn't really remember why he'd started this whole crazy business in the first place. It all seemed so very silly now, killing complete strangers then cutting them up and scattering their remains all over North London. It was just plain daft.

The only thing that made any sense was getting his own back at Hicks. How he hated that man! The whole caboodle was entirely Hicks's fault; blood was on his hands and his hands alone. That made sense. What a terrible list of problems he had to deal with. And now this poxy weather!

Back at home, making a disappointing cup of weak camomile tea and a carrot and cress sandwich, Clifton sat back shell-shocked. He realised that he was being forced back into killing again. Whether he wanted to or not.

CHAPTER FOURTEEN
BEIGE

Madness, insanity, lunacy, dementia, idiocy, crazy, bonkers, off their head, a screw loose, round the bend, mental, up the pole, cracked.

During the next forty-eight hours, thesauri were plundered by a press that itself had flipped its lid. If a story had even the remotest angle on the Cereal Killings it was made a feature spot. Jacqui Lane herself was rarely out of the public eye. She had managed to land the post of roving commentator on London lowlife for a TV news programme which was syndicated across the country and abroad. Viewers seemed to love following her cutesy-pie nose around to sniff out the stench of murder and corruption. Crime and punishment had always been good copy and made many careers, so why not hers? She was very careful to keep the case — her case — close to her dramatically heaving chest. Appearing live on primetime USA coast-to-coast screens, Jacqui's beguilingly attractive feminine charms and ever so slightly more heightened clipped British accent were now becoming familiar to new and lusting audiences the other side of the pond. They loved it while she pontificated on what she termed the 'primal screen fascination' of the case. She had become the Cassandra of crime, the Sybil of Savagery, the Vamp of the Video. Every Wednesday Jacqui hosted and successfully managed to hijack the whole show. Using her more than ample personal communication style she presented *The Six o'clock show with a Sizzle*; forty-five minutes of news, views, comment and a bucket load of gossip.

One of the first editions featured a special on the Cereal Killings. Victims' relatives, together with the police top brass, a garrulous, camply-dressed medium and a brooding American mass murderer recently released on parole took part in the *Slayathon*. There were frequent commercial breaks with all available advertising time bought up by well-known manufacturers of breakfast cereals. One had even gone so far to change their formula so that when milk was added little droplets of red 'blood' started to emerge in the bowl from raspberries hidden inside the golden corn nuggets.

It seemed that people were following the story all over the world. There were condensed reports on national bulletins in countless languages across the globe while closer to home the *Herald Review* began serialising Ms Lane's forthcoming book, *The Killer & I*. She was counting on the final denouement occurring just in time for the last chapter to be completed for optimal commercial success. Newly engaged literary and personal agents looked on approvingly as the ever-increasing and tempting lucrative offers began to materialise. In particular, there was a very keen interest from a number of huge US broadcasting concerns who were looking for a chat show host with a difference. That classy British accent sure was sexy, especially when combined with a glimpse of cleavage, a flash of sheer stockings and stories of murder, mutilation and mayhem.

Out on the streets where it really mattered, Cereal Killing mania flourished unabated. Looming over pavements and dual carriageways across the land, newly erected gigantic video advertising hoardings depicted the smiling face of DCI Hicks holding up various bits of bones, beneath which a customised logo proclaimed, 'Find the Nutter'. It was backed up by a public interest television advert portraying Dave as the last line of defence against anarchy and lawlessness. In pubs and clubs, the public sported T-shirts with various slogans: 'Catch a killer before Breakfast', 'Snap Crackle and Chop' and 'Hicks; Picking up the Pieces'. The latter design, particularly popular amongst young men, featured a caricature of the tubby detective chief inspector spearing amputated male genitalia in a park and depositing them in a bag slung over his shoulder.

Even Superintendent Jim Haigh was not immune to the media merry-go-round. He never quite understood how Hicks had whipped up the circus in the first place. Scum always rises to the surface, he knew that, but to generate this much ballyhoo was quite another thing.

And it had to happen now — just a few precious months before his well-earned retirement! Before it all blew up, he had planned a very relaxed and comfortable jaunt up to a well-earned rest. A few casual and easy-going presentations on the things policing had taught him, the importance of always playing it safe and straight; that sort of thing, but that great fool Hicks had put paid to that. The world was a different place now, and modern police work with this unending sucking up to the press just wasn't his forte. At least he'd made it plain to Hicks that he would be taking charge of all the press conferences from now on. Perhaps it was a little too late, but God knows what that idiot would come up with next if left to his own devices. One thing was sure; Jim Haigh couldn't afford the risk, and neither could his heart. He'd already noticeably stumbled on stage in that TV show, and he felt that his arteries were getting as clogged as the London traffic.

Across the country, chat in soup kitchens, burger bars, and middle-class dinner parties alike was peppered with references to the killings with the most fascinating aspect being the apparently random way in which the remains had been scattered unseen all over North London. The sheer invisibility of the killer was horribly delicious; anyone capable of carrying a bag through the streets and tossing it over a wall was a suspect. The crimes had attracted a popularity that successfully cut across otherwise rigid divisions of age, race, sex and class. Because the anonymous victims had been found in a state which made their identification difficult, the violence that lay behind the crime was easily glossed over. Even when a body had been positively identified, the relatives seemed keener to get a good price for selling their stories to the tabloids than arranging a respectfully decent funeral. It was clear that many of the dearly departed had been long deprived of love and affection and become estranged from their family many years ago. It was the utter mystery of the whole business that excited people. Some of the old girls intoned dire warnings to each other about the killer when leaving luncheon clubs and bingo halls while clutching hold of their pleated beige skirts and matching handbags. However, in their heart of hearts they knew that he wasn't in the least bit interested in them or their thin, sorry purses. The killer had become a phantom of youth in general, the spectre representing modern-day violence and evil, smirking at them behind their bolted front doors and roaring with laughter at their frailty and wrinkles.

In nice prosperous electronically protected homes, where polite dinner party conversation invariably turned to the shallow wit of sex and who had had whom, the murders were very acceptable fare, as long as they were served up just after an equally acceptable white wine accompanying the hors d'oeuvres. Almost everyone had their own story about someone who'd heard someone say or see something, which although irrelevant, unintelligible or just plain made up on the spot, proved fascinating. It all went to show that the police didn't know the first thing about protecting property, because it was surely property the killer was *really* after. It was the only thing that actually counted in life, wasn't it, even if property went so far as to include life itself.

While coffee was drained from fine bone china cups and guests prepared to leave, warnings were solemnly despatched about the menace lurking on the streets, as if the bloodthirsty culprit was in the habit of snatching well-heeled couples from the pre-warmed padded front seats of their Volvos and BMWs. The real prey of the killer, the young men hanging around late at night in a state of intoxication, were not so easily afraid.

'I can handle meself if I have to,' they said, pointing to slim flick knives tucked under the waistline of tight denim blue jeans. They were well hard and not easily frit. Anyway, he was only after poofters and turd-burglars, wasn't he?

'Are you calling me a fucking queer?'

Shop assistants were said to be instrumental in the search for the maniac. They formed an important part of Hicks's 'Third Force'; a triumvirate comprising the police, the general public and 'anyone in an optimum position to suss out people acting odd'. This 'Third Force' had the benefit of being given access to Dave's very own 'Checklist', a curious document intended, as the preface pointed out, 'to give those in the know a sure-fire lead in getting their hands on the reward generously offered by various financial and retailing concerns'. It was sponsored by a number of life insurance companies and featured advertisements placed by local businesses.

Hicks warned shop assistants not to approach the suspect themselves, but to covertly telephone a special number and use the phrase 'I was just wondering where our expected delivery has got to. I've got a case with me now, but it looks like a bad lot'. Despite the cumbersome nature of this message, the scheme had been a tremendous success, with well over a hundred faltering and embarrassing calls being made in the first three days alone. Although none of them had in fact identified the killer himself, Dave remained in good cheer.

'Just think of it!' he beamed. 'All of those calls, and any one of them could've been about the nutter himself. We're just one big happy family working together, like a great big nose sniffing out the stink in our midst.'

***

Clifton found himself plagued with doubts. Paul Craven, the irritating little creep in the adjoining office had been pestering him for some time and was now at his worst and most annoying. One morning when Clifton was attending a meeting about the installation of a new computer accounting system, he had to 'liaise' with Craven, which effectively meant sitting in his office and having to listen to a whole series of his nasty insinuations. The day had already begun on a sour note with a recurrence of one of his pubescent nosebleeds erupting just as he was leaving home.

Without warning blood had spurted everywhere and Clifton, without any spare clean shirts had to make do with sponging down his clothes before getting the Tube into work. Sitting in his own gloomy office, ashtrays as full as buckets in an abortionists', with girlie calendars on the wall, sat Paul Craven. He was evidently pretending to be very put out by Clifton's lateness.

'Take a pew, Cliff old son. Nice of you to take the trouble to pop in,' he cried out, the nasty, leering smile lingering on his thin, mean mouth. After some minutes discussing where to relocate the new workstations around the office, he then went on to make comments about where he would like to put them: ('So I can see more snatch without having to leave my desk.') Coffee was served.

Maxine Kelly, the new clerical assistant and the only black girl in the office, hesitated as she leant over Craven to put the coffee down. His hand rested on her arm.

'Wait a moment, Maxi,' he said, winking at Clifton. 'How long have you been here now, love?'

'Six weeks, Mr Craven.'

'As long as that?' he said patronisingly. 'Well let's see if you've learnt anything while you've been here. It's probably a bit different from where you come from.'

She blushed.

'Do you know what other black things I like in the morning, apart from me coffee?'

Maxine froze and shook her head.

'You don't? Well wait until this afternoon's tea and biscuits and I'll let you into the secret. He let his hand brush down the front of her smart crimplene skirt. 'After all, you do want to get on here, don't you?'

Maxine's eyes started to tear up and she nodded and left.

'There you go, Cliff, easy as taking candy from a baby. Or more like giving that baby something else to suck apart from a dummy, right?' He roared with laughter, scratching his crotch. 'I don't know why you don't get yourself in there Cliffy, they'll do anything to get on, some of these sluts, know what I mean?'

The obvious distaste registered on Clifton's face.

'Oh, yeah, I forgot. You're not keen, are you? Not on girls, anyway.'

'I think I ought to leave before I decide to report you for racial and sexual harassment. We've finished what we needed to discuss.'

'No, actually, I don't think we have,' Craven said, the smile disappearing from his face. 'In fact, I think it's you what wants reporting. There's always been something very peculiar about you, Gentle. I just want you to know that I've been watching you.'

Clifton got up to leave.

'What's that on your collar?' said Craven.

Clifton looked down. Some blood from his nosebleed had remained stuck after his sponging down and had now hardened, brown and guiltily obvious on the collar of his white shirt. He looked embarrassed.

'It's nothing. Just some blood from a nosebleed I had earlier.'

'Oh, yeah? Blood, eh? Very suspicious. You'd better go and wipe it off, hadn't you, Mr Clean?'

Clifton could not get out quick enough. What did he mean by that — 'Mr Clean'? Try as he might, Clifton couldn't escape the feeling of creeping paranoia. There was so much going on outside his control, what with Jimmy, Hicks and now Craven. He must avoid the trap. Like the Heffalump in *Winnie the Pooh*, he had to avoid the pit dug by a bear of very little brain. Despite himself he thought he heard comments from people all day long.

'I hear he's already been caught and is locked up in a nuthouse, but they don't want to admit it because he's a celebrity.'

'Apparently, they reckon it's because of what his mother did to him as a baby.'

'That policeman will get a knighthood when he catches him.'

'That wanker couldn't catch the clap.'

Whatever the truth, Clifton knew one thing for certain: Hicks's self-primed time bomb was ticking away under both of them.

***

Jimmy was starving. Starving and fed up. Ever since seven in the morning the day before yesterday, when he'd been unceremoniously booted out of his cell in Wormwood Scrubs, he had spent virtually the whole time looking for that house again. His obsession for tracking down the man who had very nearly ended his life was on the point of breaking him once and for all.

Following that weird-looking gink that night had been a bad idea. On the mistaken understanding that it was the maniac, he'd only managed to embroil himself with a plain-clothes policeman who, after first expressing disappointment that he had not after all apprehended the Cereal Killer, cheered himself with bagging 'a turd burglar'.

Jimmy was banged up, in more sense than one for propositioning and had spent the last few months inside at Her Majesty's pleasure, subjected to frequent beatings and being forced to give sexual favours for free. Jimmy had decided from now on to keep his own counsel, if not his temper, and refused to explain to the court what he thought he was doing accosting people in the street. It just meant that there was one more reason for wanting to get that bastard.

And now he was traipsing around Hackney, finally able to begin the catharsis of putting a wrong to right. He had ached for this moment every night during the past six months, and it had been the utmost thought in his mind, even when he was pinned down on the floor of Lumpy Larry Ley's cell while being gang raped by his fellows. He breathed in the stale odours that blew freely around him as he trailed a little aimlessly around yet another shabby, neglected street, poking his head into one of the less salubrious plastic pubs. The trapped vapours of second-hand smoke swirled menacingly out of the door while everything and everyone remained almost completely motionless. An old man sat alone in the corner playing solo dominoes, deep in thought about how to cheat himself. The bar staff stared up at a television on the wall where the Chancellor of the Exchequer John Major was talking about going 'back to basics'. They seemed to sway slightly with boredom while other customers murmured obscene conversations with halitosis whispers about the jumped up little grey prat. Jimmy walked across the public bar and straight out through the side exit.

Suddenly, and almost ridiculously, he emerged blinking, and knew exactly where he was. The post-box that he'd run into in his drunken, drugged exhaustion that night, the ubiquitous Asian-owned newsagent's shop, the alleyway crammed with abandoned shopping trolleys and discarded heaps of fly-tipped builders' rubble. This was it!

All the small nothings that make up the essential reality and basic identity of an area were there. He'd not been able to recall any of it until now because of the numbing ordinariness of it all. He'd fled around this corner in blind panic during his flight that awful night.

Each one of the details had registered, but his main concern had been to keep running and get away from the killer. After colliding with the post-box, he had at first run into that blind alley and painfully struck his shins on a dumped *U Like 2 Save* shopping trolley before slipping on the discarded sheets of rotting plasterboard. He had then shot out of the alleyway, run past the newsagents and just kept running, running, running to escape and to forget. And now he was back and remembered.

The maniac's house must be somewhere round the corner and very close to hand. He might just make a house call. He knew the killer was literally round the bend.

CHAPTER FIFTEEEN
AMBER

The microphone just missed his head. Ducking down quickly into the front seat, Dave Hicks slammed the car door shut and started the ignition. They certainly got up early, these press boys! It hadn't been fifteen minutes since he had personally heard the news about a discovery of another body, but here they were already, hard on the heels of the story. As he pulled away from the swarms of journalists and radio reporters camped in the street outside his house, Dave turned on the radio to hear the news report and the sound of his own car driving away with a screech up his own road.

'Detective Chief Inspector Hicks has just left his house,' shouted the reporter into the same microphone that had almost brained him a few moments ago. 'He is off to carry on the search. There is now only one week left of this fantastic deadline to bring the Cereal Killer to justice. As news breaks you can rest assured that we'll be there to bring it to you. So, until the next bulletin, I'll hand you back to the studio. This is Ian Huntley, in Hackney, for Radio…'

Dave turned it off and chuckled to himself. He was definitely the star of the show again. Now that old Jim Haigh had finally been kicked upstairs after another disastrous press conference the day before, he was free to get on and do whatever he wanted. Pure joy. After the most cursory of glances at the newly discovered lumps of corpse, this time discarded in a public toilet in the basement of a multi-storey car park, Dave first relieved himself at the adjoining urinal before emerging, still doing up his fly as he welcomed the press who were huddled around the iron railings at the top of the steps.

'Everything fits in with my previous proboscis,' he began. 'I don't think it'll be very long now before it hits the fan, and then you'll be able to interview Chummy himself instead of making do with me.'

There was the sound of slightly strained laughter.

'Now, if you'll excuse me, gents,' he continued, rising from the stench of the abyss, 'I need to leave the gents and bid you good day; I've got a little bit of a job to finish myself. I will always remain, however, at your convenience'

He moved through the crowd like a heated knife through butter, or at least like a spoon through *Bisto* gravy. Come to think of it, he *was* starving hungry, not having had breakfast yet and his tummy was screaming out for company.

Ten minutes later he was biting into a two-inch-thick bacon, lettuce and tomato sandwich, and making appreciative noises.

251

'Mnnnnnnn,' he mnnnned, 'don't you just love a nice DDT.'

The WPC forced to stand and nod while Dave devoured his mid-morning snack felt a throbbing nausea in her stomach but couldn't tell whether it arose from the sight of her boss pushing the gargantuan sarnie into his heavily whiskered mouth, or the fresh memory of the hacked-off limbs glimpsed briefly in the public toilet. Taking his well-licked plate back to the canteen she tried to shake off the loathing she felt. Still, if what she heard was right, he'd be gone soon, one way or another. The whole station had merely been going through the motions for the last few days; it was best to try and put up with him for a while longer, then perhaps things would settle back to how they were before Hicks and the killer appeared on the scene.

If the Cereal Killer was caught, Hicks was bound to be promoted, but if he wasn't — as seemed increasingly likely — well, the tubby tormentor would find himself shifted somewhere else pretty sharpish. WPC Susan Pickles' step quickened, and her humour improved sufficiently that by the time she got back to Hicks's inner sanctum, the sight of him scrabbling about with the corner of a Lever arch file to remove traces of bacon rind from his back teeth hardly upset her at all.

Dave sat at his desk watching the pretty brunette straighten her skirt and ask if there was anything else he required. If he had been one of the lads in Q Division, he'd have told her exactly what it was that he required.

252

But because he was a totally committed reconstructed police officer, determined to keep his appointment with greatness and destiny, he just puffed out his already expansive cheeks and simply asked for copies of all the daily papers. You could learn a lot that way; always listen to others. No one would ever be able to claim that Dave ignored suggestions from outside sources. Why, hadn't he followed up every conceivable lead in this case? What with the forensic tests, thorough searches, the creation of the 'Third Force' and even the time spent gazing at crystal balls with Madame Louvratska, the 'happy medium', Dave had given the term 'murder investigation' a new, more modern meaning. But now he was leaning back in his chair listening to the sound of reports being badly typed out in the outer office, Dave suddenly felt anxious again. What more could he do?

Following his now infamous announcement about the 'clue', he had been in exuberant spirits. He had completely believed the statements made to the press. At first this was quite satisfying; his prediction about catching the nutter within a fortnight was so unbelievably believable, that it had almost convinced him. But it was starting to become less persuasive. He knew that the only lead he had was his 'plan' and what made it more worrying was the slender basis upon which the 'plan' depended, namely that 'the nutter' would be plunged into such a state of panic that he'd give himself away. Or give himself up.

In the cold light of day maybe it did seem more than a little risky. Mum may have been right this time; he could be making the biggest mistake of his life. He stroked his beard, tugging at it so violently that tears formed in the corner of his eyes. At that moment WPC Pickles reappeared at his door, laden with newsprint and his anxiety temporarily subsided. People still did what he told them to, and he could see his handsome profile depicted on the front page of all of the tabloids. Life couldn't be that bad. He just had to get on with it. Nodding sagely at the headlines, Hicks muttered in a stage whisper that became a roar by the time it reached the WPC's ears.

'Read all about it. Your days are numbered, my old son. Come on my little beauty!'

***

At precisely this moment mayhem had broken out outside the *Spunky Klub* as it did almost every night — or 'Nite' as it was spelt in the lurid green and amber neon lights that flashed on and off outside the entrance. A continuous programme of information was provided by the electronic display situated just inside the door.

'A feast of Erotic morsels to TITillate your palate,' it read, 'Tonite and every Nite.'

'Club Dress Code: Cum as you are!'

Beside the door, a glass panel displayed several glossy photos depicting the promised banquet of delights; what were in the 1970s described as female impersonators but were now 'The Queens of Drag'. Their various images were displayed in all their glory, with short descriptions in fake Germanic handwriting. The photographs featured four or five young men, each dressed in elaborate costumes depicting Weimar Germany in all its most ridiculous Christopher Isherwood Teutonic fancy. Two were completely bedecked in black leather, standing legs akimbo and displaying swastika-like insignia on the seats of their lederhosen. Thigh-hugging patent leather stockings completed the ensemble, as did the little caps atop their severely shaved short back and sides. Other photographs featured on the sweaty wall illustrated similar young men with mischievous faces attempting to look coy. They were mostly dolled up in maid's uniforms; short and skimpy black skirts, tight-fitting bodices and swish black velvet chokers around their throats, although a few were dressed as more orthodox cowboys, farmhands and even policemen, complete with extremely well-endowed truncheons.

Peter Kurten studied the pictures with a mixed emotion of loathing and amusement. Two giddily excited and busy young men gently knocked against him as they swept past, giggling in dark brown voices that became tinged with obscenities as they gurgled off into the warm night air. All this vibrancy made Peter's head swoon and his thoughts turned once again to blind vengeance. He had always regarded revenge as a meal best eaten cold, but sometimes it needed heating up just a little bit to make it more palatable.

His cough came on again now, and the searing pain filled his lungs like a swarm of savage wasps, stinging and buzzing as they did so. Buzz, buzz, buzz. Hack, hack, hack. Too many fags for too many years had taken their toll and he was now being eaten from the inside out. His chest, the doctors informed him, was like a particularly mouldy piece of Swiss cheese with enormous holes spreading across his lungs as the disease feasted upon his delicious and still young body. He coughed some more, spitting a blood-flecked lump of phlegm onto the pavement. He felt the devil inside stabbing him again. What a bloody waste of a life! All those years spent puffing away on an array of cigarettes, all the time trying to imitate the image given in adverts. A mixture of confidence, calm and contentment. The ridiculous thing was this was how he felt in the first place. He had never even really experienced stress. He had never once felt nervous, lacking in confidence or displaying any doubts in his own abilities. He had never had a moment's anxiety, right up to the time he had gone for the tests. In fact, right up until the very moment when the doctor told him he only had six months to live. He hadn't shown any nervousness at all. The whole time he'd been as cool as a cucumber — only possibly, more green. Quality of life was one thing but combining it with some sort of quantity was pretty important too. He remembered the title of a 1960s television programme he'd seen as a boy — *Never mind the quality, feel the width*. How very true.

Thirty-four years old and that was that. Longevity was never more desirable than when one was going to be denied it and he felt short-changed. Yet he had everything. Handsome with a natural charm and style, he'd triumphed equally in his prep school classrooms as on the rugby pitch. In the dorms, he was the one other boys, had a crush on. At Oxford, academic and social success was inevitable. A double first, accompanied by a more than healthy sex life — with whoever he so chose. He had captained the victorious *University Challenge* college team. And now here he was, a leading architect tipped for major international awards and recognition, about to be cut down in his prime. Just one of those things. Peter had seen himself setting out to redefine the world and the way it looked. Now he'd have to destroy it first before reconstructing it in his own image; the new Genesis. He was the new creator.

Let there be Shite! And there was shite, and it was so bad, that it was good.

Looking at the tacky photographs depicted outside the *Spunky Klub* Peter was intrigued. In matters of love, or rather lust, he'd encountered very few problems. His bed was simply an extension of his ego. Always attractive to women, he'd lost his virginity to an older girl while at school three days after his sixteenth birthday. She was his best friend's big sister, and the romance was carried out under the very noses of the rest of the family whilst on a half-term visit. She was already seeing a much older boy, but Peter was quite an enticing prospect. There was always someone around more than willing to be bedded by him. In bed, as on the drafting table, he was regarded as proficient beyond the call of duty, and although commissions weren't that difficult to obtain, the blueprints usually only took one night's work. Peter called it his 'topping-out ceremony'. And now it was all going to be taken away from him. Dr Shipman the consultant had looked like a shop assistant apologising without any great sincerity about some damaged merchandise.

'I can't really give you any more than six months, I'm afraid,' he'd said, his brow professionally furrowed. 'We can't really improve on that time,'. As if it was open to negotiation. Peter shivered at the memory of the prissy consulting room.

'To tell the absolute truth, it could only be a matter of some weeks before your mind starts to feel the effects. It's not unknown for people to enjoy only a couple of months at their normal level of lucidity and intellectual capacity before they start to deteriorate. I'm sorry, but that's just how it is.'

Whatever else was said, it was those lines that remained with him. It was just how it is. Leaving the bright, new, shiny private hospital and saying goodbye to the staff dressed in crisp white designer uniforms, Peter passed the poor, broken, crippled bodies of other patients wobbling and swaying all around him, realising that they were the lucky ones. They could at least command pity and sympathy from the outside world, while he rotted from the inside while still looking like a sleek Olympic athlete. The determination that someone was going to have to pay for all this took an even deeper hold.

And now repayment was at hand. Finally leaving his sentry post outside on the street, he ventured forth into the *Spunky Klub*. He would teach them not to be so bloody happy in the face of his misery. They would suffer before it was over. Selfishness was probably the worst sin of all, and it would get the punishment it deserved. A crime against the person — that's what was needed. Any person. Lives would be taken hostage, although there was no need to wait for a ransom to be exacted. Payment would be instantaneous with extra dividends. An equitable arrangement.

Inside the velvety, luxuriant gloom that formed the essential ingredient of the club, Peter made straight for a side table next to the main stage. Young men depicted in the photographs outside steered their way around tables delivering expensive bottles of imported lager beer and more exotic drinks of varied hue to excitable customers. To his great relief Peter wasn't the only man on his own. Although his experience in attracting gay pick-ups was still in its infancy, he remained confident that his skill at picking up a wide range of sexual partners in the most unlikely of situations would stand him in good stead. A crashing of symbols announced the first show, and the brash lighting was subdued a little to lend the proceedings just enough decorum.

A troupe of heavily made-up men leaped up onto the stage and began acting a scene from *South Pacific* when the women 'wash that man right out of my hair'. The accompanying actions and expressions on the face of the artistes made it abundantly clear that what had just occurred had involved acts of gratuitous sexual abandon. Something extremely sticky was apparently being shampooed out. Peter gazed on, revelling in the seediness of it all. In between acts, music thumped out over the patrons and a number of them were exhorted to engage in the club dance 'Do the Spunk' by the equally lascivious waiters, their sinister costumes taking on a repellent autonomy. One such youth, his hair cut severely on all sides as though with a knife and fork, leered over Peter, allowing his long red tongue to loll out of his mouth, while his eyes indicated the dance floor.

'Don't just sit here alone, handsome, the management don't allow it. Get your arse over there where we can all see it.' Peter wasn't sure what he should do. He fidgeted a little, deciding against causing a scene and stood up.

'No, you've got to wait here until you've got a partner. You're not allowed to dance alone.'

The waiter looked around the room in panic. Finally, after much craning of his tattooed neck, he turned back to Peter.

'Well, it don't look like there's anyone else available at the moment, so you'll have to do it with me.' The youth held out his lily-white hand. Peter reluctantly took hold of it. It was surprisingly warm and inviting, like a chimpanzee he'd once held in Kenya, only a trifle more damp.

'What do we do?' he said.

The boy attempted a smile. 'We don't do anything; we just dance.'

The tune being belted out was a Kurt Weillian melody; all loud crashes and fairground oompahs. Within seconds, Peter was wheeled, twisted and turned to every thump and screech of the lilting listless music. Added to the couple of drinks he had consumed, it was a heady brew. The smell of sweaty dancers mingled with the foul moist air in the basement formed a most intoxicating atmosphere. And then the dancing abruptly ceased.

'My name's Dennis,' announced the youth, 'but you can call me Des. If you want anything else, you have to order it from me. No one else is allowed to serve you now, but me.' He gave a slight grudging smile, turned smartly round on his Cuban heels and trotted over to a table where three overweight men were waving for attention. They were Des's as well. Amused, Peter strained to hear their conversation.

'Three French tarts for us please.'

'I don't know what that is,' the waiter snapped abruptly, on the point of flouncing away.

'Oh, all right. Three Danish pastries then,' one of the men replied.

Peter sat back at his table and decided that it was all very well watching the world go by, but unless he wanted to go through all that again in half an hour, he would have to pick someone up pretty soon and finish what he had started.

Peering over towards the bar he saw several lone individuals and walked over in their direction. They all looked like policemen with short, tidy, definitely untrendy haircuts. Their faces shone a little too brightly, while their casual shirts looked as though they were usually worn with dirty unknotted ties. They drank white wine spritzers from tall, elegantly raised glasses, but with mighty swipes that suggested they were better suited to straight no-nonsense pints. Peter walked right past them towards the other end of the bar. Yes, sure enough they turned around, one by one, to give him the once-over. They were Hicks's men! Christ, they were onto him already. Better act quickly. Moving back to the reception room, Peter asked the counter clerk for his bill.

'Your waiter has got to give it you. You can't just get it here you know; house rules say you get it from your table waiter.'

'But I can't attract his attention and I need to leave now!'

The counter clerk pursed his lips. It was the first of many times that evening he had to explain the club's rules.

'Well, I can't do nothing about that, darling. Management policy is that bills are made up by the table waiter. What's his name?'

Peter glanced round to make sure no one had followed him outside.

'Des,' he hissed.

'Wait here, I'll go and see if I can fetch him.'

Still tutting, the clerk stood up from his desk, revealing that beneath his immaculate dinner jacket and bow tie, he wore thigh-length black leather jack boots with a red garter. Plodding unsteadily over to the black plush velvet curtains, the clerk hissed to get the waiter's attention.

'Dennissss. Dennisssssss.' Peeved, he glared back at Peter standing anxiously by the reception desk.

'You'll have to stay there. I've got to go and get him now!

This was his chance. Hesitating for no more than a couple of seconds, Peter bounded out of the reception area, up the stairs and into the street. A terrible pang stabbed him in the chest, while that awful pressure inside his head came back again. He felt it was going to explode, but knew he had to keep walking. Blast these bloody police! He would have to pick his haunts a bit more carefully from now on. Although he couldn't go on forever, he owed it to himself to keep out of reach of the grubby arm of the law as long as possible. And he wouldn't be able to do that if he hung around such obvious places as the *Spunky Klub*.

Once out on the streets the search did not prove that difficult and by midnight Peter was able to find another of life's victims to take out all of his frustration on. And there was a hell of a lot of it. At home, when it was all over, he sat on his white leather sofa listening to some Bach. They would find the body early the next morning; the bag containing the head and arm was resting up against a slide in the children's playground, just the way the other one did it. With a bit of luck, the police would never even suspect that it wasn't the work of the real one.

The music swept majestically over him and burrowed deep down into his subconscious. A bit like the cancer, really. For the first time he thought about the real killer with some insight. What would he make of all these goings on? Whoever he was he was bound to be in a state of permanent derangement by now. Just think of it, the fellow had done in about nineteen total strangers and while Peter thought that two so far wasn't bad going, it would take him a while to get up to that score. The real mystery was how to outsmart DCI Hicks; Christ, that man was on the ball. He would have to be constantly on his guard to avoid being caught. Maybe, thought Peter, it was Hicks himself who was the real murderer after all. Now that really would be something marvellous!

CHAPTER SIXTEEN
NAVY

That evening Dave Hicks gave his end-of-day orders to the 'Hicks Unit' as he had recently termed his squad of detectives.

'I want you to do everything you've done up to now,' he began, 'but I want you to do more of it and differently.' Dave had been working on his man-management skills. Looks of dumb insolence faced him across the room.

'I sometimes think that I am the only one who knows what he's doing on this case. I honestly don't know what would have happened if you didn't have me around. This case would probably be no nearer a solution than ever, with the nutter still running about willy-wisp.'

Detective Nudds could bear it no longer.

'And where exactly is the investigation at the moment, Detective Chief Inspector?' he asked.

Dave glared.

'The case, Mr Nudds, is nearing completion. There are only seven days left. I believe that you have read the press briefings. As I said this afternoon, I see this investigation,' he paused at the word, lovingly enunciating every syllable, 'as a jigsaw, and the jigsaw is starting to put itself together. There are only a few more jigs left to collect and then we'll have all the clues we need. We just have to dot our Ts and cross our Rs.'

Nudds was tempted to add, 'And talk out of our navy-blue arse,' but held his tongue.

'But what about the murders still being committed? How can we carry on while the killer is still carrying on himself?' asked another detective.

Dave got cross. That was indeed the rub, though surprisingly the argument hadn't cropped up too frequently.

'The nutter will pop up soon enough. I bet we'll even get him before he does in another one.'

Murmurs of despair swept around the room. This was lunacy far and above anything they'd heard so far, and they had heard plenty.

'Anyway,' Hicks continued, conscious that his stomach was starting to groan for his evening's dinner, 'there's nothing much we can do tonight, so why don't we all go home, eh?'

Half an hour later he was sprawled out on Mum's sofa with his great fists around an enormous cheese, piccalilli and sardine toasted sandwich.

'That'll keep you going until I can get the stew ready, all right, love?' said Mum.

Dave nodded, thinking of his next moves in the case. He didn't expect much to happen unless he forced the pace a bit; the pathologists wouldn't be able to turn up much he didn't know already, and it was no good opting for a wait-and-see approach; he was no Mr Micawber. He needed a brilliantly perceptive act to flush the killer out of his lair. While he munched away, tiny crumbs desperate to escape the giant cavern of his mouth dropped all down his trousers.

Now what would the greats do in this sort of situation? Holmes would notice something crucial but apparently unimportant like the dog that didn't bark; Poirot would mention the weather to a suspect and deduce, with the aid of his little grey cells, that from the answer given, the dislike of fish on the turn was motive enough for wanting Lord Malmesbury strangled; Sam Spade would spot the bulge in the scrawny hoodlum's pocket and know that it wasn't just because he was pleased to see him. What would Dave Hicks — Hicks from Hackney — 'The Dick from the Sticks', what should he do to catch his man? Unfortunately, he didn't know the answer at this precise moment, but he did know that when he knew it, it would be the making of him. At least he thought he knew that.

Dave closed his eyes and then considered things closer to home and asked himself another question. Would there be dumplings in Mum's stew?

CHAPTER SEVENTEEN
GOLD

On Friday evening, the notoriously smelly old man known as Pongo got onto a Piccadilly line Tube train at Kings Cross station and started pushing his way downwind and undetected to passengers further along the carriage until he at last appeared grinning and reeking by their side. Faces betrayed the horror felt as he squeezed each one in turn on the arm with his unspeakably grubby fingers and motioned for them to move aside as he continued his apparently haphazard journey along the train's packed compartments; making his way from one to another through the dangerous connecting doors while the train rattled along its predetermined route. Pongo wouldn't disembark until he had reached his goal at the end of the line. Stuck in the rush hour crush in the very last compartment of all, sweating in the unbearably non-air-conditioned stultifying late July heat, Clifton Gentle leant against the wall as he travelled home at the end of the working week.

Two stations before his own destination, Pongo arrived in the same carriage, by now sweating heavily and appearing to be in an alarmingly excited state. Within a few short moments, alerted by the consternation of other passengers, Clifton detected the sickly, putrid odour which Pongo suffused while he infiltrated olfactory senses. Like the Red Sea, bodies parted to allow this great wanderer to achieve his own destiny in his own land of milk and honey at the end of the Tube train. Clifton had of course seen, and smelt, Pongo many times before, but had never understood the true nature of the man's mania and as such was blissfully unaware until now that Pongo's mission was to take his place at the sacred chosen site at the very end of the very last compartment. One which Clifton of all people currently occupied. Bodies shuffled out of the way in what little available space there was, anxious to avoid personal contact and keen on getting out of range of Pongo's seeping, penetrating existence. Some had witnessed this scenario before and were keen to find out who today's victim would be, while others were just simply appalled at the bestial stench coming from a fellow human being. Clifton was at last face to face with Pongo, convinced that the wild look in the man's ancient, yellowy gold-encrusted eyes meant that he was going to be involved in an act of physical violence with a madman.

'Scuse me, mate, you're in my place.' Pongo gently prodded Clifton's elbow with his greasy, long fingernails tinged black with yellow undertones and finally managed to scrunch past the terrified Clifton until he at last leant languidly against the wall at the end of the train, breathing powerfully mad puffs of disgustingly rank, putrid breath all over him before attempting to shake him by the hand. This Clifton was obliged to do, since other passengers would not let him escape. He was their captive, and they could now enjoy themselves with his predicament. It was truly the end of the line.

At long last, falling out into the comparatively fresh air of Seven Sisters underground station, Clifton gratefully gulped down an early taste of the weekend before suddenly spying the front-page headline of the evening newspaper.

CEREAL KIILER STRIKES AGAIN!!
ONLY THREE DAYS TO GO

That was it, then. He wasn't going insane. It was true that there had been more killings, but this didn't improve Clifton's mood. This meant that there must definitely be someone else out there; another killer intent on stealing the show, if not his entire act. Handing over his change to the street news vendor and frantically scanning the article, Clifton's heart sank even further. Without any great surprise he read that Hicks had already categorically confirmed that the killing was 'without doubt the work of the so called Cereal Killer', and once again reiterating his firm and convinced belief that 'the nutter' would be caught before the deadline was up. Clifton dumped the paper into a nearby rubbish bin and trudged towards home. Unfortunately, due to a fault in the bin's manufacture and also because hooligans had jumped up and down on the contents the evening before, the bin had no bottom. This meant that the newspaper dropped back out and was immediately blown down the road, chasing Clifton along the pavement as a constant reminder while the front page careered in front of him in the evening breeze.

CEREAL KILLER STRIKES AGAIN! CEREAL KILLER STRIKES AGAIN! CEREAL KILLER STRIKES AGAIN! CEREAL KILLER STRIKES AGAIN!

Again and again and again!

If that wasn't enough, he remembered with a sinking feeling that he had promised Hilary to go round later that evening and meet her new man, Peter. That just about took the biscuit. He had been putting off thinking about it all day and now, with only an hour to go, it threatened to submerge him under the choking awfulness of life. If there was one thing he was really bad at, it was small talk. The only exceptions were with his victims, of course, but that was a different matter. He didn't really care what he said to them, as there was no intention to make the relationship a long-term one.

The evening's torture would last at least three hours while his entire repertoire of dreadfully tiny, small talk added up to about twenty-five minutes at most. And now there was another killer attracting attention. Someone was bound to mention the bloody murders tonight, and he couldn't keep up the pretence of polite interest in the subject for ever. It was like a busman's holiday. However, he knew that there was no getting out of it and the evening had to be endured somehow. Hilary had been a good friend, probably the only one he had ever known, but now she had met this man, Peter, it was bound to spoil everything. He was convinced that she had rushed into a relationship when she didn't know who he really was. He could be a beast of a man or even worse, a facsimile of her boringly bland ex-husband. But it was true that she deserved a measure of loyalty from Clifton and as a friend he was honour bound to support her. But what a night for a bloody dinner party!

Once inside his own flat, he picked up the post lying on the mat. It seemed to consist entirely of brown envelopes and advertising handbills. He changed into a smart dark suit he had last worn two years ago at an aunt's funeral. He then put on newly cleaned black leather shoes that pinched if he walked around in them for too long. This was all Peter's fault as well; he had been told what a smart dresser he was, and Clifton had to try and make an effort to conform. With an expression like that on the face of a condemned man at the gallows, Clifton Gentle stepped out of his flat at three minutes to seven, clutching a cheap bottle of red wine. He arrived at the place of execution at exactly one minute past. The door was hurriedly yanked open by Hilary, again wearing too much make-up, and the evening began in earnest and in the most ominous of circumstances.

***

At five past midnight, Hilary showed her guest to the door. Clifton danced down the steps, calling out goodnight in a voice that carried so far that his neighbours asleep in bed three doors up the street were sharply woken up. The pavement swayed and buckled beneath him as he made the four-minute journey in a little under eight. He had actually enjoyed himself! Hilary's boyfriend, Peter, was fantastic company, keeping them, all entertained the whole evening long, with his easy wit and ready charm. At times Clifton had literally screamed with laughter and even had to leave the room once as he was on the verge of hysteria. It was good to see Hilary enjoying herself so much as well. He'd never seen her quite like that before and she seemed so blissfully happy to have a man to call her own.

Stumbling into his flat at last, Clifton flung himself into an armchair. The room wheeled around in a crazy arc and his feet seemed to take on a life of their own as though they wanted to start capering about on the ceiling. He gripped the arms of the chair. His head throbbed from the brandy foolishly gulped down at the last minute which itself rested precariously on the best part of a bottle of South African Pinotage. His eyelids felt heavy. Favourite scenes from a Tom and Jerry cartoon came into his head and he started to giggle — there were lead weights on Tom's eyes, pulling them inexorably down. Clifton knew how he felt. With a desperate effort he rose to his feet and pitched clumsily into the kitchen where he poured himself a large vase full of cold tap water and tipped it messily down his throat as drops dribbled down his chin.

'That'll do.'

He made for the bathroom, muttering to himself. 'Bloody good bloke, that. Nice chap. Good sort.' He remembered to write something down about going for a drink the next night. Just the two of them. Saturday night. Boys night out. Hilary's miserable sister was coming round, and this would give Clifton a chance to get to know Peter better.

'Remembered to do that though; can't be too drunk; water does the trick. Good old water! Must put water back into the system.'

He went to the bathroom and urinated, still giggling.

'And water out of the system'.

Safely tucked up in bed, Clifton closed his eyes, trying to ignore the whirling sensation that still had him in its grip. Just concentrate on keeping a steady equilibrium, that was the trick. Breathe full and deep and steady as she goes was the way to go. Everything would be fine.

Thirty seconds later he rushed back into the bathroom and vomited down the toilet bowl. He really had enjoyed a wonderful evening.

He then decided to go back into the kitchen, and it was only then that he opened up his discarded post and read what Jimmy had written in the letter which he had posted through Clifton's letter box earlier that morning.

CHAPTER EIGHTEEN
MAROON

The water above Dave's head was filled by an image of huge black wings flapping around which looked like they belonged to a gigantic prehistoric bird which was trying to reach down into the depths and grab him. Enormous gulping bubbles burbled guiltily from his mouth on their way upwards towards the approaching wings, which suddenly changed shape into diving flippers. His face mask was a little smeared, but Dave could still make out other indistinct grey figures sliding through the water and moving inexorably in his direction. Suddenly from his left, one of them came straight towards him, pointing a harpoon gun. This was it; he must show a burst of speed before it was too late.

With a rapid acrobatic twist of his ample frame, Dave swivelled around in the water, wriggling in a desperate attempt to get away from the marauders, flapping his own enormous flippers behind him and clouding his view with the debris dredged up from the bottom. After swimming off a little way, he took shelter amongst the refuse lying scattered at the edge of the lake around the swirling glutinous weeds. A rusting dumped

Ford Cortina offered cover, even for a man of Hicks's substantial build, and he paddled around the chassis cautiously, searching for a glimpse of his pursuers. He had spotted two already, but it didn't mean there weren't more circling around in the oily water ready to pounce. His heartbeat quickened and the gulps of air taken from the cumbersome oxygen tank became more frantic. He listened for alien bubbles but heard none.

Suddenly, not more than fifteen yards away, two figures appeared out of the thick weeds. Their yellow rubber suits contrasted vividly with the glinting maroon harpoon guns which they both carried. Hicks ducked sharply, peeping out through the submerged passenger door window. Just one bubble of air would be enough to give him away. He was unarmed. Any bubble would be swiftly followed by a harpoon dart.

The swish of flippers got closer and the sensation that his pursuers made on the water became more resonant, as if beating against Dave's eardrums, thumping deep down inside his head. On and on.

And then they were on top of him. A third figure had come up from the rear and immediately released his missile. The water all around Dave turned crimson and he floundered momentarily, before limping off around the Cortina's bonnet, but it was all to no avail. The others had caught sight of him now and, firing their weapons straight into his chest watched as the big man spiralled out of control, massive arms and legs windmilling in the grey-green mass of weeds. His body lay still in the red swirling stew of water as bubbles rushed up from his face mask, like an assassin fleeing the scene of a crime.

'Brilliant!' Dave said, back on land and drying his hair. 'I felt just like James Bond.' He was totally exhilarated.

'Glad you enjoyed it, David,' said one of the would-be assassins. 'I thought it would appeal to someone in your line of work. It's a bit like how your prey must feel. A sort of role reversal if you will, the hunter finding himself in the role of hunted, trying to avoid the unavoidable.' There was a hint of sarcasm in the voice, but Dave missed it.

'Yes, I think you're right there. I already have a pretty good idea of how the criminal mind works. You know, how it reacts when it knows that capture is inevitable, but it's still been a most interesting insight into how the brain ticks over in a situation like this. I must write down my thoughts before I forget — everything is crucial in these sorts of investigations you know.'

The others exchanged surreptitious smiles. Pitiful really, to see how their view of the great detective differed from the reality. It all looked so very different on the telly.

'So do you think you'll become a regular member of our little lodge, David?' asked Iain Foster.

Hicks frowned, considering,

'I'm not sure that I'll be able to make it a regular thing, Iain, what with my NLSDA activities and the demands of my profession, but I'd like to come along every now and again. I'd quite like to be the hunter next time round I think, though — sort of recreating my real-life role in a different type of situation, off my own back, if you see what I mean.'

Iain did see what he meant, and so did the others, none too pleased that he'd been invited to join without their say so. At least he wouldn't become a regular member; that would have been ridiculous. It would be far too easy every week. Capturing someone within five minutes was almost unheard of. The wind picked up just as the last of the equipment had been packed away into the cars. It had been another sweltering day and the breeze made them suddenly shudder with anticipation of rain, although the sky still seemed clear.

Their club was called the London Underwater Survival Team, or LUST for short; an acronym that greatly appealed to Dave. Its members came from the most secure of the middle-class professions: a smattering of accountants, one bank manager, two solicitors, a senior civil servant, a company director or two and a unit investment broker. But no policemen so far. What everyone had in common was a longing for excitement and the expectation of something a bit out of the ordinary.

The equipment used was much the same as for conventional scuba diving, with one important addition:

the harpoon gun. With a capsule of red dye replacing the sharp steel prong at one end, it became a perfect weapon for this bloodless blood sport. The small plastic container exploded on impact and splattered the victim with glutinous dye which stuck onto clothing, even under water. The effect was always pleasing; a lifelike representation of a real hit. It was a little bit more exclusive than scuba diving, and Iain, Roger, Alastair and Gregory liked it that way. It was a means of adding a little mystique and glamour to an otherwise increasingly accessible pastime. Dave sat at the wheel of his car, his hair still damp and dripping down the back of his shirt. As usual, they'd all follow Iain's car to 'the local hostelry', as the others called the pub. Dave liked that; 'the local hostelry'. It was witty and classy at the same time, he thought. He would say that back at the station to impress the lads.

'Why don't we all go off to the local hostelry?' he'd suggest just after he'd caught the nutter. 'Just for a quick quickie.' That bloody maniac. The Cereal Killer as they all called him now. Only two more days to go now. The deadline was looming, and it would be the end of the line for him unless he delivered the goods. Fancy putting his own neck on the chopping block like that! Well, it did concentrate the mind, a bit like the scuba diving. He would have to pull out all the stops this time.

This little Saturday morning outing was intended to take him away from the pressures of the station for a few precious hours. He had been on a course at work about that once. 'Stress Management' it was called. It had been a welcome diversion, but he'd have to kiss LUST goodbye for a while. There were enough petty-minded people around who would like to see him suffer. At least that old dodderer Jim Haigh was out of the way for good, but there was sure to be someone else coming up the road. He felt like a sheriff in the old Wild West, waiting for the next gunslinger to arrive in town and challenge him. He'd seen a film like that once. Bunfight at the Okey Cokey Coral or something like that.

Iain's BMW pulled into the driveway of a large country pub, The Evelyn, complete with ivy-clad gables and teak picnic tables tucked away to one side of a tasteful beer garden. Dave was eager to get to the bar first so he could buy the drinks. He thought he'd suggest lunch there as well. On him of course. He'd have to find a phone and give Mum a ring, tell her to put the steak pie on hold. It was good to mix socially with this sort of people, much more his scene than all the plods at the station. After all, it might be his last chance before it all came toppling down around his ears.

But no, he shouldn't be thinking like that. He had to be more positive, as Mum had said:

'If anyone can catch this fiend, Davey, it's you. You've done all the hard work and it's about time that it started to pay off. You just use your wits and pin your ears back and you'll be able to see and hear him.'

Yes, that was right, he thought, it's just a matter of keeping my nerve. Tuning his personal antenna and listening out for him. After a surprisingly expensive lunch he marched briskly across the car park, the scent of cigars and steaks wafting out of the lounge bar of the country pub and up his twitching nostrils. Dave surveyed the shiny Rovers, BMWs and the odd Porsche parked gleaming outside.

'I've marked his car all right,' he thought as a grin started to appear.

Refreshed after the excitement, Dave sat back in his own car seat. The others had all made jokes about drinking and driving while they drank Dave's money away, and of course Dave had laughed along with them while sipping his orange and lemonade, all the while itching to whip out a breathalyser kit and arrest the lot of them on the spot. It was difficult being a policeman sometimes. It was difficult being Dave Hicks all the time. Even Mum had been a bit short with him on the phone when he rang from the pub.

'I'll suppose you'll not want me to cook your dinner so often when you've got more swanky friends,' she'd sobbed when he explained about lunch, 'and I thought you loved your old mum.'

Dave started up the ignition and drove out of the car park, onto the main road back into London. Back to London and back to work to catch the nutter.

***

'Oh, that's good, that's very good, Peter.'

Clifton was sitting on the arm of a chair, talking on the phone to Hilary's new boyfriend. He suddenly collapsed into fits of laughter bordering on hysterics. It was probably the pressure.

'He didn't, did he? Oh no, oh God, that's so funny, that's absolutely hilarious.' He laughed again, a little saliva dribbling out of the corner of his mouth and starting to run down his cheek. 'Oh no!' he shouted screamed joyously down the receiver.

'And that's when he discovered the toilet paper running out of the seat of his trousers,' said Peter. Clifton laughed again, but not quite so spontaneously. It was a shame, but although he was clearly very witty and charming, Clifton noticed that Peter always seemed to slightly mess up the punchline. It might have been that it wasn't quite phrased well enough, or it could have been his timing, but it was always a little disappointing.

'Listen, Peter, what about tonight?' asked Clifton, anxious to move on. 'Are you still free?' There was a discernible hesitation. Clifton imagined Peter quickly leafing through his leather-bound personal organiser, looking for a space.

'No, Hilary's already booked. My Filofax says that I've got a window. Why don't we go for a drink in town, you and I?'

Clifton had also noticed that Peter always used that expression, 'you and I'. It was almost becoming his catchphrase.

'Great, where?' There was another pause. Clifton began to wonder whether he should be so pushy; after all, they'd only met once, and when all was said and done Peter was Hilary's boyfriend, not *his*.

'Do you know the Knave of Hearts pub in Charing Cross Road? We could try for that if you like. Seven thirty?'

Clifton knew it only too well. The last time he'd been there, he'd taken someone home, knocked him on the head and sawn his legs off at the knee.

'Yes,' he said, 'that will be great.'

'Fine. Just promise you won't get me legless!' said Peter.

'What?' Clifton gasped.

'Well, you know, I don't drink much, and I don't want to get too tipsy.'

'Oh yes. Right. Fine. Well, until tonight then.' Clifton hung up the receiver. He knew that he had to get out that evening. That letter from Jimmy had been quite a shock. It would have been more of one if it actually said anything meaningful. The rent boy was apparently after money for his story. But why had he waited so long and where had he been in the meantime? Perhaps he had only just summoned up the courage to blackmail him, but it didn't really ring true. He could have had trouble tracking him down, but not for this long surely? Like just about everything else in his life at the moment, it didn't make any sense at all. Like Hilary's boyfriend, Peter, for instance, was he too good to be true?

He trudged into the kitchen, only to be confronted by an enormous pile of accumulated washing-up in the kitchen sink. With a sigh, he pulled on his pink rubber gloves and started extracting glasses and cutlery out from under the greasy mass of dirty crockery. He hated doing this. It all seemed so pointless; eating and drinking out of clean utensils when all you ever did was get them dirty again. He dredged out a pot furred with baked-on wild rice. He knew that it couldn't have been more than three days since he'd used it, yet it was already caked in a thick, hard, mouldy crust. For some reason, the sight of it made Clifton feel bitter and angry. Why did he have to be different in life, and yet still have to endure the awful banality of everyday civilisation? If he was born a freak, why couldn't he be completely different from other people, and be able to throw away all his pots and pans when they got dirty, wear special clothes that needed neither washing nor ironing, and walk about without getting dog shit smeared over the soles of his shoes?

But, of course, none of that was for him. He had been chosen by some unseen hand to be the man alone within society; a pariah at the party who was trying to gain admittance but allowed to venture no further than the kitchen. All of which brought him back to the washing-up, still sitting there.

After he had done all the dishes, he wandered listlessly back to the living room and switched the now hated television set back on. It was a cheap and desperate response against loneliness. The telly talked to him; it was his friend. Flickering images of actors dressed up as doctors and nurses came onto the screen. They were supposed to be romantically involved both with themselves as well as with the patients who curiously appeared to be bursting with health. Clifton half-dozed, half-stared, and allowed his chin to drop onto his chest. The flabbiness of his weak jawline was too often exposed when he sat that way. His mother used to go on about it a lot when he lived at home, imploring him to sit up straight so people could see how handsome he was.

And so, virtually stupefied, Clifton sat staring at the TV screen until the phone rang again. Clifton glowered at it at first, not sure whether to answer or not. It was probably Peter making an excuse about not being able to make it that evening after all. If it was him, then Clifton didn't want to know. He had nothing else to do, not even go out killing any longer. But then again, it could be Jimmy with some more sordid details about payment. He had already decided that he would tell him to sod off. He waited. Perhaps it was best to ignore it.

At last, after exactly seventeen rings, the phone stopped ringing. It must have been his mother. She always rang far too long. She knew very well that the flat was so small that you could reach the phone easily from anywhere within just six rings. Why didn't other people think like that? He did all the time. Anyway, whoever it was, they were gone now, but so was his concentration and there was no chance of recapturing the precarious mental stability of a few moments before. What if Peter didn't want to go out for a drink? What would he do then; wait for the dreaded Jimmy to strike at last?

It seemed odd to Clifton that what was once his reason to exist, to go and kill young men, now seemed so utterly boring and pointless. He had grown tired of it all and it had reached the stage where he couldn't quite remember what it was that had made him start in the first place. In all honesty, he hadn't really felt like doing it for a long time now and in truth his heart wasn't really in it all the while leading up to that Bonfire Night debacle. If it hadn't been for that blessed idiot Hicks, he would probably have given it all up ages ago.

Clifton compressed the events of his life into a few fervent images. There was the sight of his grandfather dead in his coffin; that of his own body lying in a deathly stupor on those sordid evenings alone; the various corpses he'd created along the way. It all seemed a bit silly somehow; even though he understood it was a perfectly natural logical progression, he still couldn't relate the deeds to the way he felt towards himself and to others. After all, he was a moral, caring, human being. All he needed was a little bit of understanding, and a measure of sympathy for having to be alive in the first place.

Clifton left the flat, allowing plenty of time to get to the rendezvous with Peter at the pub near Leicester

Square. If he got there too early, he could always take a look around and see how many policemen Hicks had tried to secrete amongst the fleshpots. Anyway, he hated being late. He could imagine what they'd put on his gravestone — 'Here lies a vicious and cynical murderer, a scourge on society and a fiend. But he did keep very good time'.

'He never kept us hanging around, I'll say that for him,' his ghostly victims would attest.

In the end it Peter who was late. By a full fifteen minutes. Clifton was on the verge of setting a mental deadline for when he would get up and walk away. Another ten minutes, he thought, then he would be off. Or maybe a few more. But suddenly, there was Peter, appearing through the gathering smoke of the early Saturday evening drinkers and beaming at him.

'I'm sorry I'm a little late,' he shrugged apologetically. 'I got held up dropping some things off at work. I don't usually work on Saturday, but it's needed by a client first thing on Monday. I hope you don't mind.' His smile was easy charm itself.

'Of course not,' Clifton lied. 'I didn't even realise you were late.'

Conversation soon worked its way round to Hilary.

'That's her to a tee,' said Clifton. 'She's often so bloody serious you'd think she was a real bluestocking. Sometimes she just can't see a joke; you have to talk her through it before she understands.'

'I've noticed that as well. It's not that Hilary hasn't got a sense of humour, because we laugh very easily together. It's just that she does have a tendency to be a bit, you know, over-earnest.'

'Yes, yes!' Clifton agreed a little too readily. 'She can be a real pain like that sometimes.'

Peter's smile waned appreciably, and Clifton realised that he'd once again overstepped the mark. Damn! He must try to be pleasant; it wasn't a contest. He ought to do a bit more drinking and a little less talking.

Two hours later they'd reached the far side of sobriety. Clifton was obviously more accustomed to the state than Peter.

'Come on, drink up, old chap. We're not finished yet. We've got a bit more drinking to do before the evening's over.'

'I feel a bit whoopsy already,' said Peter.

'Nonsense, you're tired, that's all. You need a few more drinks inside you. What's it to be, same again?'

'No, no, I'd like something different. Look, it's getting awfully crowded in here, couldn't we go somewhere else? Is there anywhere you usually go to in this part of town?'

The tables seemed to have been turned; now it was Clifton's shot to be the expert. He was on his own turf after all.

'Well, there are one or two places I know where it won't be quite so packed, but I'm not sure you'd feel terribly comfortable in them.'

Peter frowned, looking a trifle baffled. Confusion raged through the addled fug of his brain.

'What do you mean? What sort of places?'

Clifton relished the moment.

'You'll see,' he said. 'Come on.'

Outside, the fuggy hot night air smelt rich and clean compared to the smoky, polluted haze of the pub. Drawing in a few deep breaths of evening London fumes, Peter was surprised by the way that his head started to swim. Clifton was already some way up the road, calling back to him.

The steaming streets around Piccadilly were chock-a-block with people. It seemed that everyone had flocked there on this particular Saturday night, undeterred by the threat of more IRA bombs going off in the capital. Young and not so young trendies, some leftover yuppies from the '80s along with theatregoers, alarmed-looking American and Japanese tourists, coarse groups of overdressed middle-aged women accompanied by husbands wearing the same dark, dull suit they wore to work every day. And nearly all of them sweating away in the warm night air. Clifton and Peter pushed their way through the bubbling crowds, overhearing a bizarre surrealist cacophony of conversation merging together. Everyone was talking their hearts out, and the noise became almost deafening as they slipped through the mass of mundane and worthless lives. Clifton was always excited by crowds and loved the opportunity to participate with anonymity. It was as though he was able to retain his own character inside a crowd while everyone else took on a supporting role. His name was the one in lights.

'I don't know what it was all about; it didn't ring true to me.'

'There's gotta be somewhere decent to eat around this dump.'

'I think we need to get to the subway, honey.'

'Graham, I thought you said you were going to be nice to Mother this evening?'

'Piss off, you fucking little twat.'

'Get your cock sucked here.'

Yes, you could find all human life inside a crowd.

Arriving at the door of the *GayZebo Bar*, Clifton pushed Peter inside before he could register what was happening to him. In fact, it wasn't until he had been inside for some while that Peter fully realised exactly what sort of place it was. The large, dark room was full, but not crammed, with men. There were a lot of what his friends would have called 'types' there; cropped heads and moustaches with a fair amount of flamboyant style in abundance along with the odd anachronistic leather men in biker gear. Tinny electronic rhythmic music was playing, Miquel Brown's 'So Many Men, So little Time' rang out, but it seemed to serve only as a backdrop, and no one appeared to be paying much attention to it. An overzealous breeze was supplied by briskly turning fans.

'I'll get the drinks,' said Clifton a little sheepishly as he began to wonder if it had been a mistake. Peter certainly looked a bit shocked.

The brisk walk from St Martins Lane had sobered Clifton up and by now he was slightly dismayed by his boldness. It wasn't the fear of disclosing his sexuality that unnerved him, nor even the fact that he appeared to be coming on strong with Peter, but rather that he was doing things a little too easily. Anyway, it seemed that Peter might actually be too drunk to notice what was going on. He was simply rocking back and forth to the music in a large pink leatherette chair. Clifton ordered two large gin and tonics. Drinks in hand, the two sat quietly for a while, looking about them. All in all, there was quite a bit of mutual observation going on. Although no one seemed to be alone, there was a good deal of window shopping going on. Clifton suddenly realised that he was being watched himself. He turned to find Peter staring straight at him. It seemed an eternity before he spoke the inevitable words.

'Clifton, can I ask you a question?' he said before a slight pause. 'Are you gay?'

It had to happen one day, of course, but he didn't expect it like this. It was peculiar having to face that question, the one he didn't even know the answer to himself. What should he say? What could he say?

'I'd rather you didn't say anything to Hilary about this.'

'Of course not! I just thought you might want to talk about it, that's all.'

'Well, to be honest, I don't really consider that sort of thing.'

'Come off it, Clifton, everyone considers that sort of thing. How can you not consider it? What is it they say about men; that we think about sex once every sixty seconds or so?'

Clifton looked alarmed. Christ! Once every minute?

'What do you mean? The act itself or just the concept? I don't think I could do anything once a minute. I don't think about sex once every six months.'

Peter smiled. He still looked drunk and was leaning eccentrically to one side. With a bit of luck, thought Clifton, he won't remember any of this in the morning.

'So, you're not sure? Then why are we in a gay bar?'

Clifton muttered a few things about his feelings of isolation and anonymity but thought it wise to omit some of the more lurid details of the past.

'So, you see,' he said, 'I'm a sort of asexual; neither one thing nor the other. I don't quite seem to belong anywhere. I'm a sort of sexual half-caste. An agnostic.'

What more could he say to deflect these questions? It was all getting a bit too heavy and besides, he was tempted to blurt out too much detail. Grabbing his drink, he gulped it down, still obliged to listen to Peter's increasingly drunken rambling. At least no one else seemed to be listening.

It was at this point, scanning the room, that he noticed someone else scrutinising the two of them. At last, a distraction.

'Don't look now, Peter,' he whispered, 'but I think someone over there fancies you.' It was the perfect gambit; Peter was just vain enough to fall for it.

'Where, where?'

'Easy, tiger. Don't make it obvious. Over there by the statue.'

Peter's eyes falteringly shuffled through the swinging crowd until he picked out the outline of a seated figure half-hidden behind a black marble statue of a young boy blowing a horn. The man was staring straight back at him.

'Oh my God, I can see him!' Peter was flushed and appeared to be getting more and more excited. 'What do you think he wants?'

'Well, I can't say for sure, of course, but I'd say it was you.'

Peter looked surprised, but not, Clifton noted, very disappointed.

'Well, this certainly is a most enlightening evening.'

Now Clifton looked confused. What on earth did he mean by that; he wasn't a closet queen was he? Perhaps it was just the drink talking. He certainly hoped so.

What would he say to Hilary otherwise? Imagine it; the new man in your life, your solution to everything and your route to happiness, as queer as a coot. Well, at least that was one question answered.

More people suddenly rushed to join the dance floor as The Normal's 'Warm Leatherette' thumped out of the speakers. Clifton froze as he noticed the man at the other end of the room get up from his seat and start to make his way across the jerking dancing figures towards them.

'Hello, I was wondering if I recognised you from somewhere?' said the man. He casually slipped down into the one vacant chair beside them. Clifton watched helplessly as Peter made room for him and started to answer.

'Well, I don't know. My friend here noticed that you were looking at us, but I don't think I know you. Your face looks interesting though.'

Clifton recognised his face all right. It was the one all strangers wore when they thought they could muscle in on something that was none of their business. It was the face of an interloper, a busybody, an intruder. An entirely unwanted face.

'We don't know you, and we don't really want to, do we, Peter?' said Clifton. 'Could you move away now please? We're trying to enjoy ourselves.'

Peter looked offended, but the man did not seem to notice anything wrong.

'Would you like me to leave?' the stranger asked Peter.

'Yes,' said Clifton.

'No,' said Peter, glancing disapprovingly across at his friend, 'you're very welcome to stay, and,' he added while shooting a look at Clifton, 'I apologise for my friend's rudeness.'

'Well, that's awfully nice of you,' the stranger said, easing himself from the seat, 'but I think maybe I ought to leave. I wouldn't want to think I was the cause of a tiff.' He smiled coquettishly at both of them and gracefully got up and moved away.

Peter giggled again.

'He thinks we're a couple,' he said, 'you and I.'

How much Clifton was beginning to hate that phrase — 'You and I'.

Twenty subdued minutes and two rounds of drinks later, they were finally ready for the journey home. Clifton had become tired of Peter's constant babbling, and in all honesty, he was really beginning to get on his nerves. Perhaps it was the drink talking, he decided wearily, and not that Peter was actually boring. They had certainly drunk a lot. A hell of a lot.

Although the pavement outside was deserted, the enormous heaps constructed out of rubbish decaying openly in the street resembled angry great monsters, ready to rush out and attack them. Temperatures at night had lately been some of the highest on record, and tonight was no different, although the moment they left the club they noticed that there must have been a recent cloudburst of rain. The gutters were running with a lot of mucky water splashing onto the pavement as it collected rubbish along the way and formed little dams of detritus. The effects of the heat and humidity had turned everything rancid. Rats thrived in times like this and indeed one or two of them could be seen now, scurrying around with oleaginous greasy fur, greedily feasting on rancid kitchen fat oozing out of the filthy upturned bins. What with the constant stress caused by the recent spate of IRA terrorist bombs going off all the time the whole city seemed to be under threat.

'Well,' said Peter as he swayed off into the sticky, choking atmosphere of the street. 'It really has been a lot of fun. We'll have to do this again sometime. And don't you worry,' he added ominously, inexpertly tapping the side of his nose with an index finger, 'your secret's safe with me.' He lurched off down the road, slipping on a greasy takeaway box. 'I'm off to get a cab. See you soon, Clifton.'

With that he was gone, taking such exaggerated care not to fall into the gutter that he scraped up against the wall of the dirty book shop to his side. A few more people left the *GayZebo Bar*, nudging Clifton off the pavement. He watched Peter for a moment or two before turning and strolling off in the opposite direction to catch his night bus back home. No expensive taxis for him; he would ride home on his London Transport season ticket pass. Hearing more raucous, obscene voices he turned round to see another rowdy group spill out into the street. Clifton spotted the stranger who had come up and bothered them; it seemed that he was leaving too, probably given the cold shoulder by others in the club. Clifton watched him walk up the street in the direction Peter had taken. Good riddance. Peter would have to deal with him on his own this time.

Clifton's bus was just pulling up at the stop in Trafalgar Square and after a short sprint he managed to squeeze on and climbed the steps upstairs where he sat next to a huge, drunken Greek man smelling strongly of patchouli oil. He gazed across at the lion statues in the square and watched drunken gangs kicking more refuse into the fountains and bellowing out like beasts in the field. The oppressive sticky heat seemed to lift somewhat as the bus weaved its way up Charing Cross Road and it gave Clifton great satisfaction to feel the breeze coming in through the slatted windows on the top deck whilst perspiring inebriates stood choking on the bus fumes as it sped by.

Just as it swung round into Tottenham Court Road a slightly grubby and diminutive figure peered up from his lookout position outside the Dominion Theatre and saw Clifton Gentle gazing imperiously out of the bus window. Tearing across the road and racing to the next bus stop Jimmy just managed to clamber on board before it pulled away.

***

298

Clifton was a scream. Who would have thought it —
him turning out to be gay all along? Wait until he told
Hilary! All that stuff about a friend of hers who led such
a lonely, sheltered life and there not being many women
around. No bloody wonder! His knuckles hurt from the
scraping he had just received when he bumped into the
wall on his left. Or was it his right? He would have to
concentrate harder if he wanted to get home in one
piece. Just try to stay on the safe side of the pavement.
It had been a long time since he'd been this drunk; cars
seemed to pass dangerously close to the kerb, and in
such alarming numbers.

The whooshing noise they made on wet roads
reminded him of his childhood; living in the country he
was always astounded at the number of motor cars in
town. From his grandparents' front room, he would gaze
out at cars all day long, enchanted. At night, tucked up
in an enormous double bed, he always listened out for
the cars out and about. The swishing of rubber wheels
on wet tarmac had held a glamorous attraction ever
since; fast people in fast cars out late. Warm and snug
in the gigantic soft bed, the young Petey imagined
wondrous events in the big city, looking forward to
tasting the pleasures himself someday.

Staggering drunkenly along hot streets clogged
with even more piles of stinking refuse and foul
vegetation, he passed along the remains of Berwick
Street fruit and veg market. A sort of primitive homing

device was leading him ever onwards towards Oxford Street and salvation, in the form of a big black London cab. Something heavy landed on his shoulder.

'Hello. So, we meet again.'

Turning with difficulty, Peter saw the man from the club. 'Oh hello. I'm trying to find a cab, no luck though.'

'Well, let's see what we can do. We Peters must stick together.'

Peter nodded pleasantly, not quite understanding. What 'Peters'?

His head was spinning more unpleasantly now, making it difficult to concentrate. This chap might know what to do; better than having to think for himself anyway. Peter was led by the arm around a corner and into a narrow alley around which a number of cars had been parked haphazardly.

'What do you think of this?'

With some effort Peter stared into the gloom. He made out a large rubbish bin on wheels.

'It's all right, I suppose, but it isn't a cab, is it?'

The man laughed.

'No, silly, I meant this.' He pointed to a shiny expensive looking sports car parked beside them. 'It's mine; I can give you a lift, if you'd like, that is.'

This was more like it. Peter clambered gratefully inside; it was a flash little number with gadgets all laid out along the dashboard and they glinted when the ignition was turned.

'This is really very good of you.'

Peter Kurten smiled back.

'No, I assure you. The pleasure is all mine,' he said.

CHAPTER NINETEEN
BROWN

Clifton always woke late on Sunday mornings. And on this particular morning his head pounded, and his eyes were itchy. It felt as if they had been skewered and roasted in the night. Lying perfectly still in his pit, all he could do was groan. Focussing with difficulty on the large alarm clock, he made out that it was a quarter to twelve. It didn't matter; there was nothing special he needed to do. It had been like this since the killing had stopped. He groaned again. Maybe he ought to get himself a hobby after all. Aware that he could no longer bear staring at all the frightening shapes which were manifesting themselves on the patterns on the curtains, Clifton shut his eyes tight, flung back the sheets and tried to dangle one leg out of bed. The mental concentration that this entailed, together with the accompanying physical activity seemed to send oceans of blood rushing to the more porous parts of his brain. It hurt. The pounding throbbing in his temples became more intense. He attempted the manoeuvre again, this time in exaggerated slow motion, and found it slightly less painful, though no less futile. Why bother with all this, anyway? He remembered the reason for things being as they were and felt acute waves of depression wash over and drag him under.

The second note from Jimmy which he had found thrust into his pocket while he sat on the bus the evening before lay beside the bed, its grim threat undisguised despite the syntax with which it was framed. And what would Peter say now to dear old Hilly? Something fatuous and unkind, probably.

'Hello, darling! Guess what? Your strange friend took me to a queer club last night and tried to get off with me!'

It was just all too wretched to even contemplate. He would have to get to Peter before he said anything to her. He thought a casual jovial approach might work best.

'Look here, Peter,' he'd say, 'not a word about last night, you know. I wouldn't like to dig up all the things we said, if you don't mind. If you can remember anyway, that is.' He would laugh and try to make it sound as unthreatening as possible. Christ, what a bloody mess!

Staggering beside his bed, with one arm against the wall, Clifton put on his glasses and attempted to open his eyes. Prising his lids apart took an immense effort, but he succeeded and, still shaking, he tried breathing properly. Tea. Yes, a nice cup of thick, strong tea; that usually did the trick. The kitchen looked quite uncharacteristically clean, almost sinisterly so. Clifton scalded his thumb trying to pour boiling water into an ancient brown and white striped teapot, then dropped a carton of milk, spilling some under the fridge where it would be left to go rancid. At last tea was successfully transferred from a mug which bore the inscription 'I'm no Mug' into Clifton Gentle, who bore nothing so useful. Almost immediately the sweet tannin did the trick, teasing and cajoling long dormant brain cells into action. He started to think more clearly. Peter: he had to ring Peter!

Glancing up at the clock on the wall, Clifton felt familiar panic waves flowing again. It was now five past twelve; Peter might have called Hilary already. At first, he couldn't find Peter's number in his address book, mainly because it was entered under Hilary's. He misdialled at his first attempt and spoke briefly to an easily alarmed Miss Slot, while the right number produced no answer. Either Peter was dead asleep, or he had already gone out. Now what to do? Hilary's phone rang only three times before she answered.

'Hello, 081-349 0989.'

Clifton shuddered; why did she answer it like that? No one had given out their number since the 1970s.

'Hilary, it's Clifton.'

'Clifton!' she squealed. 'How did it go last night? I hope you didn't lead my poor darling astray. Did he get too drunk?'

Thank God. She had not spoken to him yet.

'No, no, not too drunk. Just a little paralytic.'

'I can imagine. Anyway, what are you doing ringing me on a Sunday and spoiling my leisurely wallow with the papers?'

'Oh, nothing much. I just wondered if you were going to see Peter later on today. I've got a book he wanted to borrow.'

Clifton shuddered as he said that; by Christ that was weak. He should have thought this conversation through before ringing.

'Why don't you ring him yourself?'

'I was going to, but I thought you'd be more likely to be up.'

'Well, he'd better be up; he is supposed to be taking me out for late lunch. You could drop the book over here if you want, and I'll give it to him. What is it by the way?'

'Oh,' said Clifton, trying desperately to think of something, 'it's no matter, I'll need to find it first. I'll be along in a bit, but I won't stay. I don't want to keep you from the Sunday scandal sheets; I know how much you love the News of the Screws.'

He hung up and frowned. Things were definitely building to some sort of crisis. Where on earth could that fool have got to after leaving the club? And what bloody book should he take to Hilary's?

***

Clifton spent most of the afternoon trying not to worry. It was impossible to ignore Jimmy and hope that he went away. He would either have to pay up or get rid of him. But what if he had left instructions as he'd said, 'with a mate of mine so's if you try it on, I'll get you anyway'. He was on tenterhooks. When the doorbell rang around two o'clock, he jumped and went cold, but instead of Jimmy, it was Hilary, distraught and with tears streaming down her shiny face and her eyes looking like red marbles.

'He's dead, dead,' she sobbed.

Clifton was bewildered.

'Who's dead?' He wondered if he should shake her or something. She was plainly hysterical.

'The police came round a few minutes ago. Oh God, I can't believe it. Oh God, it's terrible. He's dead, Clifton.'

Clifton tried to speak calmly.

'But who is dead, Hilary?'

'Peter!' she screamed and slumped against the door frame. 'They said they had found a body and that his sister Rose has already identified him. It was in a paladin bin in Stepney, and he had been cut up. Oh, I can't stand it. They said I wasn't to go with them just yet because it was in a mess, and they wanted time to…' She broke down into almost uncontrollable sobs, somehow managing to spit out the news.

'They want some time to clean up his body. Apparently, it was all chopped about and they, oh my

God. They think it's the work of that ghastly Cereal Killer.'

Clifton felt that he'd just been punched, hard. Nausea rose in his stomach.

'I told them you were with him last night, and they said they'd be round later to take a statement. What are we going to do?'

Clifton continued staring like a madman. Christ! He started to think frantically; trying to fathom some sense out of the mess. The trail led directly back to him. They would probably search his flat. There must be incriminating evidence all over the place; knives and such-like with small traces of forensic evidence just waiting to be detected. He had watched enough bloody television programmes about these things to know what to expect. He would be caught for the one murder he hadn't committed, the one he would never have committed. It was just too fantastic and terrible.

With Hilary sobbing into her damp cardigan, he realised with horror that he was both directly and indirectly responsible for Peter's death. Not only had he taken him to that wretched bar and got him pissed before abandoning him, but he had started all these pointless killings in the first place, and now some maniac was starting to copy his work. Worse still, the copying had led straight back to Clifton himself. The irony was simply appalling. Clifton realised with horror that he might well have been murdered himself by someone pretending to be him! The loathsome image of DCI

Dave Hicks once more steamed up in front of his eyes. He would certainly make the most of this. He would get his man after all, just as he said he would. Clifton could have wept, just as Hilary was now weeping, but he realised that the first thing he had to do was get her home and out of his flat.

'Listen, Hilly. Stop crying, love. What are you going to do now? You can't stay here. We've got to get you safe from prying eyes; you know what the press has been like with these killings. Does your mother know about this?'

Hilary nodded. 'I rang her, and she had she would be right over, but I had to see you first.'

Clifton looked at his watch. A quarter past two. There might just be enough time.

'I spoke to the police inspector who said that he'd come over himself. He said that they would give me time before they started asking questions. He was really lovely'

'Oh, really?' said Clifton. He found that pretty risible. 'All the same, I don't think they should ask you any questions today. I'll take you back home and wait for your mother to arrive.'

Taking Hilary's arm, he steered her back over the road. Of all the people to get murdered it had to be Peter, didn't it? Bloody typical of one of Hilary's boyfriends.

Clifton organised things as efficiently as possible. He found some of Hilary's sleeping tablets and persuaded her to take a couple before getting into bed with a hot-water bottle. Turning out the bedroom lights, he pulled the curtains to and prayed that Hicks hadn't tipped off the press. At five minutes to three the doorbell rang. Peeping almost comically through the curtains, he saw a white-haired severe-looking woman in a thin brown cardigan. She stared straight at him with eyes like badly peeled pickled onions. Clifton opened the door hastily.

'Hallo, Mrs Ellis, I'm Clifton, Hilary's friend.'

'I've heard all, about you,' she said, pushing straight past him and into the hall. 'What have you done with her?' Clifton felt he was being accused already.

'I've put her to bed. She's had a terrible shock. Thank goodness you could come over so quickly.'

'She should never have finished with Mark. He was a good man and more to the point, he was her husband. But, oh no, she had to go off and find someone else, didn't she? And now all this happens.' She nodded with a twitch of a neck well trained in jabs and pivotal thrusts.

'I'm not sure that's quite fair, Mrs Ellis. After all, Hilary didn't bring this on. She's completely innocent as far as...'

'No one is innocent in this world. People nowadays don't bother to think about the consequences of their depravity and lust. They make it happen, this sort of thing.'

She fixed him with those awful eyes again. 'They deserve it' she said.

Oh my God, thought Clifton, she sounds exactly like me! He stood back while she rampaged through the flat, like a rhinoceros on the warpath. Much as he regretted having to leave Hilary to the rare mercies of this woman, he knew he must get out of the flat as quickly as he could. In the few moments he had to himself before her arrival he had enough time to collect his thoughts. That stranger in the club. It had to be him! The copycat killer must have been the pushy, smooth snake who came over to their table and started chatting Peter up. It all fitted in. Desperately, Clifton tried to recapture some impression of his face, but faces had never been his strong point. They always looked the same to him unless they had something really peculiar about them, like a squint or a beard. The thought of a beard only conjured up the gristly spectral features of DCI Dave Hicks, and that made things even worse. He must focus in on this particular face, though. He had to.

At last, he had something. Blond hair, clean-cut, good-looking, white teeth: that was about it; he looked a bit like a film star. Just concentrate. The brain was still suffering from the surfeit of alcohol, but it did function. Yes, he was sure he could remember that face if he had to.

And he did have to.

'I'm going to have to go now, Mrs Ellis,' he whispered in the blackness of Hilary's bedroom, 'so I'll leave the two of you alone if that's all right.'

'Do what you want,' the woman replied. She seemed annoyed at being disturbed. 'I'm best left to deal with things here.'

'The police may call later on, but I don't think Hilary should see them; they'll only ask her upsetting questions. Perhaps you should tell them to call again tomorrow.'

'I think I'm perfectly capable of deciding what's best for my own daughter, thank you very much,' she snapped.

Clifton didn't argue. If that was all the thanks he was going to get, he'd be off. As he hastily scanned the street for signs of the police or the press, he could hear Hilary's sobbing starting up again from the bedroom. The old bitch had probably woken her up and said something nasty. As for himself, going home was out of the question. Hicks was doubtless already on his way. There was nothing for it but to set out to do something that had so far eluded the police — to catch a murderer.

Across the street and creeping out from behind a neighbour's privet hedge, Jimmy Nichols stretched off the cramp that had slowly set in during his long boring all-night vigil. After all that hunting and frustration, he'd never been so bored in his life, just hanging around everywhere waiting for the maniac to come up with the goods. He had spent most of today, for example, buying repulsive cups of weak coffee from the poxy cafe around the corner where the aggressive Greek Cypriot owner asked him at regular intervals if he wanted

311

anything else. And now it looked as though Gentle was finally going out, now that he'd left that loopy woman's flat. She'd almost caught sight of him hanging around on the corner when she careered across the road, weeping and wailing like a harpy, but seemed too much wrapped up in whatever it was that caused her to go doolally. This was certainly a nasty part of the world.

There was nothing for it, but to follow the maniac as he stormed up the road. Things were going to be resolved, one way or the other. And Jimmy would be there when they did.

CHAPTER TWENTY
WHITE

A little more subdued than usual, an openly perspiring Dave Hicks once more appeared on the TV news to give the latest on the case. He was feeling the heat in more ways than one while the questions were rattled off at him like arrows headed for Saint Sebastian's broken body. He gave out some more grisly information, revealing that the killer had left his victim in 'larger lumps than normal this time', which he explained had the advantage of making identification much easier.

'He sort of told us straight away who he is. Or was,' Dave said of Peter Borden.

A number of previous victims still remained anonymous, bearing tags attached, often with difficulty, to a jumble of limbs and joints. But this one was different. How could the police explain it?

'It's simply because the nutter's getting sloppy. His brain's on the blink. As I've said, it's only a matter of time before he's caught.'

Hicks went on to say that the police had a good idea of the man's movements up until his death and a rough description of someone the victim had been seen talking to was being circulated. More sightings were being made, although none had so far come to anything.

Did the police know the identity of the other man? Yes, they did, but he wasn't suspected of the killings at the moment. With a hint of a smirk Dave said that he was still keen to trace him and thereby eliminate him from his enquiries.

Watching from the safety of his bed whilst ebony black fans manufactured in Naples wafted cool draughts of air over his naked body, Peter Kurten snorted with derision. It was all very much easier than he had anticipated. No slip-ups this time; it was a doddle. Too drunk and too stupid to deserve to live. Why should vermin like that get to carry on when he had to die? It was all so unfair, so wrong. At least he could have a laugh at the way the police were clearly confused. And what about the stupid little fool's friend last night; the tight arse. Christ, how he hated people like that; living their whole lives on tenterhooks, frightened to enjoy every day and terrified of making mistakes. Well, he would try and choose that type for his next victim; that would give him something to worry about all right.

Peter stabbed off the TV remote control. Just one thing seemed out of place: that Hicks chap had not mentioned his 'lead' once during the questioning. Perhaps they'd edited it out as he had mentioned it every other time. It was probably something to do with the real killer after all. Anyway, the main thing was that Peter was in the clear and free to carry on for the time being.

To carry on carrying on. He had already cleared the mess up from the barbecue area in the garden. The body had gone straight into black plastic sacks and then into the boot of the Porsche after it was all over. He hadn't bothered cutting it up into such small pieces this time, but from all accounts that didn't seem to matter. In fact, the police seemed quite pleased with it that way; fitting into their theories and all that.

Now he was an established killer in his own right, what should he do next? Although he had intended to work methodically and logically, his exuberance was constantly bubbling just beneath the surface and threatening to build to a crescendo again. And he could feel that wretched headache coming on once more. He'd not been able to shift it for about three days now and sometimes his head had throbbed so badly that it felt his eyes might burst with the pressure. He checked in one of the many mirrors never too far away for visible signs. There weren't any, but Peter was still shocked by his own reflection. Something had changed; it was nothing too obvious, but there was now a sort of wild, startled look he didn't remember seeing before. And he didn't like the look of it. For no reason he laughed out loud, that absurd, giggly laugh which seemed to have developed lately. He'd never laughed like that before the cancer. Perhaps it was a symptom of the disease?

Peter peered down at the summer house at the bottom of his garden. He needn't destroy all the evidence immediately; the chance of anyone evading the Neighbourhood Watch scheme to come snooping around this particular part of Highgate in search of the Cereal Killer was pretty remote. He walked into the kitchen. Designer units met his eyes, glinting from floor to ceiling while secluded spotlights peeked out from alcoves where rare tropical houseplants thrived in optimum conditions; an Indonesian woman came in twice a week to make sure of that. He had designed the room for a feature in a woman's magazine and the job had paid for the lot. He'd even screwed the petite feature writer as part of the bargain on top of the expensive Italian marble worktop. Running an index finger along the shiny surfaces, Peter contemplated the irony that it should be him, who loved life so much, and his own wonderful life in particular, who was devoting almost every last moment to the task of depriving others of theirs. Oh well, '*c'est la vie*,' as they say. He flopped down into an outsized tub chair upholstered in blue pastel suede and tried to shift that headache with some much-needed sleep. He deserved a little nap, after all; it had been a very tiring night's work.

***

'Thank you, ladies and gentlemen. It won't be long now. Thank you, thank you.'

At the end of the press conference Dave wiped his forehead with a hanky smartly ironed by Mum and hurriedly ducked behind the dividing partition leading to his office. It was getting trickier, and time was certainly running out. By his reckoning this last one was the twenty-first Cereal Killing, and Dave had only two days left to meet his self-imposed deadline. Lumbering through the stale, stifling heat he sank with a heavy wallop into his beloved swivel chair, which wheezed at the effort. He wouldn't be sitting there for long unless something gave way.

It did and sooner than expected. With a creak and then a crash, the gigantic incident wall map covered in various photos, pins, notes and diagrams finally succumbed and collapsed onto the floor, scattering the little red flags all over the place. Hicks surveyed the scene.

'The weight of evidence is against him,' he observed with a nice line in the obvious. It was true though. Something somewhere was so obvious that they'd all missed it, even him. But what was it? Hicks would give anything to know. Two days! Why hadn't he given a different deadline; what was wrong with twenty-one days, why not twenty-eight? Mum had been right after all on that. But it was done now, and he just had to get on with it.

'I must grasp the metal,' he said aloud, stepping over the map.

What would the greats do in his position? Dave delved deep into the mists of his swirling imagination to remember storylines of the detective comics he had read. He had to empathise with the greats, feed off their uncanny intuition and crack the puzzle. Well, at least he was using the right vocabulary. The nutter would be getting worried as well; the last untidy killing showed that. He was getting very sloppy; maybe not actually making mistakes, but at least getting into a position where it was more likely that he *might* make mistakes. And what about that bloke the last victim was seen with? Not that it was him who had done him in; Dave could tell that just by looking around his flat for a few minutes earlier on. Still, the forensic blokes might turn something up. Dave hated having to admit the awfulness of the truth. The killer was after all, still at large. That had always been the basic dilemma.

Outside the streets baked like an arsonist's dream. The sun had taken its toll and the weather showed no sign of letting up. After the downpour, the night before it was hotter than ever. As the odd streetlight flickered in the fagged Sunday evening sky, a shaft of neon peeked guiltily in through the venetian blinds. Clouds of dust from the fallen map glinted around the crumpled papers and files and in the hazy light, Dave's silhouette cast an eerie shadow along one side of the wall. He looked about him and saw dirt everywhere. Ever since the case had started, he had banned any of the cleaning staff from coming into his office. It was, he said, essential that nothing was disturbed. He liked to think that this was seen as one of his little idiosyncrasies; they all had their own eccentricities, the greats. One consequence of this was that the office was now

318

incredibly unkempt and there was a layer of thick dust everywhere. Tiny flecks of paper, small pieces of skin; that's what it was, apparently. He had once read an article in one of the detective comics. You could trace a whole person from a tiny piece of dust. Something like a personal impression, all to do with hormones or something. Dave hadn't understood it properly at the time and wasn't sure if he did now, but that wasn't the point; it was knowing that this fact existed that counted.

'Large acorns from tiny hopes do grow,' he growled. He'd have to go out and find this nutter's dust; his own tiny traces. If Chummy was getting sloppy, it would show, maybe not in any obvious way, but perhaps in the minutiae of existence. He could try to track him down on his own. Undercover. Following his instincts and getting down and dirty in the nutter's filth.

A telephone call to Mum first, and then a spot of good, old- fashioned police work for a change. Perhaps that was it; just as John Major kept saying; getting back to basics. A bit of grubbing about in the muck, getting his hands dirty. He wouldn't have lost his old knack of smelling out the stench that villains give off. Dave sniffed involuntarily; the dust in the room was getting up his nose, and he stifled a sneeze. Well, in that case he would get under the skin of the nutter, burrow deep down into his pores and slough off a bit of grime for himself. The stench could be quite bad where muck collected, but he could take it. Those clubs would be a good starting point. He'd go over to plain clothes and pick up something suitable to wear. He couldn't very well go into the dens of iniquity dressed in his old grey suit and tie, could he? That was better; he was starting to think like a policeman again. He picked up the phone.

'Hello, WPC Burke,' he said to WPC Hare. 'Ring plain clothes for me, would you? Ask them to dig up something for me to wear in one of those queer clubs. Tell then I'll be round in half an hour, after I've finished up here.'

There was a faint sound like that of barely contained laughter. Dave held the receiver away from his ear.

'Can you hear me?' There was another small explosion.

'Yes, sir, DCI Hicks. I'll get on with it right away.'

'Good,' said Dave. He slammed the phone down and heard shouts of laughter through the thin partition wall.

'Idiots. Call themselves police officers? They couldn't even catch the clap.' He thought for a minute, and then smiled to himself. That was quite good. Have to use that one again, some time.

***

Two hours later he was uncomfortably seated behind the wheel of his car and dressed to kill. A fuchsia-pink shirt with outsize wing collar, over-tight lime green denim jeans, a brand new squeaky-clean black leather jacket, and, just for good measure, a black beret with white trim.

'That's what they wear, is it?' Dave inquired of the police plain-clothes fitter when he collected the outfit. The way they'd got him to walk back and forth across the room to get the whole thing just right had made him feel really authentic. The nutter wouldn't expect him to look like this, that was sure. He wasn't so much as dressed to kill as dressed to catch a killer.

CHAPTER TWENTY-ONE
BLACK

The bastards were everywhere. The old adage still applied; you can't find a policeman when you want one, but they were here now all right in droves, their car sirens echoing like banshee wails all around the city; a portend of death in the streets. One of them passed by in a patrol car, his great soppy face still replete with bumfluff. Why couldn't he have been around the night poor Peter got bumped off? Well, as a matter of fact, he was, but DCI Hicks had removed him from that particular beat to be his back up driver.

That morning two IRA prisoners had escaped by shooting their way out of Brixton prison using a gun smuggled in by accomplices and had shot a passing motorist before making off with his car. They were currently still on the run. This had prompted a massive police presence in central London as the authorities tried to limit the embarrassment at letting two desperate bombers slip out of their grasp. You couldn't move for police everywhere.

Clifton trudged on. If the police were incapable of catching murderers, then they should leave it to the experts. After all, if practice made perfect, then as a killer, and a pretty good one at that, Clifton was ideally qualified. He looked at his stainless-steel Casio digital watch; it was just after nine o'clock on Sunday night. Clifton withdrew twenty pounds from a cash dispenser, only to suddenly realise that the transaction would probably be traceable by computer link. If Hicks was onto him, he would be able to pinpoint his exact position. He was now making stupid mistakes, but he must have some cash, and they were bound to put a stop on his account soon anyway. The police would surely have been round to his flat by now and were maybe even at this very moment nosing around inside; peering in cupboards, lifting up floorboards, inspecting the kitchen drawers and implements. The very thought of it made his flesh creep.

Clifton noticed that although it wasn't quite dark yet there were already some disreputable low life characters lingering around Leicester Square and quite a few of them appeared to have been caught up in a time warp. Over by the somewhat temporary-looking green half-price West End theatre ticket booth, a few teenage greasers lolled around, trying desperately for the mean, moody magnificent look, but instead only succeeding in achieving a vague mawkishness while they dodged the pigeon droppings from the branches above. Dirty handmade scuff marks characterised their fake leather outfits not to mention their unwashed faces. Long, lank hair cried out for a decent rinse, not to mention a dollop or two of good quality conditioner. Clifton's own hair, which invariably tended to be rather oily, was usually washed within a day or two of becoming shiny, but these specimens appeared to live their whole lives in a shadow under the slimy iridescence that topped their heads.

The gang's females screeched out when ignored by their beaus or were occasionally seized in a seemingly never-ending cycle of screaming and larking about and having a good time, even though they never seemed to experience anything remotely resembling a good time. Clifton, who definitely wasn't having a good time, passed the other cliques and sub-species that time forgot, the tyrannosaurus rex and brontosauri of the new video age; scarred punks, forty-year-olds clad in over-tight denim flares, balding hippies with 'right on' slogans on their patches and bequiffed scooter lads unsure which tradition they were supposed to be upholding.

Had it really come down to this? For a man who had dispatched twenty-three people for no apparent reason to feel qualified to take the role as a nonchalant critic of current civilisation. Almost slipping and falling headlong into an enormous pile of swept up sodden refuse, stinking in the shimmering evening haze, Clifton managed to avoid the huge figure of a drunk who came lumbering towards him. Taking evasive action by sidestepping onto the abandoned remains of a greasy *Wimpy* cheeseburger, he decided to get off the streets in search of his prey. He would be an easy target for any watching policeman in the wide-open spaces that the West End provided. He ducked down one of the many alleyways lurking off Gerrard Street, and started doing the rounds of the clubs. It would be quiet being a Sunday evening, but the copycat maniac must be in one of them, he was sure of that.

At this very moment, not more than two hundred yards from where Clifton stood, Dave Hicks sat in the deep plush vinyl ersatz leather upholstery provided by the *Wild Wet & Woolly Willy Club*. Sipping his ridiculously expensive imported Nicaraguan lager and attempting to keep the froth from sticking to his beard, Dave tried hard to forget the deadline, up in just twenty-four hours. He only had until Monday teatime to get his man. Entering the club ten minutes earlier, his eye had caught the headline on one of the discarded Sunday papers lying in the gutter.

HICKS'S LAST DAY
CEREAL KILLER STILL AT LARGE

But it couldn't be his last day. He would live and fight another, wouldn't he? The press could write what they wanted, but he would still be around. Surely? All the optimism he had built up during his journey into the heart of London's vice area evaporated, and the agony of having to report empty-handed to Jim Haigh's successor, Superintendent Stinie Morrison, was too much to contemplate. He felt like the old joke of the policemen in the mysterious case of the stolen urinals; there was literally nothing to go on.

He surveyed the club once more to see if anyone resembled his own mental picture of what the nutter looked like.

Nothing.

'I don't give a donkey's,' he said into his beard. What would Mum say, though? What was worse, what would she *think*? If he didn't catch the nutter, he would be letting her down as much as anyone else.

'Christ!' he thought. 'I wouldn't be able to sleep with myself.'

All the details of his own personal nightmare were mapped out in a world without colour; all gloomy greys, pastel creams and bleak beige. He couldn't allow that to happen. He must take strength in his beliefs. After all, He was tested, wasn't He, and He managed to drag himself back from the brink. Dave focussed on the champagne fountain at the gaudily lit bar, frothing and bubbling in the lurid lights of the overhanging neon sign in the shape of an enormous scrotum, and his thoughts turned to the moment of doubt all true believers had to go through. That dreadful moment when He fell into the Reichenbach Falls with the waters below ready to swallow him and Moriarty up. Triumph amid disaster. Dave knew that he must go on; he must remain confident in his own abilities, just as brave Sherlock had done. His destiny still lay in his own hands.

'Balls to the Falls,' he said a little too loudly. The music from gigantic loudspeakers propped atop the bar unceasingly thumped along as 'Killer' by Adamski prompted some gentle gyrations from his very non-hip, hips. Dave started his method acting in earnest.

'Think like a poofter,' he thought, 'and you'll walk like one. That was the name of another song, wasn't it?' Slipping off his seat, he shimmied across to the bar, his Cuban heels clacking on the shiny marble floor.

To one side, seated in a banquette seat in a booth nearby, Peter Kurten was chuckling to himself. It wasn't such a bad idea after all, this murdering racket; in fact, it was really quite jolly. His eyes skimmed across the flotsam and jetsam that littered the dump. He had already been the subject of one approach. One of the flighty pieces of driftwood with washed-out and slightly thinning dishwater blond hair had sashayed up on his particular shore and tried to chat him up. However, despite his fey expression, Peter thought he still looked a little too well built, and probably also too well known to be seriously considered as a victim. Not that everyone in the place wasn't a victim already, with their never-ending cruising crusade for satisfaction, both sexual and aesthetic. At least he was beyond all that now. He knew what ultimate beauty was; to take another man's life.

Stepping out of the *Willy* club and into the street to momentarily escape from the pounding music it seemed that the whole world had gone mad. In the steaming, sweltering miasma that London had become in the heatwave, a couple of young and very sweaty lads were attempting to gain admittance into one of the straight clubs along the road. The dreadful painted old whore perched in the doorway shrieked at them as they lurched at her, trying to grab a piece of the action for free. These young entrepreneurs wanted more than their pound of flesh, more like a whole bosom, with nipple attached. Peter watched the grotesque pantomime with relish.

'Come on, darling, give it away for once! It won't hurt you,' one of the oafs bellowed, while his accomplice grabbed the woman's swollen and scratched breasts. As she screamed, a huge, baggy man wearing a filthy T-shirt barged out of the club.

'Get the fucking fuck,' he bellowed, punching one of the lads in the throat. The woman pulled herself free and kicked out at a groin with a sharpened stiletto heel.

'Aaaaaaaaaaaarrrrrrrggggggghhhhh you shitty old shitty, fucking, fucking, fuck... you, you fucking old bag, you spunk-filled old fuck, you fucking old...'

The man in the T-shirt turned his attention to the utterer of these vile oaths and proceeded to teach him a lesson not only in manners, but also in full-blooded swearing, abuse, and pugilism and started pummelling the youth in the stomach and face.

Standing at a safe distance, Peter realised he wasn't the only one suffering from decay. The city itself had developed its own corrupting malady and fed on whatever it could at every opportunity. As the shouting and scuffling continued, he moved past the doorway of the club, catching the eye of the old whore leering at him across the prone bodies of her erstwhile admirers.

'Fancy nipping inside for a quick shag, dear?' she pouted greasily, her face breaking out into what might once have been a smile but was now just a lacquered scar in the middle of her face. Peter quickly walked on, but not before catching sight of the lettering on the baggy man's T-shirt: 'The Cereal Killer — Go to work on a head'. Beneath the slogan was a crude drawing of a large egg cup containing what looked like a human skull being cracked open by a teaspoon.

***

In a doorway not more than two streets away Jimmy Nichols was asking a passer-by for the time outside the *Gaping Gusset Bar*. He had followed Clifton all the way back into Soho, only fifty yards away from where he'd first clapped eyes on him all that time ago. It looked like he was after another poor, unsuspecting soul to despatch. Even Jimmy had to admit that this was quite daring, given the imminent deadline that the police had given for his capture. This must have been the fifth or sixth club bar he had followed him into that evening and although he hadn't been spotted, it could only be a matter of time. There weren't that many people about although there was a noticeably high police presence in the area while the hunt for the Irish terrorists was going on. When would Gentle pick someone up? And what exactly should Jimmy do when he did?

Inside the bar, oblivious to the surveillance, Clifton looked at his watch again. A quarter past eleven. Crestfallen, he was almost on the verge of giving himself up. He was feeling exhausted, but he'd had a good run for his money. Might as well end it all now by his own hand before he sank too deeply into the beckoning mire. He had visited virtually all of the places he could imagine the copycat killer going to. After such a long time away from this world of sex shops, bars, clubs and sleazy pick-up joints they looked somewhat more menacing, like barely remembered childhood nightmares. He felt nothing but disgust for the poor, unsuspecting saps he plucked away from whatever rancid charms their sad lives possessed. Some of the people he had met had never been seen again. At least not whole anyway. Now the entire thing seemed so terribly sordid. Life shouldn't have been like that, and he was anxious to end it once and for all, even if that meant putting himself in harm's way to stop any more murders.

Clifton knew that even if he did manage to get into the right club or bar, what were the odds on being there at exactly the same time as the copycat? Time was of the essence; the next day was being billed by the press as H-Day: Hicks Day — the deadline day when he had to come up with the killer. If Clifton didn't get to the maniac who was pretending to be him by tomorrow, then one of two things would happen; he'd either be picked up for Peter's murder leaving Hicks to emerge in triumph, or a new detective would take over the case and would undoubtedly catch not only the copycat, but Clifton as well. It was an appalling fact that Clifton's own salvation depended on Hicks's continued tenure of office. He had to catch the copycat killer himself tonight. It was now or never.

Clifton thought of Hilary, and of her vile mother.

'First divorce, then murder, and now queers!' she had yelled at Hilary when Clifton had left her house.

It was too awful to contemplate. He looked around him at the dreary, forced jollity that the fleshpots of London were able to muster on a miserable Sunday evening. If the worst did come to the worst, it might not be an absolute disaster. The great brooding animalistic city wasn't the greatest place to be, especially in this heat and stifling, muggy humidity. And there was always the continuous filth, the rancid stench of takeaways and the foul choking air from the traffic. And that was without considering the disgusting manners of people swarming all over the place, blocking your path at every turn. Perhaps it wouldn't be quite so bad to be locked up in prison; at least solitary confinement would allow one to escape all this.

He suddenly felt himself becoming unbearably enraged. He had to pull himself together. Looking around he was aware that people at the next table were nudging each other and motioning towards an outlandishly attired looking character in the corner. That beard, the belly, those glasses, that gargantuan pair of flapping lime green trousers. The disparate, desperate images of Detective Chief Inspector Dave Hicks once again swam before his eyes. Hicks! That bloody moron Hicks! If it wasn't for him, Clifton felt sure things would be different. All the unnecessary killing would have stopped long ago when it all became so pointless. It was Hicks and Hicks alone who had caused the whole bloody mess. It was Hicks who had set off this other copycat maniac, it was Hicks who had led Peter Borden to his death and it was Hicks who had ultimately ruined his life. Clifton's eyes flickered around him as the heavy thud of itinerant truths started falling about all around him.

And then he saw what he was looking for.

The copycat maniac was sat, chatting to a slim, bedraggled figure hanging flaccidly onto the bar, not thirty feet away. He must have come into the *Gaping Gusset Bar* in the last few minutes along with Hicks. It was definitely him, although he looked a little different from when he had seen him with Peter. He was wet; soaked through. Little rivulets of water ran down his face from saturated blond hair. He must have been swimming, thought Clifton. But then he noticed one or two other people standing around, chatting excitedly while water dripped from their clothes. It looked so unusual, after the long, dry period to suddenly see people out in public looking wet. Under the bar's hot lights steam began to rise from the heads of the other newly arrived customers and it seemed as though their very brains were simmering. Clifton glanced back at the copycat maniac. If he looked back at Clifton, would he recognise him? Last night with Peter, the maniac had looked straight into his eyes, but you never could tell what he registered. If he was mad enough to start this whole obscene charade, then he might be too unhinged to know what he was doing. He was probably high on drugs anyway. Clifton continued staring at him.

The maniac didn't seem suspicious or wary at all while he continued chatting to the listless youth who seemed to find what he was saying incredibly amusing. In fact, the more Clifton looked at the copycat the more normal he appeared. Only more so; more handsome, more urbane, more assured. More everything. He didn't look like a murderer at all, but then Clifton didn't know what a murderer was supposed to look like. He didn't think *he* looked like one anyway. He must act quickly if he were to grasp the slim lifeline of escape on offer. This could be it; his last chance to finally emerge from the nightmare.

'I must grasp the metal,' he whispered before realising the solecism.

Peter Kurten felt a tap on his shoulder and stiffened a little before turning. It could be anyone; the boyfriend of the youth he was attempting to lure, another interested punter, or even the police. But it was someone else entirely; someone quite inconsequential looking.

'Hello, I hope you don't mind; I was wondering if I could buy you a drink?' Turning back to the youth, Peter excused himself.

'I'll see you later, Bruce, I just need to catch up with an old friend.'

Clifton thought he'd been rumbled. The maniac had recognised him after all!

He quickly ordered two drinks from the bar and sat at a small private table against one wall, looking directly at the copycat.

'Thank God for that; I never thought I'd be able to get away from him. He was boring the arse off me.' Peter beamed a smile. 'Well,' he said, inclining his head forward a little, 'aren't you going to tell me your name, my saviour?'

'It's Clifton.'

'Lovely to meet you, Clifton. I'm Peter. I haven't seen you before, have I? I'm sure I'd have noticed someone so charming.'

Clifton inwardly sighed a mixture of relief and dismay at the weakness of this chat-up line.

'No, but I have been here a few times before. I used to come here quite a lot before it got all tarted up.'

Peter looked at the unfashionable cut of Clifton's casual jacket, his dull shirt and altogether uninspiring air and recognised him as another willing victim. Although still a novice at this game, he could spot a sucker when he saw one. It was all going wonderfully well. If only that persistent buzzing in his ears would go away.

Clifton didn't know what to say. The silence seemed to scream at him. The maniac seemed to be on the verge of leaving. It had never been like this before, but then he had never hunted someone who in turn was hunting him.

'Do you come here often?' he said, but as soon as he had uttered those words, he realised what a fool he was being.

'God,' thought Peter, 'I've got a right one here; he's practically begging for it.' He gulped down his drink. 'Why don't you let me buy you the next one; what's your poison?'

As he watched Peter Kurten walk confidently up to the bar and order more drinks, Clifton's mind raced. He must get him out into the street, take him somewhere secluded, whop him on the head and then call the police. It was a slender enough plan, that was plain enough, but it was all he had. Somewhere secluded in Soho; where? He had to concentrate. At least the maniac was obviously too deranged to have recognised him; he would at least have the element of surprise.

Glasses refilled, the two fell into an uneasy conversation, each with thoughts of the other's entrapment. Clifton decided to be direct. Putting his hand on the hand that had killed his friend Peter, he leant forward.

'Why don't you come out the back with me, after we've finished these?'

Peter Kurten was taken aback. 'Well, you're a fast worker. How do you know I want to go out the back with you?'

'I just do, that's all. I can tell with your kind; even though you think you know what's happening, you're new to this sort of thing, and you wouldn't have come over here with me in the first place if you didn't want something else to happen. If you thought you could get off with that boy over there you wouldn't have bothered with me, but you're still not quite sure of yourself are you, so you'll settle for the safe plain ones like me.'

Clifton sat back and smiled pleasantly at the maniac. He had worried him; that was clear.

Peter Kurten dropped his guard a little.

'Where shall we go? It's absolutely pouring with rain outside now you know.' He paused. 'I've got a better idea, Clifton. Why don't we go back to my place? It's not that far from here and we can get to know each other in comfort?'

'No, I don't fancy that, some other time perhaps, but I feel the need for a bit of rough this evening. If you don't fancy it, we could drink up and see if someone else turns up.'

'No!' Peter said quickly, 'I don't mind. It's just that I don't want to get caught. We are in the middle of town, you know, and there are police crawling about everywhere looking for those escaped IRA bombers.'

Clifton smiled. He had evidently lost none of the old magic. It was quite amusing to see the copycat maniac falling over himself to get into position. Experience always told in this game.

'There's a place around the corner in a turning off Poland Street. It's boarded up, but you can get in; I've done it before and it's safe.' He smiled at Peter Kurten. 'As safe as a bit of rough can be, anyway.'

All Clifton needed now was that they weren't seen by Hicks as they made their exit. Both men tried to feel as cool as they could in the circumstances, while ironically Vanilla Ice's hit 'Ice, Ice Baby' cut through the stilted atmosphere as subtly as...an ice pick. They made their way up the stairs of the club and into the night.

Jimmy shivered as he watched them leave the bar. By now he was almost shaking with panic. He knew that he had to do something, but what? It was now just past midnight although the street had suddenly become uncannily busy; a lot of people had ventured outside just to watch the novelty of the downpour of rain falling and feel the cooling breeze blow again after so many weeks of unrelenting heat. Should he tell one of them, or try to accost Gentle himself? He could scream 'that's the Cereal Killer over there, let's grab him' but he knew that wasn't the answer. Up until now Jimmy had thought about trying to get some money out of all this and start a new life away from the filth and brutality of selling sex. But now faced with the prospect that the killer was setting out to commit another obscene crime all he really wanted to do now was to stop him. He wouldn't sell his soul to the Devil, no matter what others did.

And then Jimmy spotted a figure lumbering up the steps onto the pavement. It was the silhouette of somebody he recognised although he looked a lot different than usual. He ran over towards the large, bearded figure, hesitating slightly when he saw the full, bizarre nature of the clothes he was wearing.

'Detective Chief Inspector Hicks, my name is Jimmy Nichols and I know who the Cereal Killer is.'

Dave Hicks eyed him keenly.

'How?' he said simply, a paw clutching at the walkie-talkie stuffed in his purple shoulder bag.

'He tried to kill me last year and I've been trying to track him down ever since and I've finally found him tonight. He's just left that bar with another man, and I think he's planning to kill him. I know where he lives and everything. If you'll just follow me and...'

After the first few words all Dave could hear was what his trained ear told him was the break he'd been looking for ever since the case began. He acted decisively.

'James Nichols, I am arresting you for the murder of twenty-one persons. You do not have to say anything unless you wish to do so, but what you say may be given in evidence.'

'But, but you don't understand. I'm trying to help you,' Jimmy protested even as the handcuffs were slipped over his thin, scarred wrists and he looked all the while into that beaming bearded face underneath that ridiculous beret.

***

Now that the drought was truly over the downpour of rain had washed the normally filthy London streets strangely fresh and the roads glinted with a sheen that television advertisements would have described as 'brand spanking new and clean'. Every single scrap of paper, every discarded piece of rubbish, each lump of dog shit and human detritus had been swept away by the cataclysmic cloudburst, flushed away down the drains and along the sewers. Everything ended up there one way or another, and now the very cares of the world seemed to have been washed away for good. In the still falling drizzle, the asphalt road surface shone like polished black marble while windows reflected newly cleaned passing car headlights which resembled beautifully cut crystals. And it was at long last mercifully cool.

Clifton allowed the raindrops to fall freely on his upturned face. This was the way the world would be from now on with no more filth and lies or killing. Just purity. London was to be cleansed once and for all and become somewhere people could live, liberated from mess and worry and free from scum like the copycat maniac killer. And Clifton would be free from Hicks.

339

Hatred and animosity would become a thing of the past, and Clifton could at last wave goodbye to the Devil and take back his own hand.

He held up a piece of corrugated sheet metal halfway along the alley and the two men entered the deserted building in Poland St. Inside it was quite dank and dingy, with the floors thick in ancient dust. Rubble was strewn about on the floor and there was a distinct contrast to the disorder within from the now sparkling streets. Clifton had been here before and was slightly shocked that it was still accessible.

'We'd best go into one of the rooms up the top,' Clifton said calmly. 'We shan't be disturbed there.'

Peter Kurten started to climb the rickety staircase, but suddenly seemed to hesitate and check himself, as though making sure he'd brought everything with him. Clifton, following on behind, prepared to make his move. The two men stood on the landing and Clifton pushed open a stiff, creaking door that led into what looked like an old stock room. Some sagging cardboard boxes disintegrated gently in the corner of the room as rainwater dropped in through a crack in the ceiling.

'Why don't we get comfy here first?' Clifton said tenderly, slipping off his damp jacket and unbuttoning his shirt, running his fingers through now wet hair.

'I'm a bit cold, actually,' said Peter. 'I think I'll leave my clothes on for a bit.'

They listened to the disconcerting sound of raindrops dripping onto the floor. Peter moved over to the window and just as he peered out of the grimy casement, he felt a smack across the back of his head. At first, he registered only a mild surprise, but turning, saw Clifton wielding a thick piece of wood, apparently once part of the flooring. It hit him again, this time straight in the mouth.

'Right, you maniac, I've got you now. You killed my friend Peter Borden and now you're going to bloody well pay for it.'

The pain in Peter Kurten's mouth was excruciating. With his tongue, he felt what seemed to be a broken tooth swimming around in his own blood. This time the plank hit him on the shoulder, followed swiftly by a sickening kick in his midriff which took the stuffing out of him.

'Don't, don't, no more; I'll admit it all!' he said, the plank thumping him again on the chest. 'For God's sake, just arrest me, and get it over with; I'll come quietly, I'm finished.'

Clifton suddenly stopped in mid-swing and laughed.

'Who do you think I am? I'm not the police, you bloody fool.'

'Well, who are you then? Aren't you one of Detective Hicks's men?'

Clifton saw red in redder hues than he'd ever seen before and for a moment considered finishing Kurten off straight away with a well-aimed blow to the top of his head. This was too much.

'I'm not with bloody Hicks, that great steaming idiot. The police couldn't catch the killer in a million years. They haven't got the slightest clue and don't know what to look for, but I do, and I've got you.'

'Then who are you?' he whimpered. 'I didn't do *all* the murders, you know, I've only done three. The thing is, I've not really been feeling myself lately.'

'Don't you worry who I am. That's not important.' He had to be careful, he didn't want to say too much if he was going to hand Kurten over.

Peter's voice betrayed panic in its insistency.

'Then who are you?' he implored again.

'And who are you, sunshine?' said another voice behind them.

Clifton froze, his features momentarily contorted with confusion. There in the doorway of the squalid room was the frame of a large man dressed outrageously in an ill-fitting costume, his bright blue spectacle frames glinting in the half-light above a full, bushy beard. Clifton had to say something quickly.

'This man,' he said, pointing with the end of the plank towards the crumpled figure lying prone on the ground, 'is the Cereal Killer. I've tracked him down and caught him for you; his name's Kurten. Peter Kurten.'

DCI Hicks looked extremely impressed, and marched further into the room, peering at the forlorn figure slumped on the floor.

'And so,' he said addressing the cowering form, 'it looks like it's curtains for you.' Dave chuckled and looked over at Clifton for a sign of hilarity which never came. 'He's given me quite the run around, I can tell you. Well, his little game is up. The bottle has certainly hit the floor now.'

Hicks turned around to face Clifton and held out an enormous paw invitingly.

'I must congratulate you on a fine display of public service, my friend. I've always said that the public would prove to be my greatest ally in this case, and that together the police force and those they seek to protect would work hand in glove to solve this case and catch the killer. And once again it looks like I've been proved right.'

Clifton managed to restrain the temptation to spit and instead he smiled and in turn held out his hand.

'Thank you, Detective Chief Inspector, that's very kind of you. 'My name is…'

As the handcuffs were expertly slipped onto Clifton's wrists, Dave finished his sentence for him.

'Your name is Clifton Gentle and I know all about you, chummy. And my name is Dave Hicks. Hicks from the sticks and this…' Dave beamed broadly and gave Clifton a cheeky wink, 'Well, at last, this is *my* case.'

*

THE END

*

Acknowledgements II

Thanks to my good friend Kate Edmunds from www.eggnogg.co.uk for the cover design which perfectly captures what I wanted it to look like.

Thanks to my great friend David Brown for the photograph which unfortunately also perfectly captures what I look like.

Thanks also to my wonderful friend Keith Hicks for marketing expertise. Although he bears no resemblance to his namesake, he's always on the case.

Printed in Great Britain
by Amazon

70207975R00206